BITE

OF

THE

WOLF

BITE

OF

THE

WOLF

WADE WALKER

World Mythic Entertainment

First printing, October 2022

ISBN: 979-8-9871084-1-3

Contents

BITE

OF

THE

WOLF

Author's Note:

All of the following reported in this manuscript is true and derives from classified documents received and decrypted via Q-Wave quantum computing transmissions. These files have been pieced together as a manuscript to tell this exciting, strange, and true tale, straight from these leaked intelligence documents.

Some the names have been changed to protect both the innocent and not-so-innocent.

1: THE WOLFSANGEL

Nothing feels quite like the stinging tingle of a boot straight to the face. The bottom of the steel-toed boot smashed into his nose before he could think once about it, let alone twice.

His name was Val West, and he could have been just another tourist enjoying the sights and sounds of Transylvania's annual Oktoberfest celebration. He could have been just another middle-aged businessman, smartly dressed in his light brown worsted three-piece suit with cream shirt and olive tie. Or, he could have been an international criminal using the din and distraction of Brasov's premier event to arrange illicit acts.

As it happened, he was none of these... some, or all of which could get you kicked in the face for any number of reasons. Instead, he was a secret agent for a secret organization and his secret was apparently out. Struggling to shake off the dazed haziness, his muscle memory from countless fights took over. With a rapid knife-edged chop to the throat, he sent his attacker to the ground, gasping for air. After one more chop to the back of the neck for good measure, he knew the fellow who had been following him since he left the Acasă la Dracula hotel minutes earlier would not be waking up soon.

Val West checked his face, straightened his tie and went back to his business. What was his business, exactly? Stepping out of the shadows and over the unconscious attacker, he went looking for a gypsy.

Not one who could tell his fortune, but one who could tell him his immediate plans for the future.

Twenty-four hours earlier, Val West had walked down the sidewalks of a neglected old London neighborhood littered with the remnants of once prosperous businesses. Orange sunlight bounced off the window fronts, the glare obscuring the faded and decayed displays. West's destination was a decrepit storefront, known as Rare Lampshades Unlimited, a store specializing in rare and imported lampshades. He thought the addition of "unlimited" was a bit ridiculous, but despite this, it was never designed to be profitable and had never seen any business, aside from the occasional curious tourist to be shooed away or, in some rare instances, actually sell a lampshade to.

Rare Lampshades Unlimited was just another one of International Command's stations and IC stations were almost always located in front businesses such as this one. There are always businesses you wonder how or why they were started, let alone make a go of it. This is why: they are not designed to be profitable or viable. The previous station West reported to was under the cover of manufacturing electronic dog polishers.

The scent of dusty must was hanging in the air before he even entered. The old bell attached to the door by a string jangled while West struggled with an uncooperative entrance door. It would be a few moments; it always was, as they played this game of storekeeper and prospective customer.

"Coming, coming," bellowed a voice from downstairs. West looked around at the store and was slightly amused that not a thing had been changed since he first began reporting to this station nearly ten years ago. By the look of the décor, with its faded, lumpy wallpaper and scuffed wooden floors covered by patchy orange and green rugs, nothing had been changed, or cleaned for that matter, since at least the mid-1970s. The shopkeeper, Henri de Balsac, was an old agent who had gone senile but still spoke in code quite well; so well in fact, that it seemed he could only speak that way. The old man hobbled over toward West while carrying two lampshades, dust filling the air with each step, which cause a great sneeze from Henri.

"Good day, monsieur. I was just bringing up these absolutely wonderful new acquisitions: these rather exquisite 1920s barbola boudoir lampshades. And I'm sure you will appreciate this particular beauty." He held up a rather ugly, moth-eaten lampshade with a floral print, made with what looked like decomposing carpeting. "An Italian paralume from the 1930s with beautiful appliqué dark and light green decoration on a beige background. The inside of the shade has its original paper protection which contributes to its beautiful soft light."

"How about a lamp to go with it," West inquired, continuing to play this part with Henri. One never did know who might be listening in, especially with the recent opening of a Bulgarian VCR repair shop down the street.

"We only sell lampshades exclusively, monsieur," said Balsac, running his fingers along his waxed grey mustache.

"That is unsatisfactory. Surely your storeroom has the special type of lamp I'm seeking."

"Harrumph…. Well, if you insist, monsieur. A lamp is better than a candle."

"But both provide illumination," replied West, using the code speak Henri still delighted in using.

Henri led West to the stairway and said with a wink, "Straight down and to your left. It is the door marked, 'Employees Only' but we'll make an exception in your case." West thought that may have been a good-natured dig at his work ethic and smiled to himself, as he knew not too far from now these exchanges with Henri would come to an end. Even though Henri seemed to love it, West decided that no matter what phase of his career came next, he would be damned if he would spend his remaining years playing the part of a shopkeeper for some dusty International Command fake storefront.

He went through the swinging back doors into the storage area. A vintage desk lamp provided the only light in the dingy room. He went over to it, pulled the drawstring to turn it on and off, using one short and three long pulls. The wall opened up to reveal a hallway with a thick metal sealed door at its end. West walked toward the door and felt a flutter he wasn't used to feeling. He was nervous, knowing he either was getting a new mission or perhaps was finally being deactivated as a field agent.

There was also another feeling, an even more sickening feeling, that IC had become rotten, slowly taken over by those who seemed to have other—possibly sinister—interests. Despite the required shadowy sketchiness of a secret intelligence organization, this was the first time Val West had ever wondered if he was on the right side anymore.

This was also his first time meeting his new commander, Major Flanagan. His previous commander, Mr. Mulvaney, had been in intelligence for decades and had once been a top operative, which made him an effective spymaster. He hoped this Major Flanagan had the field-tested toughness needed for the job.

West had spent most of his career under the command of Mulvaney. Even though he had been assigned low-level assassinations lately, he knew it was IC policy directives, and not the opinion of the tough-but-fair Mr. Mulvaney driving those decisions. He stood before the door as an infrared scanner identified him and opened to a large installation filled with computers, maps, graphs and other highly sophisticated equipment used in the current state of espionage.

"Mr. West. Please come in," a pleasant female voice called out from a partially open office door. Through the doorway he saw a pair of shapely legs wearing a navy-colored skirt. He peeked in and saw the very attractive sight of the owner of the legs, a brunette with hair pinned up, focused intently on the papers on her desk.

"Well, I must say the Major definitely has good taste in secretaries," West said as he leaned closer and looked her up and down. "I approve."

"I do not," she replied with her cold, narrowed eyes meeting his gaze. "I am Major Flanagan. I would like to say it's nice to meet you, Mr. West, but already I have my doubts about that."

West straightened up. "Ma'am."

Major Flanagan motioned to the chair in front of the desk. "Please sit down."

West could feel something unusual in her tone, besides the irritation from their introduction, and with it, he felt butterflies of anxiousness about what was to come next. She took out his file and began reading his stats out loud, keeping one eye on him to verify their accuracy. He averted his gaze toward the gold curtain covering the wall behind her while she read, trying to stay cool and composed.

International Command Personnel File:

Valentine Reilly West
Race: Caucasian
Age: 44
From: Bear Lake, Manitoba, Canada
Drafted via Camp X-9 in Ontario.
23 years of service in International Command

She looked him up and down. "Five foot, eleven and a half inches tall. One hundred eighty-five pounds." Looking at his gut to confirm, her eyes seemed to say she was not quite convinced. Continuing, she compared his file photograph with his appearance as he sat before her. "Eyes: Light brown. Hair: Medium brown, usually side-parted, combed back." She paused to look at him, and then scribbled onto a notepad. "Note: add hair growing whiter in color on sides."

"Actually," West interjected, "I prefer the term 'growing blonder.'"

Major Flanagan ignored the comment and continued. "Rugged features, with square, masculine jaw and dimpled chin. Small mole on upper left cheek. Quite a nice write-up. I'd say it's also quite accurate."

"Thank you, ma'am," West said, blushing slightly.

"As is standard operating procedure for field operatives of a certain age, your recent assignments have become less demanding. Your file shows high marks, and I see your previous commander has recently had you on routine sanctioning missions."

"Yes, ma'am, although I am still quite capable of more than that."

"That's what I was hoping. A situation has come up. With our current caseload, I need someone with experience who can be relied upon." She dropped a heavy gold bar onto the desk.

"Have you seen one of these before?"

"If you mean a gold bar, yes, of course."

"I assumed you would know at least that much. Look at the symbol." Expecting to see a Nazi swastika, a common marking on vintage gold bars of this type, he saw it was a mark with which he was unfamiliar. It looked like a sideways, inverted 'Z' with a vertical line in the center: (*as pictured in Figure 1.1-- Editor.*)

Figure 1.1: The Wolfsangel Mark

"I'm sorry, ma'am. I am not familiar with this particular brand mark." He wished he had known, as he was now thinking maybe he wasn't being sent to an office job, but to be sent on an assignment that required more than just being a glorified hitman.

"It's a Wolfsangel. German for "wolf's hook." British Narcotics, working with Interpol on a planned drug bust near Belgium, instead found a smelting operation of gold bars. Nazi gold bars. Not just Nazi gold bars but marked with this—the Wolfsangel. These bars were rumored to have been produced by certain divisions of the Nazi SS during World War II, but until now, not a single one has ever turned up."

"Where do we come in?" West asked.

"Normally this would be handled by Her Majesty's Treasury, but since this bust, large amounts of newly melted gold have been making its way into various European markets. We have reason to believe this is an international operation and the Chief Secretary to the Treasury has requested MI6 defer this case to International Command. We have received some intelligence reports from Transylvania, which suggest a connection to this gold influx. Being we are short-handed at the moment and in spite of your most recent medical report, which is, shall we say, questionable, I think you can handle this, in a hands-off capacity."

"Hands off?"

"Yes. I want this strictly to be an intelligence-gathering assignment. No fisticuffs, no car chases, and no killing and NO GUNS."

"Doesn't sound like much fun at all."

"You're not here for fun. This is a different time than when you first joined International Command and to better reflect the current landscape, we want to remake IC's image as kinder and gentler, as well as inclusive."

"This is a secret organization, ma'am. I don't think public image is all that important."

"Well, I do, so if you want this assignment, I suggest you get going. Otherwise, we have an Albanian supermarket location that could use a new door greeter." She placed a folder marked with the designated 'top secret' symbol on the desk. "You'll find what you need in this briefing, including credentials to get you into Transylvania. Your flight leaves for Brasov early tomorrow morning, where you will meet with the other assigned IC operatives—a local contact, and an IC agent being sent over from The Vintage Telephone Book Emporium—the Florida bureau office."

She handed him the dossier, which he placed in his briefcase. West bowed politely with an added "ma'am" and exited the office. On his way back up the stairs he reflected on how he was relieved to still be an active agent, but still felt uneasy about the direction IC was heading in. His was a dangerous world, not concerned with politeness, correctness, equality and inclusiveness. It was especially not concerned with fair play or the perceived intolerance of a well-placed bullet. Even with his reservations, he was relieved to be on an active field mission, such as it was.

He rounded the stairs and walked back into the main floor room. Balsac was busy stacking assorted lampshades into a display. As the day went on, he would take it down and start again several times to pass the hours.

"Monsieur," Henri called out as he noticed West leaving. "Did you find the lamp style you were looking for?"

West looked the old man and let out a sigh. "No, Henri. I am afraid not."

Henri shook his head. "That is regrettable indeed."

"It is," West said with a barely disguised bitterness. "I shouldn't have expected to find clear light in such a shady business."

West bid goodbye to Henri and walked off down the broken lonely sidewalk. He wondered what lay in store for him on this mission to what was known as the land beyond the forest: Transylvania.

2: GYPSIES, SPIES & WILDEBEESTS

A bloated orange moon rose over the Transylvanian city of Brasov as it celebrated the coming of October. Soon, Val West would rendezvous with fellow International Command agent Thomas Hedison, Codename: Wildebeest. He had worked with Tom in the past, and being a few years younger, he was still enjoying the prime of his career as a field operative. West found him to be quite jovial and as close to a friend as one could have in the business.

The two of them would be meeting with Dacia Zabor, known in International Command as Double Agent Gypsy. West saw a photograph in the mission dossier and was favorably impressed with what he saw. She was a beautiful Romani gypsy who worked as a personal assistant in the Transylvania National Alliance security office of General George Ferenc. Unbeknownst to Ferenc, she also worked for IC, relaying information. Although she was a traitor in the Transylvanian government's eyes, she owed both her life and her father's to International Command and repaid that debt every chance she could with valuable intelligence.

Feeling oddly energized after his scuffle with whoever had been tailing him, West walked down the festively decorated street. He did tweak his bad shoulder a bit, but some of the Transylvanian wine he heard so much about would help with that. He breathed in the crispness of the autumn air and listened to the furious fiddling of traditional Transylvanian folk music growing louder with each step. In this crowded festival atmosphere, the three agents would be able to pass along information freely, being one of the rare situations where the Transylvanian agents could not keep tight surveillance.

Entering the heart of Oktoberfest, small and large tents and stages covered the town square. Men in Alpine hats and lederhosen danced around with large steins of Transylvanian beer, lusting after the desirable young women in Bavarian dirndl dresses who seemed to be everywhere. However, despite the natural distraction, West was only looking for one woman in a dirndl: Double Agent Gypsy.

He walked the cobblestoned streets marveling at the magnificent backdrop of the mountains beyond Brasov, coupled with the last red splashes of a spectacular sunset. He was looking for the agreed rendezvous point, a wine tent called "Cort de Vin." He ignored his rumbling stomach and the zingy sweet pepper odor of Paprika Chicken-on-a Stick wafting through the air.

Around a corner near a fortune teller's tent, he found the Cort de Vin and was struck by his first sight of Dacia Zabor. She was even more striking than she appeared in her file photograph, and he had to remind himself he was here on business. She had also been briefed on his appearance and upon making eye contact, she approached him with a goblet of wine.

She danced around him flirtatiously and handed him a goblet of Transylvanian wine. She then spoke while holding hers up, the glass covering her mouth. "Only speak about business while you are appearing to take a drink," she instructed. Though she spoke with a thick Transylvanian accent, her English was impeccable, and her long dark hair matched her distinctive and attractive Romani features. She was wearing the traditional Transylvanian dirndl with a tied apron knotted squarely in the middle and lace blouse, which was struggling to restrain her ample bosom.

West nodded that he understood her instructions and tipped his goblet back and told her once Wildebeest arrived, they would need to find some place quieter and with more privacy. She nodded, and he led her over to a small table. Once seated, she took the glass away from her lips to speak more conversationally. "You have been to Transylvania before?"

"No, I've never managed to sneak in here," West replied with a smile. "It is quite lovely country."

Gypsy thought for a moment and responded with "Lovely, but dangerous." West thought the same thing of her as she continued. "The Transylvanian wilderness can be dangerous at night, especially on nights with a full moon." She reached under her apron and passed something to him under the table. By feel, he could tell it was a knife of some kind.

West put the goblet to his lips. "Thank you, but I am armed."

"It is a silver dagger. You may find your gun will fail you, and it could save your life."

"I appreciate the gesture. I have seen a lot of strange things during my time, but I don't believe in superstitions."

"It doesn't matter if you believe in superstitions or not. You are in Transylvania, and they believe in you. Please take it, I insist."

West reluctantly accepted. He did think a dagger was always a welcome addition, so he took it as a practical item, but mostly out of politeness to her. He quickly palmed and placed the sheathed dagger inside his suit jacket. His hand still inside, West felt a slap on his back. Could the Transylvanian secret police be on to him already? Did they find their sleeping friend he had laid out earlier? Turning around, he was relieved to see the almost always-smiling toothy grin of Agent Wildebeest, Thomas Hedison.

"Val West, how the hell are you?" Hedison said through a mouthful of Paprika Chicken-on-a-Stick. "It's gotta be at least three or four years since we last worked together." Gypsy gave a disapproving glance at Hedison for his loud and careless attitude to what was a very dangerous situation for her. She gave them the directions to a gypsy encampment just outside of the festival area, where they could speak more freely. She left first, followed a few minutes later by West and Hedison. They knew which way to go to get to the encampment, but still took a roundabout way through backstreets, doubling back a couple of times as a precaution, but mostly out of habit from having been in the spy game for so long.

Arriving at the camp, they spotted Gypsy standing near a covered wagon. They all climbed in, and Gypsy took out a map and spread it on the small table between them. She spoke in whispered tones, always with the belief they may be under surveillance.

"A week ago, two men came to General Ferenc's office. One was a short, thin man with curly hair and large nose. He was a loud Australian, with an even louder Hawaiian print shirt, and did most of the talking.

The man with him—who the Australian seemed to be working for—was tall, maybe six foot five. He wore a black suit and tie, with black overcoat, and he carried a large briefcase. He had slicked back hair and appeared to be in his forties. His face had a hard look—a stone face, but the thing that stood out most was a scar that ran from his left ear down to the chin, marking the left side of his face. The scar stood out enough, but there was a look in his eyes that was cold... and terrifying.

"The x-ray installed in the doorway revealed neither were carrying firearms. They barged in past the entryway to the reception area and the Australian started talking very fast to the other receptionist. She explained he needed an appointment, and that General Ferenc was a very busy and important man. The Australian stressed that it was matter of national importance. At this time, I took the opportunity to take some photos."

"Can we see these photos?" West asked. Gypsy sighed and explained that the camera device is implanted and would need to be removed and sent to IC for processing.

"Now the next part is what was most unusual. The scar-faced man opened up the briefcase and held up a gold bar… marked with the Wolfsangel symbol. The receptionist called in to Ferenc's desk and once he heard about the gold bar, he was of course very interested in meeting with the two men. Ferenc came out of his office, practically drooling over the thought of the gold bar. He is a pig in all things. I am sorry… I digress.

"He greeted them warmly and invited them into his office. I was able to hear most of the conversation through the hidden microphone IC gave me to place in Ferenc's office. It didn't all come through clearly, but I was able to make out that a deal was struck between Ferenc and the two men for what they termed as an 'ecological study.' The two men then left Ferenc's office. On their way out I overheard the scar-faced man say to the Australian, 'It's amazing who will see you when you arrive with a gold bar to start the conversation.' He had a gravelly, whispery, hiss of a voice."

West had been taking all of this in and as promising of a lead as this was, he hoped she had more. She did.

"I was able to see the billing and manifests of what Ferenc was arranging for them. There is billing for heavy equipment movers and other construction machinery, along with building materials, shipping trucks and personnel—some even from the Transylvanian military—all under the account and orders of General Ferenc, as 'official business.' This equipment is all going to an area northwest of the village of Vklana." She pointed to Vklana on the map and used her fingernail to trace a route approximately to the position she had described.

"What do you know about the area where they are bringing all of this equipment?" West asked.

"There is nothing there. It is an undeveloped, unpopulated woodland area, property of the Transylvanian government. The area they are bringing everything to is about a half kilometer from the base of the South Carpathians. Beyond it lie the Cozia, Lupului, and Vâlcan mountains."

West thought for a few moments and then turned to Hedison. "What do you suggest for a route to sneak in and do a little snooping around?"

Hedison stroked his chin and looked over the map. "There's a small river here, running along this ridge. We can come in at the outskirts of Vklana and hike to the river. Looks like approximately a three-to-four-kilometer walk. Nice night for it and with the moon as bright as it is, we should be able to get away with minimal light use. Then, we'll follow the river up to this point here, right before it widens. The cliff is lower at this spot, so we'll go up there and move in to take up positions." He pointed to the outer perimeter of the site, which was ringed with forest. "This looks like good enough cover for us to see into their worksite, and if we can, move in closer for a better look."

"Splendid," West said as he further studied the map. "Let's plan to leave for Vklana in an hour. Gypsy… Dacia, you have been a tremendous help. Now, get along back to the festival so your alibi will stay intact in case you are questioned when you go in to work on Monday."

Gypsy wished them well and kissed them both on their cheeks, which gave West a tingle he should have expected, but had not. He was impressed with what a brave and resourceful young woman she was and how International Command was fortunate to have such an asset. And what a marvelous asset indeed.

West drove Hedison in his rental car along the winding country roads to Vklana, a tiny old traditional Transylvanian village. After parking, they shed their overcoats and the two, clad in the standard issue black spy suits of International Command, took the small amount of equipment needed: night vision binoculars and climbing gear, along with the equipment they weren't supposed to bring. West had his trusty Glock 19, chambered in 9mm and Wildebeest had his old, scuffed Sig Sauer P226 pistol. Before they left, West grabbed the silver dagger Gypsy had given him, and strapped it to the equipment belt strapped across his chest.

Hedison laughed with delight. "So much for being 'non-lethal observers.'"

West was glad they agreed about the impractical absurdity IC was trying to impose on them. "I don't know about you, but if I'm going into the wilderness in the dead of night, I plan on taking a weapon or two. Let's just try and not kill anyone for once, if only to save on the endless paperwork that IC requires now."

Hedison chuckled again and the two friends started off through the thick underbrush. To pass the time, they made quiet conversation.

"So, what code name do they have you using these days," Hedison asked.

"I don't get to use it much, but I'm officially listed as Z-10."

"Z-Section?" Hedison shook his head. "What the hell is that about? You're too good to be muddling about in Z-Section, doing low-level sniping jobs."

West shushed him for talking too loudly and in a low tone explained that he agreed. "I also have about five years on you, so let me know if you're treated as well when you start reaching mandatory retirement age."

"Not me. I'm getting out before that. I joined for the adventure, but now I think I've had my fill. I got a gal back in Wichita I'm planning on settling down with. I'm going to do some farming, and maybe have… oh, I don't know, eight or ten children. If nothing else comes up between now and the end of the year, hell, this may even be my last mission."

"I envy you, being able to walk away like that."

"It's just a job, my friend," Hedison said. "But my family and my future family are more important these days than chasing skirts and scumbags across the globe. Soon it will be time to sit back, enjoy the country life and write my memoirs… that no one will be able to read. Secrecy Act, you know."

Faint sounds of trickling water affirmed they were on the right course. They soon reached the river, the waters shining brightly under the full moon's illumination. On the other side was the high, rocky cliff, topped with trees. The cliff ran along the river, and they followed it until they found a low spot in the river and made their crossing.

Continuing along the riverbank, they found what they were looking for: The cliff line ended and was now a sizeable, but much easier to climb, hill. Upon reaching the hilltop, they slowly and quietly walked through the woods until Hedison stopped to look at his infrared compass.

"Ok, let's split up here," he said. "The edge of the woods is still another three hundred meters or so. You go up that ridge, and I'll go down in the swamp."

"Fine. Radio silence until 2400. That is, if you can go that long without talking."

Hedison grinned. "Hey, it's going to get lonely in that ol' swamp. Didn't bring a flask, so I might have to break radio silence for a sing-along to keep entertained."

"You go right ahead. I'm going to be doing the old sniper go-into-a-trance trick and zone out until I see something interesting."

"You're no fun anymore, but alright. Radio silence until 2400... I guess I can make it for another couple of hours or so."

"Enjoy your swamp. I'm going to find myself a nice tree with a good view to settle into."

And that's exactly where Val West found himself. Up a tree. Very fitting, considering his uncertain status with IC.

Shafts of autumn moonlight broke through the dark forest canopy as the night settled in. West prepared to spend the bulk of this evening in the discomfort of a gangly old tree trunk.

He rubbed his aching shoulder and thought about the fight he had had earlier in the evening with the Transylvanian agent who had attacked him. Luckily, he was able to end it quickly, because the longer the fight, the less chance he had these days. Now, reduced to a simple "non-lethal observer" as his new boss had put it, stuck on a routine case like this, he feared his days of action and adventure were coming to a close. His past injuries may have been catching up to him—this was evident by the way his knees creaked while climbing up the tree—but he still felt he could hang with the younger agents.

Every mission left its scars, as his recent medical report had shown. Time may have been catching up with him, but experience was more important than physical ability and with his level of expertise he didn't have to work as hard. That's what he told himself, although he wasn't quite convinced.

Leaning back on the tree branch, he heard a rustling in the thick underbrush and looked down to see a rabbit leap out, followed by a hungry wolf on the hunt. West knew the feeling as he watched his fellow hunter in the darkness. Even if he didn't agree with the "observe only" orders of this directive, it was still a hunt, and he was on it. More importantly, he could feel the feeling of the hunt, the taste of the wild blood that never leaves. It was all he could taste at the moment.

He looked at his watch and saw it was getting close to midnight. Soon he would contact Wildebeest and report the uneventful last hour. Maybe he would have something of note to relay. The moon was still shining bright, but clouds were periodically darkening the view. A thick, low fog had moved in. It was low enough not to have an effect on his target, as he was about eight feet up, but it would be hell to navigate through once ready to head back. He looked out from his perch to the site area, still shrouded in blackness.

Then the blinding light hit him straight in the eyes.

3: BEYOND THE FOREST

The harsh light shined in Val West's eyes, and he immediately and instinctually froze in place. Based on the light's movement and the distant sound of tires crunching on gravel, he realized it was vehicle headlights. Standing on his tree branch, he breathed a sigh of relief. Even though the lights seemed directed at him, there was no way he could be seen amidst the thick and tangled foggy woodland where he was watching. The vehicle, a Hummer H2 limousine, pulled up and parked next to one of the newly constructed buildings. An outdoor motion light came on and West was glad he and Wildebeest had remained in position and not triggered the motion lights or any other security measures that were in place.

West put up his binoculars. No night vision was needed as the outdoor motion light illuminated the entire construction site and penetrated into the edge of the woods. Scanning the area from his tree branch vantage point, he was able to see two large metal pole buildings, both of recent construction, as well as the heavy equipment Gypsy had seen on the billing documents. He could spot a number of earth-moving vehicles—backhoes and rear-end loaders, along with large cranes. On the other side of the cleared area were large shipping containers and numerous semi-trucks with cargo trailers.

The limo doors opened and the first person he saw was a gawky, thin man with a poof of frizzy, curly hair and a bulbous, beak-like nose. Upon exiting the vehicle, the man nearly fell into a mud puddle and shouted, "Chroist!" That would be the Australian. Keeping him steady was a mustachioed man in a military uniform. West could see it was the uniform of the Transylvanian National Alliance.

Even though they had never met, West knew this to be General George Ferenc by his jowly appearance, and from what he could tell from this distance, his cheap hairpiece and poorly dyed mustache. From what he knew of him, he wasn't surprised Ferenc was involved. If there was a dirty deal going on, he was sure to be involved and profiting from it. He figured it wouldn't take too many gold bars to get Ferenc to put his own interests above Transylvania's.

Apart from the two was the third man, the one Gypsy described as the "scar-faced man." Just as she described, he was wearing a long black topcoat over a black dress suit with black necktie. West focused the binoculars more intently and saw the man had dark, slicked-back hair, a thin, dignified mustache, and that scar—a gruesome mark starting below his left ear, crossing the cheek and running down to the bottom of his chin. He had an intense look in his eyes and seemed to be in his own world while the other two talked loudly to each other.

The scar-faced man soon rejoined the Australian and Ferenc and the three continued talking while gesturing off in the distance, in the direction toward where the mountains lie. The scar-faced man again broke away from the other two and softly walked towards the woods, towards the direction of West.

Could he have seen me? West wondered, with the little internal pitter-patter which always accompanied the potential of being discovered. West didn't think it possible. He was five hundred feet away, through thick woods and a fog adding further concealment. Was there something on him that glinted in the moonlight, perhaps? Something that attracted this man's attention? Before he could think to make his next move, the man stopped. West watched him, waiting for him to do something. It was an interminable few seconds before the man looked up at the full moon shining through the clouds, sniffed the night air and walked back to the other two men, who were now inside the pole building.

West decided it was time to break radio silence. He activated his wrist communicator to signal Hedison.

"Wildebeest, come in."

The communicator crackled with static. "Hey there, good buddy," Hedison responded. "I can't see a damn thing through this fog. How about you?

"I've been up a tree."

"Sounds about right."

"Indeed. You probably couldn't see it from down in the swamp, but a vehicle just arrived near my position. I saw the three men Gypsy described. Once they leave, we can move in for a closer look. There are some motion lights we'll need to watch for. Just hang tight and stay quiet for now."

"Well, I hope this fog lifts by then. Otherwise, I'm going to have a hell of a time even getting to your position without getting lost a couple of times."

"I'm going to move down to a lower branch. I should be able to see the headlights when they leave from there and…"

The wolf he had seen earlier came bursting through the fog, along with the rabbit and several deer, all in tow.

"Come back on that, you were cutting out," Hedison said.

"Sorry, just had some wildlife come racing through. A wolf chasing a—" All West heard next through the receiver was the sound of Hedison screaming in terror, a dreadful sound that echoed through the swamp all the way to the tree where West was crouched. Through the receiver, amidst the garbled screams, he could hear a horrid snarling in the background. Whatever was attacking Hedison, he had to go and try to aid him.

West began climbing down when the growls and a howling bounded through the thick undergrowth toward him, twigs and branches snapping as it advanced. Could it be a grizzly? There were many roaming the wilds of north Transylvania. Whatever it was, it was bursting through the wood like a storm wind. He moved back up the branch and was over six feet off the ground. West was reaching for his gun when the beast leapt through the air, knocking him off the tree branch.

Instinctively, he backflipped out of the tree, a move he had not used in years. His left knee instantly paid for it. The beast jumped down from the tree branch and West fired, emptying his entire clip. It was unfazed by the bullets rippling into its torso and began charging towards West. Ignoring his throbbing knee and relying on all the adrenaline he had coursing through his body, he ran.

West knew he had some kind of hellhound on his trail, and he ran like hell through the tangled thickets, blood running down his face as the sharp branches tore through his clothing, then into his flesh. Unaffected, the beast pursued him through the brambles and the brush, leaving a path of destruction in its wake.

Painfully jumping from rock to stump to low branches, swinging himself forward, he used his speed and momentum to power him through. West needed to find something—anything—to give him some cover away from what had to be a rabid wolf of some kind. With the thick forest and fog, he couldn't see more than a few feet in front of him, let alone see anything he could use to shelter himself. He pushed himself forward, with the beast so close he could practically feel it breathing on him. It stopped suddenly. West could now hear the distant sound of the rushing river and realized this was the end of the line as he remembered the cliff drop down into the gorge.

It was in this last split second of realization while sliding off the cliff edge that he grabbed hold of a small, knotted fir tree. He wasn't sure it could support his weight and while looking over the cliff edge to see where the wolf was, he also felt around for places to grip.

The wolf did not retreat, and it slowly crept toward him. Through the mist, he could see the glowing red eyes as the moonlight glistened off the white fangs, the rest shrouded in darkness. It inched closer with its open maw of champing teeth. West knew he only had one chance left. He felt for the silver dagger Gypsy had given him and while holding himself over the cliff edge with his right arm, an exhausted, aching arm, he used his left to unsheathe the dagger.

With an agonizing effort, he pulled himself up with his right arm. The shining red eyes and fanged mouth rushed at him. West swung his left arm up at it with the dagger and struck it in the chest, and he felt it dig in and make its mark. The beast howled in pain and clamped its fangs down hard on West's right forearm. The pain was immediate and severe and with it, West lost his grip.

As he let go, all he felt was the feeling of falling into the darkness far below.

4: *lupus hominarius*

Val West's battered body plunged deep into the rushing river. He surfaced, perhaps voluntarily, perhaps by instinct, and was swept downstream, smashing into rocks and tumbling down rapids, carried away by the current. The night faded into dawn and as daybreak changed the foreboding appearance of the Carpathian Mountains, a small ripple appeared across the now calm surface of the river. The ripple moved along with what looked like a massive bird flying down the river's path, its quiet, but strange insect-like hum scaring off wildlife in its wake.

Miles away, in a quiet clearing in the Transylvanian forest, sat a large gypsy caravan covered wagon. Inside, a short, hunchbacked man with prematurely gray hair with a mustache and beard fashioned into a Van Dyke sat in front of a computer screen, furiously working the controls of this drone which was disguised somewhat unconvincingly as a large bird.

Special Double Agent Gypsy, Dacia Zabor, entered the wagon and brought a warm cup of tea to the man. He continued working the controls, oblivious to Gypsy's presence, while using his free hand to fiddle with his waxed mustache points.

"Any luck yet?" Gypsy asked in her thick Transylvanian accent, which sounded like a sweet sing-song melody to the man named Dr. Hector Borge.

"I took the drone up as far as I could get to the construction site without being spotted and couldn't find any traces. From the data I intercepted from the wrist com-link, no vital signs were being transmitted. I'm afraid based on that and what was retrieved from the last audio transmission, Agent Wildebeest is dead."

"The other one... Val. You said you had a fix on his location."

"I did, but the com-link is no longer on his body. I used the drone to fish what was left of it out of the river about a half hour ago." He breathed out a sigh. "All I have now is that he was in the river, but exactly where may prove impossible to determine. Thank you for the help... you best get back to Ferenc's office before anyone gets nosey. And Gypsy..."

"Yes, Dr. Borge?"

"Thank you for the warm tea," he said with an equally warm smile. "It's quite chilly this morning and I very much appreciate it, as well as all of your assistance."

"You're welcome, sir. I hope you find Agent West and, for at least closure, that you find Agent Wildebeest."

"Dacia, you are too kind and too good for this rotten business. I'm afraid our purposes are not so much for closure and respect for the dead, but for more practical purposes. Heartless, but practical. And necessary."

Dr. Borge went back to his drone, feverishly scanning through its camera viewfinder to find a trace of West. After another hour, he maneuvered the drone from the river's edge to a swampy area where a small tributary slowed to a swampy trickle. Following the tributaries path, he let out a yelp, and quickly zoomed the camera in farther.

In a green pool of slime was the face of Val West, lying partially upright on the bank in the shallow swamp waters. Borge immediately scanned for vitals and found the faintest trace in the prone and unconscious body. He sent the drone in closer and positioned it over West.

26

Two long pincer-like arms extended out of the drone body and reached, gently picking up West under the careful control of Borge.

"Commander," Borge's voice announced with excitement over the transmitter. "We have found him. No, sir, we are just in time if anything. Tell Cedric to have transport ready at the border crossing. I will be there soon with the cargo."

Borge got up from his seat and left the wagon. Outside, he opened the door to another wagon and entered in a code on a wall keypad. A large glass cylinder, large enough to hold a man, emerged from inside, placed on a platform which extended with it.

Minutes later, the drone arrived, carrying the near-lifeless body of Val West. A whooshing sound of depressurization came from the cylinder as its air-sealed gaskets released, opening the main panel of the glass coffin-like capsule. Borge directed the drone to gently place West inside the capsule. After doing so, the drone then flew into the other wagon and collapsed itself into the shape of a metal shelving unit.

Using a surgical knife, Borge quickly stripped off West's wet and tattered clothing, making note of the external injuries West had sustained. After monitoring the faint heartbeat and shallow breathing, he attached a breathing tube and electrode pads to various parts of West's anatomy. Looking him over one last time and verifying the monitoring signal was satisfactory, Borge pushed the control buttons on the cylinder keypad, which air-locked the chamber and filled the cylinder with liquid. Pushing the cylinder back into the wagon, he shut the door and donning his gypsy clothing, climbed aboard the stagecoach. With his two wagons in tow, Borge prodded the horses with his buggy whip and started down the forest trail.

***

Sir Cedric Kenton was waiting impatiently for the gypsy wagon to arrive. The tall, clean-shaven man with snowy white hair adjusted his tinted glasses and checked over his uniform. Even though he loved the rush of adventure of wearing a disguise and crossing the Transylvanian border under the guise of the Red Cross, he did feel like maybe he was getting too old for this sort of thing. The Kentons were aristocrats, with Cedric's family line having secretly served covert intelligence operations since the nineteenth century. Although he would try to deny it, he knew it truly was his life's work. It wasn't just out of loyalty to the Commander that he kept himself in the action.

Sir Cedric knew the Commander would be there in person if he could be, and in his stead, Cedric answered the call of duty. He also preferred to work directly for the Commander, because he also felt the sense that International Command proper was no longer the same global intelligence cooperative he had once believed in.

So far, he had encountered no problems, but he still wanted to get back over the Transylvanian border as quickly as possible. Then, it was on to Budapest, where the Commander had arranged to have a cargo plane waiting. After that, he could relax with a drink and Borge could bore him with a whole lot of technical talk. Despite their different backgrounds and approaches, he had come to appreciate and respect Borge. He was also extremely curious about this latest plan by the Commander.

Off in the distance he could see the coach and wagons lurching nearer and began readying the van for a fast getaway. Borge stopped the wagons near the ambulance and stepped down, greeting Cedric with a smile.

"Good news," said Borge. "We got him just in time and his vitals are holding steady."

"Which one?" Cedric asked.

"West," Borge replied. "Agent Wildebeest is dead, unfortunately."

28

Cedric knew of Wildebeest but did not know him personally. Val West was someone he had worked with on a several missions over the years for International Command. He had heard from others that Thomas Hedison—Agent Wildebeest—was a fine man, but he had hoped if it turned out only one were found alive it would be West. What he was uncertain of, though, was what kind of future Val West would have and maybe he would have been better off not surviving.

Under the dark of night, the cargo plane touched down on a private airstrip outside of London. Soon, Sir Cedric, Dr. Borge, and the capsule containing Val West, arrived at their destination: Swain's Lane in London, home of Highgate Cemetery.

Perched on a hill overlooking London, the old Victorian graveyard, called a 'Victorian Valhalla,' is known for having 'the finest funerary architecture in the country.' Plagued for years by persistent rumors of ghosts and vampires and all other sorts of paranormal activity, the one thing that is true, and not known in the rumor circle, is underneath an unmarked mausoleum lies the location of a secret intelligence base.

Borge and Cedric carefully carted their crated cargo through the older and mostly disused section of the cemetery, past lonely avenues of crypts surrounded by thickets of skeletal trees. Upon reaching the mausoleum, Cedric walked up the crumbling stone steps to the door. Next to the doorway, he flipped open a moss-covered stone decoration concealing a keypad. Cedric paused to look around, and then entered the numbered code. The false entrance doors slid away to the side, revealing the passageway inside.

Dr. Borge waited with the capsule, hoping no adventurous teenagers or would-be ghost hunters would be traipsing through the graveyard this night. Moments later, a nearby crypt and several old headstones disappeared under the ground, the space opening up to reveal a rampway leading down. Cedric drove a small, motorized cart up the

29

ramp. He and Borge placed the crate onto the cart and all three made their way down underneath the cemetery, with the false gravestones cover sliding back into place behind them.

The two long shadows cast by Cedric and Borge descended the sloping labyrinthine tunnel, moving past parts of tree root systems and the occasional neighboring underground burial working its way out. At the bottom, an electric door opened, bringing them into a brightly lit laboratory filled with state-of-the-art equipment and computer systems.

They moved the cart with the capsule containing Val West over to a platform. Dr. Borge removed one end of the crate and the two heaved it upright. The capsule's base locked into the platform and a power source activated, while Borge carefully pried away the rest of the crate. West gently floated in the solution, covered in wires and tubes, all working to keep him alive.

Their work done for the moment, Borge and Cedric sat down in the desk chairs of the large control panel and monitor system, the mainframe of the headquarters. Sir Cedric opened a panel in the wall and a bar top extended out, with glasses, ice, and a selection of very expensive whisky and liqueurs.

"Drink, doctor?" Cedric asked Borge, while tumbling ice cubes into his glass.

"Normally I'd abstain and be highly annoyed that you somehow had this cocktail bar installed without my knowledge, but considering the heavy lifting we just did, I'll take a double."

"That's the spirit! And of what, dear boy?"

"A nice cool glass of potato juice would hit the spot right now."

Cedric shook his head. "It's an insult to put such health-fad rubbish into one of these fine glasses... aside from the type of strong potato juice the Russians make."

"You don't know what you're missing," Borge replied as he took out a can from his stockpile of vegetable juices. "This is far more beneficial."

"That depends on what benefits you are looking for. We did a hell of a job today, so here, make an exception and enjoy this quite ultra-smooth vodka made with hard winter wheat. It is $5,000 a bottle, so please indulge a little."

Borge crinkled up his nose. "I'll stick to wheatgrass, thank you."

Before either could get in a sip of their well-deserved drink, an alert sound came over the combination oscilloscope and amplifier positioned near the control room deck. The amplifier came to life with a hum and the scope waveform began moving in a zigzag pattern. "Good evening, gentlemen," the electronic voice announced. "Pity I can't join you in a drink. Since I can't, let's get right into the debriefing, shall we?"

"It has been an evening indeed, sir," Borge responded. "Cedric and I must be in better shape than we thought, although I'm sure my hump will be feeling it tomorrow."

"And our patient... how is he?" the voice asked.

"He is completely stabilized right now, sir," Borge replied.

"What did the examination scan find?"

"More than a fair number of cuts, bruises, contusions, some broken ribs, and a broken knee... and the two puncture wounds in his right arm. He was hypothermic and unconscious at the time of recovery and is now in an induced stasis until ready for recovery."

"Will you be operating tonight?"

"I wasn't planning to, sir, but I can."

"Yes, do that. And save the drinking for after. That will be all. Good night, gentlemen."

The speaker and oscilloscope screen powered down and Cedric, who was already on his second drink, looked at Borge.

"Clearly he only meant you, but I doubt your choice of beverage will cause any impairment." He poured a second glass of vodka, clinked the two glasses together in a toast and said, "To a damn good job today and to you, doctor," and then drank from both glasses while Borge heaved a sigh and began preparations for a long night.

***

Val West awoke with a start. He felt as if he had been dreaming endlessly or maybe it wasn't very long at all... of floating in the darkness, drifting along peacefully. The thought occurred to him that he might be dead. His blurry eyes only saw a soft, dim light. Once they started to adjust, his vision slowly came into focus, and he lifted his head to look around.

After the grogginess began to clear, he realized he was dressed in a patient gown and was lying on what appeared to be a hospital bed, his body covered in monitoring electrodes. Once he noticed this, he froze his movements. He wasn't sure where he was, but he was almost certain he was alive. The real question was who had found him and were their intentions of hospitalizing him good or bad?

On the surface, most people would think it was a good situation to be in, but his world was different and almost nothing was ever what it seemed. He slowly turned his head to take in his surroundings. It looked like a typical hospital room. He could see words printed in English, although that wasn't sufficient enough evidence to prove he wasn't in a fake English hospital room in a Transylvanian secret service installation.

It all seemed a little off. The room was meant to look as much like a typical hospital room as possible, but it seemed a bit too spare. He felt strange, and assumed he was on some type of pain medication, although he also felt a weird energy he couldn't place. Whatever he was on, it made him feel better than he had felt in a long time. Considering all the connected test leads that were monitoring him, he expected someone would be coming to check on him soon. He would get answers, one way or the other.

Feeling a strange animal-like energy he hadn't felt since he was young, he decided not to wait and began ripping the electrodes off his body. This produced the desired effect and within seconds, he heard footsteps coming toward the room.

Dr. Borge rushed in and was startled to find the bed empty. He found himself quickly being grabbed by the shoulder, whirled around, and pushed on to the bed where Val West stood over him, eyes ablaze.

"Hello, 'doctor.'"

Borge began to sweat and fumbled for words. "Yes, uh, nice to meet you, Mr. West."

West grabbed him by his collar and slightly tightened his grip. "If you don't mind, I'm not so much in the mood for small talk as I am in the mood for answers."

"Okay, just hold on, no need to get nervous," Borge said, regretting he had come to check on West alone.

"It's not nerves, my humpbacked friend," West said through gritted teeth. "In my line of work, I find it advantageous to be distrustful. Now, who are you and where are we?" He noted the doctor's accent was Danish—not easy or even necessary for the Transylvanians to fake. Maybe he was legit.

A voice came from the doorway behind him. "Even though it is now evening, I guess I should say good morning, Mr. West." The voice sounded familiar to West. He turned around slowly to view the speaker. Recognizing the dapper man with the dignified tailored-suit and gleaming white hair as Sir Cedric Kenton, he felt a slight reassurance of the situation.

"Nice to see you again, Cedric. If you don't mind, I would like an explanation before exchanging any more niceties."

"Completely understandable, my good man," Cedric said, trying to calm the situation. "I can give you the briefing details and then I will leave the technical details to our dear friend, Dr. Borge."

West eased up his grip on the terrified Borge and turned toward Cedric, who calmly recounted the details. "We knew you and Agent Wildebeest were in Transylvania, thanks to the efforts of Gypsy. You see, she works for us as well."

"You mean you aren't with International Command?" West asked.

"In a manner of speaking, yes. This is ParaCommand, an overlooked and underfunded division of International Command. It's basically forgotten for the most part, and we like it that way. We—and by 'we,' I mean Dr. Borge—fished you out of the river and together, we brought you here. You've been comatose for nearly a month."

"Under whose orders did you bring me here? What about Major Flanagan and my London station?"

"Yes, we'll get to your former assignment later. As for right now, you are here under the orders of Commander 7."

"As in *the* Commander 7?" West asked, with a certain amount of incredulity. He had, like all other agents, known of Commander 7 and assumed he was long dead or long retired. He wondered why someone of Commander 7's status would be in charge of an operation like this. Of course, Sir Cedric was here, and he was always known to be a very valuable field agent in his time. Even though West still had his natural suspicions, the names of Commander 7 and Sir Cedric Kenton brought a high level of credibility.

"Right then," Cedric continued. "Now, while you were in a comatose state, Dr. Borge was able to examine and observe how your body is reacting."

"Reacting to what?"

Dr. Borge stood up, moved nearer to the two men, and held out a still-trembling hand toward West. "Mr. West—glad to meet you. Dr. Hector Borge, at your service." The two shook hands and Borge turned on a view screen. The screen showed numerous scans of West's body. He zoomed in on a magnified blood sample. "This is your blood type: O-Negative." He then switched the screen to show another sample. "This is your blood type now. The recombinative DNA mutagens have created this alteration, which has produced a synthesized metamorphological state. It is very similar to an unobserved quantum subatomic particle state, with the observation in this case being the introduction of Wave Length Frequencies. These high energy protons produce a photosynthetic effect on the pliable nature of the L-DNA, which your blood is now comprised of. It's very exciting stuff, I must say!"

West stared blankly at Dr. Borge for what seemed like an interminable few seconds. "That's all very scientific and maybe even 'exciting' as you say, but what the hell does it mean, in normal human terms?"

Borge began to explain further but Cedric put a hand up and cut him off. He gently stepped closer to West and looked him straight in the eyes. "It means that normal human terms no longer apply to you. You are now *lupus hominarius*.

In short, my dear fellow: You are a werewolf."

5: CAN'T FIGHT THE MOONLIGHT

During his time in the secret service, Val West thought he had seen and heard it all. With Sir Cedric and Dr. Borge claiming he was now a werewolf, he realized he was wrong. It was an absurd notion, and all of his rational thought told him it was nonsense. What were these two up to, exactly? Were they even who they said they were? Sir Cedric seemed like the same old Cedric he had known and worked with on past missions. West knew of the possibility of very convincing enemy agent impersonators, and in his mind, the possibility just became more likely. The thought crossed his mind that it could still very well be Sir Cedric Kenton, though perhaps captured and brainwashed.

There was also the fact he didn't know this man, Dr. Hector Borge. They also still had not told him where he was, other than what they called a 'ParaCommand station.' He decided to play it cool for the moment and carefully observe his surroundings and the behavior of Cedric and Borge. West had showed no reaction when Cedric had stated he was now a werewolf, and that was by intent. He noticed the looks of concern on both men. They knew they were dealing with a highly trained and highly dangerous man, werewolf or not.

"I'm sorry to blurt it out like that," Cedric said, fidgeting nervously. "It's a strange thing to have to tell someone and I figured you would appreciate the honesty... which, as you know, is not always common in this business."

"Yes, I do appreciate that, even if I don't believe you," West replied. "As far as honesty and transparency go, you could start with telling me exactly where we are and when I can leave." West saw the solemn looks on both men.

"I'm sorry but you will have to stay a while longer," Cedric said. "I know this all must seem highly suspect and quite frankly, crazy. However, the Commander will be speaking to you soon."

Borge cleared his throat and stepped forward. "Mr. West... tonight is a full moon. This is why we chose to bring you out of the coma at this time. I know this is a lot to throw at you, but please, stay in this room. Even if you don't believe us now, even if you don't believe the Commander, once the moon rises you will have no choice but to believe."

Dr. Borge and Sir Cedric left the room, closing the door behind them. West turned over in his mind all the outrageous things he had just heard. The werewolf business was crazy talk. He wasn't sure what to make of it and why they would even claim such a thing.

Even though Commander 7 was supposedly going to explain everything, West wasn't planning to sit around and wait for him. He looked around the hospital room and noticed the space at the top of the walls. Not even a real room, he thought, and looked around for cameras. He found what he was looking for and moved a chair just out range of the camera trained on the bed.

He sat in the chair and scanned the rest of the room. Seeing no other cameras, he slowly eased his arm over to the door. Locked. Not usually a sign of good intentions, he thought to himself. From his seat he was able to open a drawer in the cabinet near him and found a paper clip.

While fashioning the paperclip into a lock pick, he noticed he did feel better than he had in a long time and his bum knee did seem to be much better. Also... no aching shoulder... or elbow... and so on, as he went through the list of chronic aches and pains he knew all too well. From what he was to believe, he was also in a coma for the last few weeks. Maybe the extended rest had something to do with it. He thought that seemed unlikely without a knee replacement, and he also thought he should feel some effects from having been comatose. He left those thoughts, as his lock pick was now ready.

Reaching back while still seated in the chair, West worked the pick and quickly sprung the door lock from the jamb. Slowly and silently, he rose from the chair and flattened himself to the wall. Peeking through the crack of the door, he saw the room was a cordoned off part of a larger laboratory.

Easing out of the doorway, and with no alarms triggered, he began moving along the wall. No one was in the laboratory, and he was able to observe the tall rows of blue metal cases housing panels of switches with countless flashing, blinking lights, alongside waveform monitors displaying ever-changing patterns. Among the rows of machines, electrical laboratory equipment with colored lights shining out through glass globes, crackled, and sparked. The whirring sounds of reel-to-reel tape machines doing computations filled the lab, spitting out tickers of paper with coded symbols of what he supposed was top-secret information.

This was standard in International Command, as well as any legitimate spy agency. These seemingly primitive computing methods were untraceable, with no location tracking or digital paper trail, unlike modern computer systems. No respectable or even semi-respectable intelligence organization used the internet or mobile phones, as they are the most unsecure and easily hacked forms of communication ever devised. They were meant for tracking and spying on average citizens and low-level criminals who thought this was a safe and secure way to store and send communications. West continued to look around and saw there was also a newer than state-of-the-art Q-Wave

Quantum computer. He didn't trust those either, but only because they seemed too powerful and potentially dangerous.

West kept close to the wall as he crept along. He noted there was not a single window, and he assumed this base was underground, but how far? This wasn't his first time being captured and it also wasn't his first time escaping. A corridor branched off to his left. To reach it, he would have to cross an open area in the laboratory, an area with a wall of view screen monitors and what appeared to be a control center. He darted across and into the corridor.

Once inside, he saw it was a tunnel, with exposed packed earth above him. He rushed up a cement ramp and thought this seemed promising as an escape route. Through the darkness of the sparse lighting, he saw what looked like a door up ahead. He ran toward it and an alarm sounded. With a loud click, the door auto locked and behind him, a thick glass barricade came down from the ceiling, trapping him.

The alarm stopped and Sir Cedric and Dr. Borge appeared on the other side of the barricade glass. West flashed his teeth and let out a deep growl. Both men backed away, even though the glass was six inches thick. West found himself backing away as well, surprised at his reaction. It was a strange and a powerful feeling he had never felt before. He ran up the tunnel to try the door anyway, when a static noise came over a speaker mounted near the top of the tunnel wall.

"Mr. West."

Val West stopped and listened to the voice coming through the speaker. It was not coming from either Cedric or Borge.

"I am Commander 7. I regret not being able to be there in person, and this will have to do. I assume you have heard of me."

As Commander 7 was legendary in the espionage world, West felt a little star-struck and stumbled over his next words. "Of course, sir. Your mission files are required reading at the Academy and every agent knows of your work."

"Good. Then hopefully you will believe me, even though we can't give you proof just yet. I know what you're thinking. I've been in these types of situations before as well, and I would also be attempting to escape. Today is October 1st. The sun will set at 7.48 p.m., British Standard Time, and the full moon will rise at 8:04 p.m. It is now 6:40 p.m. Will you at least give us that long to prove we aren't enemy agents trying to play mind games with you?"

West had never met or spoken with Commander 7, but something about the way he spoke felt credible. It was the gut feeling, which, while wholly unscientific, had proven so valuable to him so many times in the past. With a sigh, he answered yes to the Commander. He nodded to Cedric and Borge and the glass barrier drew back into the ceiling. Despite his gut feeling, he still had major reservations and hoped he wasn't making a mistake as the three walked back into the laboratory.

Over the next hour, West paced around the mock-up hospital room, thinking of all that had happened. If he didn't turn into a werewolf when the full moon rose, he had to have a plan. He still couldn't believe he was actually considering the idea of being a werewolf. If he didn't, then he had to assume that Commander 7, Cedric, and Borge were either impostors—perhaps attempting to brainwash him into being an assassin for them—or just plain crazy. In the case of either event, he would be leaving whether they liked it or not.

If this really was Commander 7, then he felt he at least owed it to him to stay another hour or so. Still trying to determine whether he was in actuality a prisoner or not, he noted the cyanide contained in a false tooth had been removed. Oddly enough, a new tooth was in its place. His tongue felt around the tooth. It felt real but had to be some kind of implant.

As the clock ticked closer to sunset, he sat in the examining room chair, filled with nervous energy. Sir Cedric and Dr. Borge entered the room.

"Well, it's getting close to the moment of truth," Borge said.

"I hope it turns out you're lying," West replied. "On the other hand–if you are–know that will mean even more trouble for you than you ever bargained for."

"Val," Sir Cedric chimed in. "We know of your capabilities as a top-level agent and assassin and believe me, we do not want to be on your bad side."

West clenched his teeth and spoke curtly. "Believe me... you're getting dangerously close." He had been trying to keep his cool but found a wild aggression in his words and action, one that he couldn't stop.

Dr. Borge instructed West to lie down on the examining table. After taking his heart rate and blood pressure, he began attaching test leads and other monitoring equipment to him. Borge pushed a button and backed away. Solid steel restraining cuffs sprang from the examining table and wrapped around West's wrists and ankles. He immediately and instinctually fought against them.

"So that's the game, is it?" West barked. "What next, injecting me with drugs to continue the next phase of your brainwashing?"

"Dear fellow," Cedric said calmly. "If we truly had bad intentions, would we have not just killed you when placing you in a coma, or brainwashed you then, when at your weakest? Now you said you would give the Commander this time to prove what we are trying to tell you. It shan't be long now. Please just to try to remain calm."

West shot a frosty glare at both men. Deciding further conversation would not help at this time, they left the room, locking the door behind them. The clock now read 8:00 p.m. and West felt queasy. He would know within minutes if there was any truth to this werewolf story.

Twilight gave way to nightfall and the moon was on the rise. The room West was in also began to rise. The floor beneath him was on a platform and he could hear its hydraulic system turning, raising it up from underground. The lift stopped and he was now in a mausoleum with open-air windows, reinforced by steel bars. He looked out over the cemetery, the details slowly vanishing in the fading embers of sunset. He turned his head and could see the first glimmer of moonlight creeping in from the window on the other side.

The moonlight was now shining on the examining table. West looked at the big, brightly shining satellite and it transfixed him. A hypnotic feeling came over him and he found he could not look away. The sound of his own heartbeat grew louder and louder to him, and he tried to calm himself, using spycraft techniques taught to him long ago. The techniques did not work.

He finally broke his trance to look down and saw his hands were pulsating, the skin rippling. An electric energy coursed through his body in a rush he had never experienced and could not possibly explain. Before his disbelieving eyes, he watched his hands turn into claws growing long, sharp fingernails with hair rapidly covering them. At this point, all the training to stay calm in tense situations, all of the techniques to survive torture—in short, everything he had learned and had experienced to keep his mind sharp in every possible scenario failed him.

The energy flowing through him was a pure, raw, and primal power. He heard a guttural growl come out of him he didn't know he made, and the last thing he thought about was how thrilling the bright moon was as everything went red.

In the control center, Dr. Borge and Sir Cedric watched the transformation over the monitor. They had been prepared for this, but once they saw it happen before their eyes they were never as glad to be watching it on a screen and not in the same room as they were at that moment. The moon continued its triggering effect, and they watched on in astonishment.

West's ears extended and grew pointed, quickly covered by thick brown fur. His face contorted and his nose reshaped into a snout-like appearance, while his eyes had turned golden with blood red pupils under a thick protruding fur-covered brow. The contortions stopped and they could clearly see his shredded clothes were hanging in scraps off the enlarged muscular body, now fully covered in brown-grey wolf fur.

The transformation was now complete, and Val West was now a werewolf.

The werewolf turned to the camera. It snapped its mouth filled with fanged teeth in rage, letting out a horrifying howl that reverberated throughout the graveyard. Both Dr. Borge and Sir Cedric couldn't help but shudder at this thing that seemed so unnatural, yet it was natural... it was *super*natural. The monster raged against its restraints and in the next moment, caused true alarm for Borge and Cedric. They were both awestruck and terrified when they watched the werewolf flex its arms and legs, breaking the heavy steel restraints.

"That was unexpected," Dr. Borge noted.

Cedric furrowed his brow. "Yes—quite. At least the crypt walls are steel reinforced concrete and the rebar on the windows should keep him busy until sunrise."

As soon as Cedric made this observation, the view screen showed the werewolf jumping off the examination table and thrashing about inside the mausoleum. It jumped and grabbed at the window bars, growling and howling with a growing fury. Lunging into the air with a great windup of momentum, it launched itself at the wall. With a great crash, the werewolf erupted through the wall in a cloud of dust and rubble.

"You were saying?" Borge remarked to Cedric as they both rushed to figure out their next move. Cedric grabbed a net-launching gun used for wildlife capture and Borge grabbed a tranquilizer rifle.

"Don't think those will work on this beast, mate," Cedric said.

"These will. I have colloidal silver solution in the darts—different strength levels in each. We just have to hope they will only incapacitate and not kill him."

Cedric and Borge ran down the corridor with their equipment and rushed out to the cemetery grounds.

Running between the tombstones, Borge fumbled with a flashlight, while Cedric reached inside his sport coat, producing a revolver from his shoulder holster. "If your darts don't do the trick, then I'm afraid we'll have to resort to more lethal methods. I had it loaded with silver bullets just for the occasion."

"That will kill him," Borge said. We just want to capture him, remember?"

"I am aware and would be quite disappointed in having to kill Val. But if it comes down to him or us, then I'm afraid it's going to be him. And in that case, you'll just have to try and extract the bullets and see if he revives."

"And you can explain to the Commander why you killed his pet project."

"Now, now, let's just focus on finding him and worry about who is to blame later."

Sir Cedric and Dr. Borge scrambled through the large cemetery grounds, desperately hoping to find the beast before it escaped over the high walls and out into the busy London nightlife.

On the far side of the graveyard, near a winding avenue of mausoleums, a young couple ran along the pathways of the necropolis, giggling as they tripped over crumbling gravestones. This was a common occurrence at Highgate Cemetery on full moon nights. A less common occurrence was that of werewolves prowling the grounds. The young man and woman engaged in passionate—and most likely drunken—kisses, stumbling their way to a flat-topped marble coffin crypt.

With the loud beating of their own hearts, along with heavy breathing, they failed to notice the sounds of other heavy breaths coming from above the tombtop adjacent to them. "You beast," she said in ecstasy as he mock-growled and continued nuzzling her throat. She moaned and turned to look up at the full moon shining brightly down on them. The growling grew louder.

"You animal…"

"That wasn't me, love… I thought it was you… whuh??"

A dark silhouette moved in front of the moonlight, then leapt down at them. Her moan turned into a scream that got caught in her throat. Her scream broke free when they saw the real beast bounding toward them, growling with drool dripping from its shiny white fangs, the red eyes glowing in the shining moonlight.

They both screamed in terror and dismounted the crypt, as well as each other, and stumbled down, attempting to run while still frozen in panic. The beast came at them, and the girl saw the beast's arm raise up with its sharp-clawed fingers, ready to strike. The claws grabbed at her ankle while her boyfriend kept running. She fell onto the ground and the animal licked its lips and went in for her throat.

The girl's screams echoed through the graveyard as she helplessly watched the red eyes and white teeth flash before her face. She continued screaming even as the creature jerked straight up into the air with a cry of pain and fell backwards away from her. She sat on the grass, paralyzed with fear. Two shadowy figures moved toward the beast and in the brilliant light of the moon, she could see the beast was slowly writhing in a net. Her feeling of dread grew as the figures moved closer and she could see they were carrying rifles.

"Sorry about that Miss," Sir Cedric said cheerfully as he walked closer, his features becoming more distinguishable in the moonlight. "Animal Control. Someone lost an unruly German Shepherd, but we've got him under control now." She didn't think this thing had looked like any German Shepherd she had ever seen, or even a wild dog or wolf, for that matter. Dr. Borge checked on the fallen werewolf form of Val West, subdued and quivering under the net. He walked over to the girl and helped her off the ground.

"Now, let's get you out of here," Borge said as the girl blankly nodded. "You do know it's illegal to be in here after hours?" The girl slowly nodded again, and Cedric took her gently by the arm and led her toward the cemetery wall. He helped her up and over the wall, to the streetlit safety of Swain's Lane. "Miss," Cedric said with a smile. "Please be more careful from now on. You may also want to consider dating someone else as well," noting her boyfriend had continued running after reaching the other side of the wall. The dazed girl silently nodded again and slowly made her way down the street, looking over her shoulder until Cedric lost sight of her.

"How's our German Shepherd?" Cedric asked Borge.

"He'll live. The silver darts hurt him, but the levels are only enough to stun him temporarily... which means we better get him back to the lab before the effects wear off."

Borge waited for Cedric to come back with a motorized cart, with the silver tranquilizer gun trained on the prone werewolf—ready in case it were to surprise with its immense power and strength again. The silver tranquilizer held, and they carted the werewolf West back to the ParaCommand laboratory, where they placed him in a cage and hoped to not have to go hunting again that night, no sleep coming for either of them until the first signs of dawn.

6: WOLF IN THE FOLD

Val West was having a hard time remembering the evening before. He remembered the strange, hypnotic beauty of the bright moonlight transfixing him, then his heart racing and a strange panic coming over him. Maybe he had been drugged. He did have a vague recollection of what seemed like a hallucination—his body pulsating and changing, and then...nothing. Now, he found himself confined by chains in a small, windowless room.

West wanted to trust Cedric and Commander 7, if that's who he really was. He wasn't sure about Borge, the hunchback doctor, but in truth, he wasn't ready to trust any of them at this point. There had to be a rational explanation.

Maybe he hit his head during the fall off the cliff, and the head injury was causing concussion delusions. It wasn't post-traumatic stress disorder. All IC agents had been trained to overcome mental weakness, to walk it off and move on. This was different. He was contemplating the situation when the door creaked open. Dr. Borge and Sir Cedric entered.

Cedric walked over to West, and with a weak smile, offered a simple "good morning." West stared back blankly, now having gone back to the methods all IC agents were taught when captured as prisoner. He would offer up nothing until he could find a tactic to either gain more information or buy time for an escape. Still, there were certain little red flags he had been trained to detect when being held in a deceptive captivity situation, and these, both consciously and subconsciously were not there. This werewolf idea was still too much to entertain, but he did feel in his gut he should at least play along and try to unravel what the real game was.

A visibly nervous Dr. Borge turned to West. With West's background as a high-caliber agent, Borge knew he could try an escape attempt at any time, and it could go very badly for all involved. "Please come with us to the control room. We have video footage from last night to show you. Commander 7 will also be joining us remotely."

West nodded with an insincere smile and gestured for the two men to lead the way. He wondered if he should act now and take out both of them but decided to retain his usual gentlemanly facade and watch this footage. He could always kill them afterward if needed. Sir Cedric motioned for West to take a seat near the wall of monitors.

Dr. Borge cleared his throat. "The footage you are about to see is from the cameras placed in the observation room. It was recorded last night at moonrise. Perhaps you will be able to tell us what you remember of the experience."

The video began playing and West saw himself on the examining table with the restraints around his arms and legs. He saw Dr. Borge and Sir Cedric leave the room, followed by his reactions as the moonlight began shining through the barred window. The film footage continued, showing West going from hypnotically enraptured by the bright moonlight, to the horror of realizing his hands were becoming fur-covered claws.

However, it wasn't only in his mind as he remembered it. The video showed the reality of the transformation on the view screen in front of him: His face contorting, the nose becoming a long muzzle for a mouth filled with fangs, the ears elongating into tall sharp points, thick fur growing out of the skin, and the flashing yellow eyes with narrow red vertical slits for pupils.

At the transformation's climax, the monstrous head reared back and let out an inhuman howl that sounded like neither man nor animal. West saw his beastly self-rage and with another great flex, break the restraints, bursting straight through the wall. Could this thing actually be him? The idea was just too strange to accept.

At this point, the video was stopped, and Sir Cedric and Dr. Borge looked to West for a reaction. He remained blank-faced. After a few awkward seconds which felt like minutes, West finally spoke.

"How am I supposed to believe this isn't a doctored video?" West asked.

"My dear boy, we do not have these capabilities," Cedric explained. "This is not a film studio. We aren't NASA. And we certainly aren't spending our time making werewolf pictures, either."

"Then this is obviously some sort of psy-op*," West said.

"We're also not the CIA."

West knew in his heart it was not film special effects and that it was the truth, no matter how bizarre it seemed. At some point while watching the video, it clicked that it was all true. He could feel it inside. It was in the way he couldn't stop himself from staring at the moonlight. The way he knew he really did see his hands transform before his eyes. The way he felt the strange, primal, animal energy overtake his body. He had no doubt.

He was indeed an actual, real-life *lupus hominarius*.

He was a werewolf.

West hesitated, turning away to gather his thoughts before he spoke. "You're right, Cedric. I do apologize—to both of you—and to Commander 7. It wasn't just seeing this video that finally convinced

---

*Psychological Operation. Commonly used by covert intelligence agencies and the mainstream media.-- *Editor.*

me. It's that when I watched it, I felt it… I felt the experience. But how is this at all possible?"

"Well, now," Cedric replied. "This is a lot to lay on anyone, and if you had not expressed doubt, I think I would have expressed doubt about your sanity. Dr. Borge can explain the mechanics of it. As an added bonus, he is promising to explain it in an understandable manner."

Borge ignored the jibe and pulled up various charts and figures on the screens of the control room monitors. "Obviously, being pronounced as a werewolf sounds illogical, so I would like to show you what we know about the science behind it—the science of lycanthropy, which is what werewolfism really is."

Borge continued to fiddle with his presentation materials as he further explained. "Now, the science involved is admittedly narrow as there hasn't been a lot to go on, at least from a laboratory study perspective. I will tell you what we know here at ParaCommand about how it happens and how it fits into what we would call 'werewolf lore.'"

"Before we get into all of this," Cedric said, holding up a glass to West. "You may want to have a glass of this quite excellent brandy."

"I'll pass," West said, and then added, "For now."

"That's a bit out of character for you, but while you keep your mind sharp, I will work on dulling mine," Cedric said, as he poured a second glass for himself.

Normally, West would sit through briefings half glazed over, just waiting for the main details and a point to be made. However, with this particular briefing, he was all ears. Dr. Borge brought up two photos on the monitors. Both were screenshots taken from the video footage of the previous night.

"On this monitor you can see a digital image file of you. Tell me, what is a digital image file made of? By this, I mean your jpgs, pngs, and etcetera."

"I'm sorry... I don't know," West answered. "I'm not a computer science expert by any means, so please explain."

"Right then. In what may be a bit of an oversimplification, all image files are ultimately a combination of binary code: ones and zeroes, arranged in a way that presents the image of you we are seeing. Our bodies, and everything for that matter, are constructed in a similar fashion. By that, I mean we are made of atoms, which are made of electrons, protons, and neutrons. Very basic high school science class stuff I know, but it is important in explaining the shapeshifting aspects of lycanthropy.

"At the most basic vibrational level, our bodies are just a collection of vibrating subatomic particles, arranged in the shape we recognize as human beings. Now, in your case, that of a lycanthrope—also known as a shapeshifter or werewolf—these arrangements shift to a different combination, creating another form, in your instance as that of a wolf-like humanoid creature.

"Getting back to the image file example: On this monitor is an image of you in human form—an arrangement of ones and zeroes that make this an image you recognize as yourself. Using this photo viewer, I will now click to the next image. In this image, you see yourself in werewolf form. This is also, as is the last image, an arrangement of ones and zeroes now arranged to show you as the image of a werewolf. So, just think of these images' binary ones and zeroes as your vibrational cellular compositional structure and you can see how these shapes can shift by simply changing the combination... the vibrational state of the arrangement of the atoms. There's also a quantum level all of this works on, of which I can go into further detail if you would like."

West turned to Cedric. "Pour me a tall glass of that brandy."

"Gentlemen, we are not quite done yet," said Borge. "Now, if I may continue. Werewolves, of course, have long been part of both myth and history. Until you, and of course, whoever bit you in Transylvania, the last credible reports of werewolves were in the 1940s. As the paranormal research and espionage division of International Command, we have investigated any and all reports of werewolves in the hopes of being able to capture one for study to confirm our theories, as well as advance our knowledge.

"I was able to study your physiology and determine there is a lycanthrope mutagen that is transmittable by a type of 'venom' secreted in the werewolf chelicerae—that is, the canine eyeteeth, or fangs. Once this mutagen is transmitted into a living body, it then affects the human DNA by causing a mutation, which allows the combined human vibrational structure to shift its form. This is involuntarily activated by the effects of Wave-Length Frequencies on the altered DNA. What are WLF frequencies, you may ask?"

West did not ask that question, but he did ask Cedric for another brandy.

"WLF frequencies are light frequencies emitted by lunar rays, also known as moonlight," Borge continued. "There may be other triggers, but at this time all we know is that at a certain density level, the WLF rays will cause the shapeshifting to occur, hence the full moon's ability to trigger a lycanthropic transformation due to its high level of WLF rays."

West drank down his glass of brandy. He then asked Dr. Borge what he hoped would have a satisfactory answer. "Is there a cure?"

Borge paused and then carefully chose his reply. "It is theoretically possible. The werewolf venom containing the DNA mutagen could potentially be reverse engineered. But it would need to be from the infecting werewolf, and that werewolf would need to be alive, in order to obtain living venom samples. This, of course, has never been attempted, and is purely speculative."

"If I bring him to you," West asked with a glimmer of hope, "then you can create a cure, yes?"

Borge fidgeted and thought for a moment. "It's not that simple... but yes, again, it is a possibility."

"Then it's settled. I will track this creature down to the ends of the earth if need be. And when I bring it back—alive—you can use it to synthesize a cure, so I can go back to normal."

Borge looked around uneasily, uncertain how to respond. Commander 7 chose that moment to make his presence known as the waveform monitor positioned in the control room lit up and his voice came over the attached speaker.

"Mr. West," the Commander said. "Once your mission is completed, we may be able to make those arrangements."

"My mission?"

"Yes. And after your mission, you may decide you don't want to go back to how you were."

"First off, I haven't agreed to any mission, other than hunting down the werewolf that bit me and getting cured, and then I plan to go back to my missions with International Command."

"That is incorrect," Commander 7 replied. "You work for me now. As far as IC knows, you are working a desk job back in your hometown of Bear Lake, Manitoba, Canada, as part of the IC Northwoods division. Your work reports and whereabouts have all been arranged by me. International Command is such a bureaucratic mess that it will be years, if ever, before they realize not only were you not stationed there, but that the office doesn't actually exist.

"I've wanted a werewolf operative for a long time, which is why I sent Borge and Cedric to Transylvania once I received credible reports of sightings. You just happened to get the luck of the draw by being bitten."

"Bad luck, it would seem."

"Perhaps. Or perhaps not. I will agree to explore having a cure generated for you, should you bring back the werewolf alive. You well know, as a spy for many years, that the odds are greatly against you now when it comes to finally catching a fatal bullet. As a werewolf, you can beat those odds and live a longer life, with better quality.

"Don't tell me you haven't noticed the changes in yourself. How's that knee? Haven't noticed the nagging pain of it have you? That's because after twenty years of bumps, cuts, bruises, lacerations and all of the other physical damage which is part and parcel of being a field agent, you now have the regenerated physical body of approximately twenty-five years of age. I would give everything to be able to have that opportunity again, even with the side effect of being a werewolf."

"It doesn't matter. I'm a man, not a beast and I want a cure," West said to the speaker box standing in for Commander 7. He didn't know if the attached waveform scope was able to see via camera, but he looked straight at it as he made his conditions known. "Once I bring the werewolf back alive and you use it to cure me, then I want to kill it. That's not for me. That's for Wildebeest. For Tom."

"Fair enough then," Commander 7 replied. "The mission, first, which Cedric and Dr. Borge will begin preparing you for."

West bristled at the idea. "How do you prepare for being a werewolf? There's no way to control this," he sighed. "My being a werewolf is of no use to you."

"That is where you are wrong, my dear wolf-man," Cedric said with a slight hiccup. "The good Doctor Borge has created something quite intriguing, which we are all very curious to see in action."

Before West could continue his protest, Borge whirled about the room excitedly. "Yes, indeed! It's come along quite nicely and with

54

the new data from last night's transformation, the calibration should be fairly close to accurate. We will need to do much more testing, of course."

Borge gestured the men toward the mechanics lab, a dingy little area burrowed out of the catacomb walls. The lab was filled with more blinking, whirring machinery, and illuminated by the crackling light of strange electrical devices. In the center of the lab was a standing pedestal, covered by a sheet. Borge walked over to it and pulled it off, revealing a modified suit with wires and electrical leads running through and over it.

The suit itself looked like the sleek, form-fitting standard black International Command spy bodysuit. There were two crisscrossing straps and at their center point, in the middle of the chest, was a v-shaped triangular device, with a pulsating red glow. It had the usual built-in padding and cargo straps on the arms and legs and the suit was topped off with a strange partial helmet atop the display stand's head.

"Mr. West," Dr. Borge said proudly, "This is your new tactical field uniform. With this, we can control you in werewolf form. How, you ask?"

"I didn't, but go ahead," West said.

"Yes, well, because your transformations are triggered by the moonlight, or technically speaking, WLF rays, this suit is designed to, through the use of its neural connector, use stored WLF photons to induce transformation, regardless of a full moon. You can see the veining along the suit, which has lunar crystal injectors to facilitate the process. It can also, depending on the level selected, infuse smaller amounts of WLF, enough to make you transform, but wear off after ten-to-fifteen minutes or so.

"Now, to reverse the transformation, these "arteries" along the suit carry liquid colloidal silver. In the correct amounts, this will keep the WLF rays from being able to trigger a transformation. In the wrong amounts, it is deadly. We will be calibrating these amounts as soon as we begin training.

"You'll find it to be quite comfortable, like a second skin. It's made with a new biosynthetic polymer nanite material and will respond to your body temperature once you've been wearing it for a time. When in regular use, it is, as you see, the standard black. When in werewolf form, it shifts to a red color. Of course, it's all biochemically monitored by an internal computer system. It employs a device called a Chemotrode and is controlled by a neural uplink we call the NeuraComlink, to the ParaCommand satellite, allowing me to view and control you in the field..."

"Whoah, let me stop you right there," West said, glaring at Borge. "What do you mean by allowing you to view and control me in the field?"

Dr. Borge stammered a bit, visibly uncomfortable by the combative tone from West. "Um, yes. This head piece allows me to see through the eyepiece and then control your movements, with this controller."

"That's a video game controller."

"In a sense. It was, but it has been modified to work with this suit and neural controls. At least I think it will work, but we'll know for sure once we test it in the field," he said with a chuckle.

At this, West instantly flew into a fury and grabbed Borge by his neck and pinned him to the wall. With fire in his eyes, West growled at him. "This isn't a game." Cedric grabbed West's arm. West went to strike, then as he turned and looked at Cedric, he regained his composure and released his grip on Borge.

"My apologies, Dr. Borge. My animal instincts appear to have gotten the better of me. But I do want to assure you that this is not a game and I'm not here to just be a pawn for you."

"Understandable, understandable," Borge said, backing away from West before continuing. "I do want you to know, that being a hunchback, I am naturally lousy at hand-to-hand combat, but as a video gamer, I'm quite good and I've won multiple game-playing championships as a legitimate e-sports athlete. So, I do ask you to put your trust in me, if only in that regard."

West rolled his eyes. He pointed to the red glowing triangular chest piece. "Alright. Moving on then, what is this for?"

Borge explained. "That is the heart of the suit, so to speak. It's where the WLF photons are collected from the lunar crystal and then introduced into your system. It's also where the colloidal silver is distributed in the same manner. It is made of quite indestructible metal material we obtained, possibly off-world in origin. When the biometric sensor on the face of the cover is given the code by thumb print it also acts as a kill switch.

"A kill switch?"

"It will inject all of the suit's colloidal silver at once, killing you if you've been compromised."

"Just like the false tooth you used to have with cyanide in it," Cedric interjected.

West felt around in his mouth. "It's gone... and a new tooth has grown in its place."

"To be expected," Borge replied. "Regeneration is part of the metabolic makeup of lycanthropes. Now, before we get started with training, I want to show you this last part, the head piece. Until we get the remote transmitter working properly, for now the head piece connects you to the NeuraComlink satellite uplink system via the jack implanted into the back of your head."

West felt the back of his head and was extremely annoyed when he felt a round metal circle.

"You drilled a hole in my head?"

7: LONEWOLF

An exhausted Val West sat down on his bed in his tiny room at Para-Command base. He had been training for weeks with Dr. Borge controlling him in the suit. Though he was not consciously aware, he did watch the training session videos afterwards and as crazy as it all seemed, it could possibly work.

He had also watched footage from the camera-eye view of Borge using the joystick controller to manipulate his movements. Borge had put him through the paces, making him run, jump, flip, dodge rubber bullets, all with an increasing level of skill and accuracy. He also saw his werewolf-form sprayed with various poison gases, subjected to high volume ultrasonic frequencies, including a high-intensity dog whistle, and all other manner of things he would prefer to never come across in any form.

So much had happened so quickly, and he was only just recently coming to terms with it. Despite his acceptance of the current state of things, he was still as resolute as ever in wanting to be cured. He lay back on the bed and brushed the white lock of hair out of his eyes. Another side effect from his lycanthropy, the streak in the front of his hair was a reminder of all the physical changes he had experienced. As a long-time secret service agent, he understood where Commander 7 was coming from in wanting a werewolf super-agent. He just didn't want it to be him. West was a man and he wanted to remain that way.

He could not deny the effects, however. When he looked at himself in the mirror, the man looking back looked at least ten years earlier. That is, apart from the silver streak in his hair. The feeling of restored youth—no more accumulated aches and pains chipping away at him, the curiously heightened senses even when not in werewolf form—these things all made him consider whether being a werewolf wasn't so bad after all. Ultimately, he always came back to wanting to live and die as a man, not a beast.

A knock and a greeting from Sir Cedric disturbed his thoughts. After the understandable paranoia of his arrival, his cold feelings toward Cedric had returned to the warmth they had shared in years prior, and he welcomed the visit. He trusted Cedric, and over the last few weeks, he had even developed a sense of trust-bordering-on-respect for Dr. Borge. He still didn't know what to think of Commander 7 though, with his only interaction thus far being with a speaker and waveform monitor representing Commander 7's remote involvement.

Cedric entered the room with a bottle of Scotch and soda, and without a word, poured a glass for each of them. Even in an underground secret hideout, Cedric always managed to be dressed as if he was going to a high society soiree. He probably would be going to one of these affairs, perhaps even later that evening. Nevertheless, he would always rather be at the base and involved in the action.

He sat down in a small rickety chair and fixed two glasses, which they raised together in a toast. Tasting the Scotch, West pronounced it near perfect and Cedric agreed. Years ago, when West was a new agent, he was sent to Sir Cedric Kenton, a true expert in the finer things. Cedric was charged with teaching the young agent West how to be a sophisticated man who could hold his own in the best restaurants and casinos in the world, alongside the wealthiest jetsetters that populated them.

Cedric had taken him to fancy dinners, showed him how to walk, how to talk, how to eat, and what was maybe the most important aspect to show you were one of them: how to drink. Now they were sipping very expensive Scotch underneath a cemetery. Added to the fact was West was now a werewolf, and the two men couldn't help but have a laugh.

Cedric shook his head. "It is all a bit barmy, isn't it?"

"It is," West said in between sips. "I still don't think being a werewolf is becoming for a supposed gentleman, even one that's a spy."

"Neither is sleeping with women to gather information or killing whomever you are told to, but we always ignored those pesky little details," Cedric said, holding his glass up to the light, examining the golden caramel color. "The fact is, projecting a classy veneer was always a good way to hide that we are monsters. I suppose it's a bit harder when you're literally sprouting hair and fangs."

"Touché," West said, emptying his glass. "So far, Borge's been doing a good job of teaching an old dog new tricks. A couple more weeks of training and he may have me civilized yet."

"Perhaps... if we had a couple more weeks," Cedric said. He stood up and paced the room. "Commander 7 will be giving a briefing and you're heading out on the first flight tomorrow morning."

"What?" West felt a shock go through him. He thought he still needed more training. Or maybe it was the realization he was hesitant about actually doing this. "Flight to where?"

"That I can't say. Even if I did know, I wouldn't say anything before the Commander did."

"Is he coming here?"

Cedric let out a slight sigh. "No, he never meets in person anymore. But I know what you're thinking: in a business like this, built on deception, how do we know this is actually Commander 7?

"The thought had occurred to me."

"Naturally, as well it should. All I can tell you is, I've known him many years, going back to when he was an agent being sent out to stop global threats, and I can tell you without a shadow of a doubt, he is who he says he is. He is a good spymaster, and if he could, he would still rather be the spy."

"So… he sees me as the opportunity he wished he had."

"Something like that. He, of course, worked for the Admiral, a spymaster's spymaster if there ever was one. So, I assume, now that he is in that role, he thinks it best to approach the job and his agents in a similar manner. Once you can read between the lines of his cold exterior, you know that he cares very deeply about everyone he sends on a mission, knowing he could be sending them to their death. He likes you. I can tell. And I suspect he sees something of his younger self in you."

West knew a compliment when he heard one and the opportunity to serve under Commander 7 was a great honor for any special agent. "Things seem to be getting rotten in International Command these days. For years I served under Mr. Mulvaney and I'm proud to once again work for a real spymaster."

"Try to remember that when he gives you orders you don't like," Cedric said with a chuckle as he finished the rest of his drink. "He'll be calling soon, so we best get to the war room with Borge."

Designed for mission briefings, the war room had a wall made of a bank of monitors, with global maps adorning the surrounding walls. As West and Cedric entered, they found Borge waiting. Before they had a chance to greet each other, the speaker with the waveform monitor atop it crackled to life and tuned in to Commander 7's voice.

"Gentlemen," the amplified voice intoned. "Please, be seated. You are about to be briefed on what is being called *Operation: Wolfbite*. Mr. West, you are now being assigned the official moniker of Code Name: LoneWolf. This is also the operating name for your beastly form—a weapon under the direction of Dr. Borge. I also understand 'Lone Wolf' was your codename in your early days in International Command, and will be quite fitting, as if you complete this mission, you will be the only living werewolf."

"That is," West interjected, "Until I bring in the werewolf that bit me and a cure is generated."

"You keep reiterating that point," Commander 7 responded, the voice becoming lower and firmer. "I do understand, and yes, we will honor this part of the agreement. But for now, you're undivided attention will be appreciated."

West sheepishly looked down, like a school pupil who had just spoken out of turn. The Commander continued the briefing.

"LoneWolf, you will be leaving for Tangier. Travel arrangements have been made and credit cards and other forms of identification have also been prepared for you in your briefing kit."

"With all due respect, sir, I believe Transylvania is where I should be going in order to track down this werewolf."

There was a pause. Commander 7's voice volume rose. "If you were truly being respectful, you would simply say 'yes, sir' and get on with it."

West paused to remind himself of whom he was talking to, and then replied with a simple, "Yes sir."

The Commander continued. "That's more like it. Now, I know why you want to go to Transylvania, but as you can see on this map Dr. Borge was so kind to create, there is a connecting pattern. The trail of reported "animal attacks" with the murdered victims' throats being ripped out, leads from Transylvania to Serbia to Andorra, along with another recent case in Gibraltar which seems to fit the profile.

"Intelligence obtained by Double Agent Gypsy in Transylvania suggests a connection between the gold smuggling case you were originally assigned, and a treasure hunting firm based out of Tangier.

Gypsy sent an unclear photo image taken with her breast-camera of both of the men you described. Dr. Borge has identified the man with curly hair and prominent nose as Burt Digby, proprietor of Dig This Treasure Hunting, Ltd., located in Tangier. The man with the scarred face has not yet turned up in any databases, and the photo image is too unclear to make a match.

"German authorities have an interest in Digby in connection with a rumored illegal dig in the mountains of Wewelsburg, Germany, a little over two months ago. Our intelligence suggests the site you and Wildebeest were investigating in Transylvania was just a gold cache excavation site and there is no reason to assume they would return. I am not ready to make a determination yet, but I believe there to be something more at work than just the smelting and smuggling of Nazi gold… possibly something much worse.

"It won't be long before every international alphabet agency makes the same connection with Digby and the Wewelsburg investigation. You need to be there first. Your flight leaves at 4:00 a.m. Cedric has arranged all of your luggage and travel details. You are to go to Tangier and engage with Burt Digby's firm, find out what they are up to and where they are going. And along the way, you may just find the werewolf that bit you."

West had more to say about the "may" part of finding the werewolf that cursed him but trusting Commander 7's instincts and knowing his role, he managed only to respond with, "Yes sir."

"Now that we understand ourselves, LoneWolf," Commander 7 added, "Both Borge and Cedric will be in contact with you in field once more information is established. And one more thing: Best of luck to you, Val."

And with that, the Commander's waveform monitor powered down and the speaker went silent. West thought to himself how the Commander used his Christian name. He must think more of him than simply a deadly weapon, and that little touch helped him have a little more faith in the mission he was about to undertake.

Knowing he had an early flight and still needed to prepare, West began walking out of the war room only for Borge to stop him.

"Before you leave, Mr. West, there is one more item, one that isn't in with your other travel items." West looked at him curiously. "Because a wolf's sense of smell is known to be roughly one hundred times greater than humans, it stands to reason a werewolf's scenting abilities are similar, or greater. I haven't been able to fully test this yet with you, but I have something that may help keep your cover when tracking this other werewolf."

Borge took out a large tube of lotion. "You will need to apply this to your entire body, at least one every twenty-four hours."

West took the tube and opened the cap, sniffing the contents. "It smells a bit like a cheap musk aftershave."

"Well, yes, I added that into the mixture as an additional cover."

"Why?" West raised an eyebrow. "What are the rest of the ingredients?"

"Oh," Borge squirmed nervously. "Just a mix made from the scent glands of human cadavers, along with some scatological materials."

"I assume you mean— "

"Yes, yes, urine and fecal matter, but it's been highly processed and distilled, along with added extracts of ambrette seed, galbanum and angelica root to give it a rather nice musk scent."

"Rather potent," West said as he turned up his nose. "Like something from an old man's toilet kit."

"Actually," Borge replied, "More like his toilet, to be technically accurate."

West shook his head, pocketed the tube, and gave a slight bow to Borge and Cedric before making his exit.

There would be a lot of preparation before the morning. He had to prepare mentally for this new assignment.

It felt like his first assignment and in many ways, it was, all over again.

8: DIG THIS

It was a muggy, hazy eighty-four degrees when Val West stepped off the jetway in Tangier, Morocco. He was wearing a nicely tailored summer suit (interesting, since he had not had measurements taken while at ParaCommand. He would have to speak with Cedric and Borge about apparently measuring him for suits while unconscious) and didn't exactly mind the change in climate from the damp cold of the English autumn.

Just as with International Command, at least in its better days, everything was prearranged so he could focus on his mission. His clothes, luggage, hotel, identification (several) and finances were all in place and after checking in at the Le Royal El Minzah Hotel, West planned his visit to the office of Dig This Treasure Hunting, Ltd.

Old Tangier is cluttered with claustrophobic cobblestone streets and rows of crumbling dusty shops, with those still in business nearly indistinguishable from those long abandoned. The air of the African midday thickened with humidity and the variety of smells became more pungent. Even more so than in England, West began noticing how much more his senses were developing while in human form.

The first stop at the address he had been given proved fruitless. Upon further inquiry, it turned out Burt Digby had been evicted for non-payment of rent. He continued his search along the streets overlooking the waterfront and finally found what he was looking for. It was a small, rundown building with a faded, hastily attached sign reading Dig This Treasure Hunting, Ltd., written in both English and Moroccan Arabic. As it was still early afternoon, West knew he had plenty of time to take in details. He walked across the street and sat down on a short stone wall, keeping one eye on Digby's office, while pretending to keep the other on the view of the rotting, reeking old fishing docks on the opposite side.

West tried to enjoy the afternoon and ignore the overpowering smell of dead fish. He was curious as to whether it was actually that noticeable or whether it was just his newly enhanced sense of smell. He shrugged and decided it was time to pay a call to Dig This, as there had been no activity since he had arrived.

From the cracked slanted sidewalk, he looked through the dirty front window to see the office appeared to be open, if not exactly welcoming. West opened the heat-swollen door and entered, an old bell on a string clanging to announce his arrival. He thought perhaps that Burt Digby himself would be greeting him. To his surprise, the scent he picked up indicated something else entirely.

While he waited for service, he took in the surroundings. The office was more rundown than he expected, even for someone with as dubious of a reputation as Digby. The flickering shadows of an overtaxed ceiling fan broke up the harsh lighting coming from bare lightbulbs. No security cameras to be found and no evidence of any type of alarm system. He wasn't sure the front door even closed all the way. Important details to know for his planned after-nightfall return visit.

There wasn't much more to note, as the office was barely decorated outside of a couple of moth-eaten worn-out chairs in the open waiting area. West approached the counter along the back wall, hoping to get a glimpse of some paperwork left in the open, and found the source of the curious scent. He knew it well as his experience over the years had landed him in the bed of many a conquest. It was the unmistakable, but now greatly amplified, senses-scrambling scent of a woman.

"Can I help you?" a soft female voice asked from the back room.

"I certainly hope so," West said, craning his neck to find the face behind the voice.

Before she even appeared from the doorway of the back room, the rush of female pheromones overwhelmed his sensitive sense of scent, and he lost his focus. West took a deep breath to compose himself before the woman came out to the front counter. Her scent was a great indicator of her looks. She was blonde, with shoulder length hair, maybe five-foot-six if in heels, and appeared to be in her mid-twenties. She wore a bronze button-down silk blouse tied at the midriff, with denim hotpants. West suddenly felt like he was fourteen again and had to hold his briefcase in front of himself so as to not give too much of himself away.

To his embarrassment, his voice cracked when he began to speak, which he covered by clearing his throat. "I'd like to speak to Mr. Digby about a site I have access to which may contain a quite sizable amount of treasure."

"I'm sorry. Mr. Digby is not here, and he is booked up for quite some time."

"When do you expect him to be back?" West asked, wiping the building perspiration off his forehead.

"I don't know, and we aren't taking on any other jobs at this time." Her practiced politeness went cold. She moved around to the front of the counter and gestured West toward the door.

"But you don't even know what the job is?" he protested. "Are you Mr. Digby's secretary, Miss—"

"Nimble. And I'm not a secretary. I'm a treasure hunter in my own right."

"My apologies... Now that I know your credentials, might you be able to help me with..."

"I can't help you." West noticed her put-on air of authority, which showed some cracks at the seams. "I'm sorry, but you'll have to come back when Burt is here."

"When will that be?"

"I don't know. I'm... I'm sorry."

"Well, I'm sorry, too." West looked her straight in the eyes and she averted his gaze. "Sorry to have bothered you, Miss Nimble." She turned away from him and went back behind the counter.

West bid her good day, then turned and walked out the door. He had seen the slight quiver in her lip, along with the hesitation in her voice. Matched with the language spoken by her eyes, he knew she was playing a part she didn't want to play. There would be a very good chance he could get more out of her on his return visit tomorrow. But tonight, he would be visiting the office again... alone.

A sweltering night fell over Tangier and the busy streets of the old town section of Medina had become quiet. Val West slipped out of his hotel room and navigated the narrow winding alleyways to his destination. He wore his black trench coat over his new spysuit in the thick, sweaty night and was very grateful for the suit's temperature controls. It wasn't exactly the second skin Borge had billed it as, but he was getting used to it.

He ducked into a misty dark alley obscured by humid steam wafting up through the grates. Twisting around a tight corner, West walked out into a small empty lot and almost didn't notice the two young Moroccan men armed with machetes standing before him. Not now, he thought. He needed to get to Digby's office and didn't have time for machete-wielding teenagers trying to act tough.

The toughs leered at West, their blades glistening under the pool of the lone streetlight. West didn't want to deal with this, and decided retreating and losing them in the labyrinth of connected alleyways would be the best option. He turned around to see three others, also dressed in similar street gang fashion, blocking him from going back into the alley. Taking a breath, he scanned the group to decide his strategy. He didn't fear them, especially now that he felt a youthful energy of his own once again. He was more concerned with attracting unwanted attention.

A loud crackle in his ear interrupted his thoughts. A voice transmitted into his ear through the NeuraComlink. "West, I read you!" It was Borge. Before West could respond, the eyepiece of the spysuit deployed, telescoping out and into place over his eye. "Ok, I have visual now."

"Borge, what the hell are you doing?"

The gang members looked on with curiosity as West's temper flared, unsure of who West was speaking with. Keeping an eye on the street gang, he watched as they began flashing the machetes and circling closer. "I was alerted by the NeuraComlink when your heart rate elevated," Borge explained.

"I don't need your help with these punks."

"You don't. But I need the live-action practice."

"Now hold on a sec..." West felt the rush from the surge of WLF photons coursing through his body. The gang members gave confused looks, commenting to each other about what kind of drugs this *Turista americano* was on.

The change came on quick. The spysuit changed from all-black to red and the trench coat ripped apart as West's body grew into the larger, animal muscled LoneWolf. The punks watched in disbelief at what they were seeing. LoneWolf threw his head back with a ferocious growl. Borge focused the view through the eyepiece and readied the controller for action. Before he could turn to face them, the sound of a single machete clattering on the ground was the only evidence the gang was ever there. Borge reached for the deactivation controls and let out a sigh of disappointment.

The transformation back was equally swift, and West jolted back to consciousness with the same feeling as waking suddenly from a dead sleep.

"Not a very tough gang, I'm afraid," Borge said as West reoriented himself. "They ran off before I could even get any practice in."

"That's just too bad, now isn't it? And you can turn off those alerts. Just because my pulse rises a bit doesn't mean I need you in my ear. You also owe me a new coat."

"But I thought you…"

"No. You didn't think, you just acted. I want those damn alerts turned off and how about this: Don't call me, I'll call you. Got it? Good. Over and out."

Borge knew better than to offer a response. In an instant, West heard the hum and crackle of the NeuraComlink go quiet in his ear. He swore a few times to get it out of his system, and then returned to his plan.

After arriving at his destination, West waited for the night to grow quiet again. Satisfied, he chose his moment to slip inside the Dig This Treasure Hunting, Ltd. office. He had cased it from various points of distance earlier in the evening. He did observe the lights go dark but did not see Miss Nimble leave before he went back to his hotel. That meant there must be a rear entrance he could find and enter, which would make this much easier than the planned forcible entry.

Running past dim streetlights, he ducked into a darkened alleyway behind the office building. The level above the office appeared to be unused and abandoned, with missing windows and a general sense of neglect, although he could not be certain as most of the buildings in this block had this appearance.

West crept through the shadows to the back door. He tried to open it gently just in case there was an alarm he hadn't noticed. He gently worked the door handle and thought more about the alarm. If he did manage to trip an alarm, would anyone even respond to it in this neighborhood? It didn't matter, as he could tell the back door was barred from the inside. Looking around, he saw his way in was up—a series of small ledges between each stacked-on story of the crumbling stucco building. It would be a rough climb—tight, with not much grip, but he had made rougher climbs.

The first leap up was much easier than he was expecting, a welcome side effect of his lycanthropy. His body felt enhanced beyond just looking and feeling younger. He negotiated his way to the roof and slipped in through one of the empty open windows. His night vison had also improved considerably. Scanning the open area for the stairway, he found a trapdoor in the floor. Despite his best efforts to move as silently as possible, the warped wooden floors creaked and moaned under his feet.

West slowly opened the trapdoor. There was only blackness, except for the faint slivers of streetlights projecting patterns through the window blinds. He looked around for a ladder and found none, and instead grabbed hold of the trapdoor frame and slowly began lowering himself down. West paused for a moment to prepare for the drop. He knew his feet were only about four feet above the floor level, but he wanted to ensure that his landing was noiseless. His nostrils began to flare as he again picked up the attractive scent of Miss Nimble, apparently still lingering throughout the building.

A beautiful woman's scent always drove him wild, but it was difficult to get used to it being this distracting and disorienting. As much as he appreciated the heightened sense of hormonal intoxication, he would have to speak to Borge about this, although once Borge was able to generate a cure, he wouldn't have to worry about it anymore...

or any of the other changes he had been experiencing and adjusting to for that matter. He positioned his feet to land on the balls and let go.

The scream when he landed was not part of the plan.

West had not landed on the floor as intended, but on a small bed, which collapsed on impact, leaving him laying atop its occupant. His ears heard the clearly female scream at an amplified level, the scent sent his senses awry, and the sensation of danger jolted through him. All of this at once alerted him to the fact he had just landed awkwardly on top of Miss Nimble.

The swooshing sound of an aluminum baseball bat came at him, and he flipped backwards onto the floor, her swing just barely missing. He rolled himself forward with the intent of calming her down, although he wasn't sure how that would be accomplished. The bat bounced off the floor with an echoing clank. West began trying to explain, but stopped once he heard a clicking sound. It was on a trigger, but not of a gun. He ducked and a blast of mace sprayed past his head. It was clear that he could see better in the dark than she could, his entrance notwithstanding.

"Wait! It's not what you think."

"What am I supposed to think, creep? You're here to either rob me or rape me... or both."

"I can explain. Turn on a light and we'll talk." Her fingers fumbled in the darkness for the bedside lamp. Instead, the lights went out for him as the ceramic lamp shattered off the side of his skull.

Val West thought he was good with the opposite sex. He normally was, and he was quite proud of his track record, a statistical tally he kept to himself but was pleased with, nonetheless. Now, as he groggily came to, he wasn't so sure he could either charm or explain his way out of this. He looked around and found he was still lying on the floor, broken lamp pieces all around him. Groaning, he rubbed his aching

74

head and sat up to see where the girl had gone. A harsh light switched on and he turned around to a gun barrel in his nose.

"My, you have quite the arsenal," he said, trying to be both literally and figuratively disarming. "You could have started with the gun and saved us both some trouble."

"It was under my pillow, and I couldn't get to it because some pervert came down from the ceiling and landed on my bed."

"Yes, I hate when that happens." He examined the gun pointed directly in his face. ".38 Colt Police Positive revolver. A classic and an antique at that. I don't think you want to go dirtying it up on me."

"Don't count on that." She pointed to the corner of the room. "Over there. Sit down." West inched his way across the room and plopped down into a soiled old chair. With the lights now on, he could see her makeshift sleeping arrangements in this back room filled with old, dusty junk, along with the remains of her now flattened bed.

She kept the gun trained on him and looked him over. "Oh, it's the Canadian with the 'big treasure scoop'."

"That is true, but how do you know I'm Canadian."

"You don't hide your accent as well as you think. Plus, I once dated a Canadian hockey player, and he was almost as stupid as you are."

"Well, now that's an unfair generalization. I don't even play hockey."

She paused for a moment. This man was abnormally calm and seemed unthreatening. He also had a certain charm, which she found somewhat irritating, especially at this hour. Definitely not your typical Tangier rapist-type. Still, just because he was a smooth operator didn't mean he wasn't trying to lull her into a trap.

"Alright, enough. I want answers," she said, pointing the gun for emphasis. "And if I don't get them, I'll splatter your brains all over the wall."

West craned his head and looked at the stained, peeling dirty wallpaper behind him. "Do you think anyone would notice?" She turned her head to suppress an amused chuckle. In an instant, West grabbed the gun from her hand before she even realized it was missing.

"Ok, now let's do this a bit differently," West said, gun in hand.

Tanya sat down on the edge of the broken bed and sighed. "I knew it was too good to be true to think you might actually be a halfway decent person."

West unloaded the bullets and tossed the revolver to the far side of the room. "I said we were going to do this differently. Now, before I start with who I am, let's hear about who you are."

Confused tears welled up in her eyes. She decided that this man could have already robbed, raped and killed her by now. Her intuition told her he likely wouldn't, but she wasn't sure she could trust it anymore.

She breathed deeply, hoping she wasn't making a mistake. "You already know my name: Nimble. Tanya Nimble. My boyfriend—most likely soon-to-be-ex-boyfriend that is—Burt Digby, owns this business. We're both treasure hunters. I'm also an archaeologist, well almost. I'm really close to getting my Archaeology and Historical Studies degree, and I am a licensed metallurgist, but I really want to be a treasure hunter.

"Burt's the real treasure hunter but I think he's probably better at being a con man. He said he had a big lead and needed me to stay here and mind the office, and that he'd be back in a couple days to get me. Then he called and said it would take longer, but that he had a line on an even bigger treasure site and that we would go to this dig together. I don't know… I just don't think I trust him anymore. I probably never should have."

She looked away, unsure she should be saying any of this, but felt she had to tell somebody. "All this started after he went on a secret dig

76

in Germany. Then, this strange man showed up with him here and Burt wouldn't tell me anything. They took *The Bootylicious*, his treasure hunting vessel, and went off to salvage this treasure the man told him about, and everything's been super weird ever since."

"Tell me more about this man."

"Well... I didn't actually talk to him, except when Burt yelled at me to bring them coffee and the man refused it. Burt never introduced me to him or told me his name. He had a German-sounding accent from what I could tell. But what I remember most is the creepy feeling I got from him. He had these intense, piercing eyes and an ugly scar that ran along the side of his face, all the way down his chin."

"What else do you remember about his appearance?"

"He was clean-shaven, except for a thin mustache. He had dark brown hair, slicked back with a gray or white streak at the temples. His dress style was very dignified, with a black dress suit and a black tie. He wore a white dress shirt, but everything else was black. And he just sat there while Burt made calls and arrangements for their expedition. Burt made me stay out front in the reception area and I couldn't hear much else."

"Any idea where the site is that they went to on *The Bootylicious*?"

"Now hold on... are you some kind of a cop? Why are you after Burt? I knew that treasure story you came in with was bullshit."

"Fair enough on that point. I'm not interested in hiring Burt for a treasure dig. But I am interested in this scar-faced man you told me about. I don't know who he is yet, but I have reason to believe he is part of something Burt doesn't want to be involved in. From what you've told me about him, he seems to be in over his head, whether he realizes it or not."

"Burt isn't a bad man... but he is a something of a sleazebag. And it turns out, his Archaeology degree is bogus, so I have that bone to pick with him as well. As his 'Office Manager,' I've had to pay all the bills, which really means avoiding bill collectors. He's deep in debt and I'm sure he thinks this job will get him back on track."

"Yes, perhaps. Like many people, the lure of a big payday is too powerful to resist and I'm betting this stranger isn't going to hold up his end of the bargain. I've seen too many cases where someone with skills like Burt is used, and when his usefulness is up, he'll be eliminated along with any other evidence tracing back to this scar-faced man."

With that statement, Tanya began bawling hysterically. "All I wanted was to be a treasure hunter and find beautiful antiques and make discoveries and now I'm stuck here in this shithole, with no money and no way out, and now you're going to arrest me as an accomplice, aren't you?"

West moved closer to her and tried to sound as comforting as he could. "Listen. I'm not going to arrest you." He watched as her sobbing slowed and a perfectly formed snot bubble rose and popped from her nostril.

"You're not?"

"For one, I'm not a cop. My name is Val West. I work with an international organization, and I assure you, the scar-faced man is of much more interest than Burt and his office manager."

Tanya flew into a rage and pushed him back, "I'm an archaeologist, almost... not an office manager!"

"My apologies. And I'm sure you were a damn good archaeology student as well."

Tanya blew her nose and tried to collect herself. "Top of my class, University of Ohio. And in the three years since dropping out, thanks to Burt, I've managed to accomplish nothing in the treasure hunting or archaeology fields." Her lip began quivering again, but she held back her tears.

"You've got plenty of time for that later, but we're running out of time right now. I knew about Burt, and you can bet I'm not the only one on the trail. Tangier is about to be crawling with agents from various organizations, if it isn't already. You aren't safe here."

"Yes, it seems just about anybody can come bursting through the ceiling at any time."

"Quite. You can come with me to my hotel and then I'll get you out of here first thing in the morning."

She looked at him with a hint of disgust. "What is this, some kind of line?"

"Yes. A lifeline. You can either take it, and take a chance with me, or stay here and take your chances with the other uninvited guests about to show up. And I can't promise they'll be as gentle or charming as me."

"Well, you haven't killed me yet... although the night isn't over yet. Okay, I'll go.

"I assure you by giving me your help now, you're doing a great service. I need to find out where *The Bootylicious* is. I need to see any files, manifests, anything Burt has that will give me a lead to where they've gone."

"There's nothing here. He took his laptop and a small safe with his files in it. You won't be able to get any marine data either. *The Bootylicious* isn't legally registered. But I have some information that may help."

"Great, let's hear it."

"Only one on condition... that I come with you."

"Tanya, this is very dangerous work, I–"

"I'm going, or no deal. And you wanna talk about dangerous... let me tell you, it's going to be very dangerous for Burt once I get ahold of him."

"Far be it from me then to get in the way of a woman scorned. Okay, let's hear what you've got."

"I'll let you know once we're on the way."

West gritted his teeth as he considered his options. This was the best shot he had at tracking Digby down, whether he liked the idea or not.

He looked at Tanya and smiled, replying with just a hint of insincerity.

"Splendid."

9: ¿Qué pasa ahora?

The following morning Val West and Tanya Nimble went off in pursuit of *The Bootylicious*, captained by Burt Digby and the mysterious scar-faced man. A trained pilot, she had attempted to charter a seaplane but discovered to her embarrassment, but not to her surprise, Digby's credit card was declined. West found a willing renter in one of Tangier's seedier ports and made use of the gold reserves in his ParaCommand-issued briefcase.

A dozen extra gold Krugerrands insured no questions asked, and in West's mind made the plane's return optional. The old Cessna 172 Skyhawk was rickety, and West wondered if it would even make the flight to their destination, let alone return. A little over forty-five minutes later, they were over the Alborean Sea. As it widened into the Balearic Sea, he decided it was time for Tanya to provide a bit clearer direction.

"Ok, Tanya. We've been flying for over an hour, and I think it would be good to know where we are going."

"From what I can tell—and this is only from what I overheard—they are somewhere off the coast of Mallorca."

"You do realize that leaves quite a lot of area to cover."

"I know, but it's all I had." West suppressed a frown as Tanya revealed her less-than-specific information. "That and a call from a bill collector from Alcúdia, looking for payment on some supplies."

"Hmmm. I guess that does narrow it down slightly. We'll dock the plane near Alcúdia and see what we can turn up."

West piloted the Cessna over the soothing blue of the Balearic Sea and began lowering the altitude. The oceanic scent filled the cabin and for a moment, both West and Tanya allowed themselves to feel the luxury of the relaxing atmosphere. It was a place for love, not war, but as always, a sense of inevitable violence was hanging in the air.

West knew this feeling. The strange contrast of the beauty of the exotic destinations his missions sent him, underlined by the creeping death always lurking in the shadow world he inhabited. Tanya did not have this type of experience jading her, and he hoped to leave her safely behind once they reached Alcúdia on Mallorca's northeast coast.

He slowed his approach as the green-topped cliffs of the Spanish island came into view. Tanya looked out the passenger window and marveled at the sight of the boats dotting the Mallorcan coast. When viewed from above, the clearness of the water made the boats appear to be floating in the air over their shadows cast on the sandy ocean floor. West descended toward the Port de Pollenca just north of Alcúdia and brought the plane into the harbor.

The Mediterranean breeze was warm and pleasant, a welcome change from the stifling, claustrophobic heat of Tangier. West found a quaint old hotel not far from the port, but yet far enough off the beaten path. While checking in, he conversed in Spanish to the hotel clerk. To West's slight annoyance and amusement, Tanya objected, also in Spanish, to his taking the Honeymoon Suite, which he took for them anyway.

Before entering into the dangerous territory of tracking down *The Bootylicious*, West and Tanya took the time to enjoy a dinner of Mallorcan cuisine, as well as sampling more than a few glasses of the local Calimandria cocktails. West found her company enjoyable and with

82

the revitalization he was experiencing, he almost felt like they were a young couple on their first date. She was intelligent and also quite a spitfire, he decided. He almost forgot he was on a mission, and that he was also on the clock when it came to his true priority: being cured of lycanthropy. They left the restaurant, for it was time to check in with ParaCommand and then gracefully, and somewhat regrettably, ditch Tanya at the hotel once he had secured a charter boat.

In the suite, West took out a battered suitcase and opened it to reveal an even more battered shortwave radio transmitter given to him by Dr. Borge. He thought a phone call would suffice, but Para-Command had their ways. He uncoiled a shortwave antenna and opened the large French windows to place it on the outside ledge. Tanya was laying down after a glass too many of Calimandria and watched West with curiosity as he connected it to the back of the transmitter.

"What is that thing?"

"It's a transmitter," West replied, over the hum of warming transistors. "I have a call to make."

Tanya sat up and narrowed her eyes at him. "Couldn't you just use the phone?"

"Now darling, in my line of work we don't do that sort of thing... not secure enough."

She thought about it some more. Looking at the beat-up metal box, it all seemed more complicated than it needed to be. "Why not just use the phone, but talk in code?"

"Yes, well..." West paused and looked away. "That's why I'm in intelligence and you are not."

Feeling rebuffed, Tanya turned over and relaxed in the cool breeze coming through the windows. The sound of her light snoring moments later meant West wouldn't need to speak in code to Borge and Cedric after all. He turned a few knobs and with an electric hum, the old transmitter popped and crackled to life.

"Scorpio E-X-1 calling TERMINUS 1234," West repeated over the transmitter microphone several times before he heard a fumbling noise on the other end.

"Allo there!" an overly jubilant voice responded. It was happy hour back in London after all. "How's things in old Tangier? I had quite a few escapades there back in the day, once with this very nubile young double agent with the cover of a contortionist prosti–"

"Cedric, never mind that. I'm in Alcúdia now and working on a lead. It's not much, but it's at least something to go on. Anything developing on your end?"

West heard a garbled sound and a tumbling noise punctuated by a muffled "Give me that! Really!" which sounded like Borge, off-microphone.

"Borge Here. I do have some official information for you, which we picked up from the International Maritime Database. It is unconfirmed, but there was a report of a vessel which could be *The Bootylicious* having made port at least once in Port Hercule, Monaco. It was registered for marine study, with authorization from Corsican authorities."

The microphone was fumbled about again, and Cedric's voice came back over the air.

"I say! Or as I was trying to say before Borge so rudely took the microphone, is that my Mediterranean sources chimed in with some information that the ship in question had been spotted in connection with some known Corsican mobsters, which in his opinion, would be important in moving the Nazi gold bars throughout Europe."

"Yes," West said. "My source thought they were possibly in Alcúdia, and I don't have any reason to think they weren't here or that they couldn't come back. I'm going to be looking for a local charter

84

service to take me around between the eastern tip of Alcúdia over to Monaco and see what we can find, under the guise of a fishing expedition. I'm also leaving the girl—my source, that is—at La Posada Largo in Port de Pollenca. See that she gets safe transport back to Tangier."

The microphone popped and crackled as Cedric explained. "I'm afraid that's not possible. Word's out and it looks like Tangier is hot right now and it's not just the weather. According to local police scanner reports, Digby's office was trashed, thrashed, and burgled this afternoon. Unless that was your doing."

"What kind of animal do you think I am?' West replied.

"Well..."

"Never mind. Don't answer that."

"Animalistic tendencies aside," Cedric continued, "Whoever did this is undoubtedly on to your trail—and the girl's—and you should expect they'll be finding their way to you soon. They could be friend or foe, but you know there aren't many friends in this business. And we certainly don't want whoever your successor is in IC to go cocking things up. What are you going to do about the young lady?"

"I guess I'm going to have to keep her with me for the time being."

"That's too bad for you, old boy. I'm sure you'll find some way to make it work and being cooped up in a hotel in Mallorca... it could be worse."

"Indeed, but unfortunately it will get worse if we don't keep moving. I'll check back in with you as soon as I can."

"About the charter boat, I can get a good contact for you. Check the numbers broadcast on 7205 at 1800 Zulu. Borge and I will make plans to travel to a nearby, but rarely used and unfinished Para-Command cemetery base at Cimetière de l'Est in Nice, some 30 minutes from Monaco. This will be very exciting! I haven't been to the Riviera in quite some time and to this base in particular."

West wished he could share Cedric's happy-go-lucky enthusiasm. He signed off and powered down the transmitter. Over on the bed Tanya was fast asleep, on her side with her back turned to him. He decided to let her sleep after the events of late. This was all matter of course for him, but a completely new world of danger had just thrust itself into her life. He reasoned she would be safe for now, and unless anything turned up in Digby's office to suggest Alcúdia as the next link in the chain, she would be safe for the time being.

1800 Zulu time rolled around, and West walked through the French doors to the balcony of the suite. Twilight was setting in and the night was coming to life as Tanya snored away. He had brought out a portable transistor shortwave radio and set it on the railing. Working the dial, he found the specific frequency: 7205, as relayed by Cedric earlier, and soon a monotone voice began broadcasting, reciting a string of numbers. West wrote the numbers down and then opened the new codebook issued by Borge to decode the sequence. Spelled out was the name CARDONA MALLORCA CHARTERS.

West left the sleeping Tanya and walked the short distance from La Posada Largo to the marina. A sun-faded sign gently swayed in the evening ocean breeze, its peeling letters reading "Cardona Mallorca Charters." A small canopy stood in for an office, and docked next to it was a lone fishing boat. It looked seaworthy, but that was the best he could say about it.

An old man with a well-worn straw hat over his face sat underneath the cover of the canopy. West strolled up to him and greeted him in Catalan with a friendly "bon vespre." The man snorted as he was jarred awake and quickly tried to compose himself. He was a native Mallorcan with a leathery weather-beaten face. "Bon vespre, Senyor." He rubbed the sleep out of his eyes and examined West. "Ah! An Englishman."

"Canadian, actually."

"Molt bé! We don't get many visitors from exotic parts of the world."

West smiled. "I don't know if I'd go as far as to say that."

"It is exotic to someone who has never left Alcúdia! It is a bit warm for you here, no? We don't want you to melt, like a how you say, man of snow?"

"No, we wouldn't want that. What I do want is to rent a boat for an expedition."

"Cardona Charters is the best in Port de Pollenca! You have come to the right place. I am Capità Marco Cardona, of the vessel ¿Qué pasa ahora?, at your service. You don't want the other charters- just a bunch of French frog-eating men who have moved in- they all think they are the next Jacques Cousteau or something. The other locals, they don't know the real good spots like I do. You wish to go out to sea first thing in the morning?

"No. First thing after nightfall."

"A bit unusual. What are you fishing for?"

"I'm not sure yet. But I will once I see it."

"Uh huh. I do not do night charters though. My day rate is just $800 American. We go in morning, catch you big tuna, and you go home happy, sí?"

"I'd like to go tonight." West palmed two of the one-ounce pure gold Krugerrand coins from inside his belt. It was standard issue for IC agents to wear a belt lined with these coins, which usually helped one get what he needed, no matter the country. "Here's payment." West handed the gold coin to the surprised skipper, who promptly took one of the coins, then softly bit it.

"That's some fishing you must want to do, Senyor. What time you want to be leaving?"

"I'll be back as soon as it's dark enough. And the name is Val West.

His eyes brightened. "Ah, sí, Senyor West! I don't know what you think you are going to see in the dark, but you are the customer."

"I don't know either, but let's hope that in this case, the customer is always right."

Captain Cardona pocketed the gold coins and gestured toward the boat. "Let us go aboard and discuss details of your expedition."

West followed Cardona aboard the fifty-foot fishing vessel. Once inside the small cabin, Cardona offered a chair, and he sat in his captain's seat and swiveled to face West. "The Commander contacted me a short time ago to let me know you were coming. A CIA man and the Italian secret service have also been sniffing around lately. They stand out worse than you. Secret agents, hah! Anyway, I won't talk to them and when they come around. I put on the stereotypical Catalan local act. The Commander is different, though. I owe my life to the Commander, going back many moons ago.

"I can take you out near where you're interested, but not too close. That ship, *The Bootylicious*—she's been out there, but not under that name."

"Yes," West replied. "Registered for marine study with the Corsican government."

"In a manner of speaking. There's been Corsican mob vessels coming back and forth through that area. I don't want to be tangling with them if I don't have to. Another skipper I know runs a contraband smuggling ship at night and the Corsicans almost sank him."

"That sounds fine. I have a few things to take care of and there's one other thing: There'll be a passenger—a young lady—coming along, and you'll need to put on your best stereotypical Catalan local act."

"Aww, Jesucrist!"

West gave a grin and a salute to the old skipper and climbed down onto the dock. On the short walk back to the hotel, he thought about the plans for the night. He didn't want to take Tanya, but for her sake the best course of action was to get her to Monaco. Once there, Cedric and Borge could arrange to get her somewhere safe. For now, he would keep her nearby and hoped to keep her out of the way. Maybe, in the best-case scenario, she could prove to be an asset. The stars were starting to shine over Alcúdia as West made his way to the hotel entrance.

It looked like it would be a clear night. Clear enough for fishing... or hunting.

10: BOOTYLICIOUS

At La Posada Largo, Val West walked silently along the hall to his hotel room. Long ago, he had developed the habit of keeping an eye out for anything that may seem even slightly out of place. He was used to being followed and ambushed and he almost felt more suspicious when he was not. Placing an ear to the room door, he customarily listened in for any unusual sounds. The bright waxing gibbous moon was now in the phase between a half moon and full moon, and he could already feel its growing effect. He could smell Tanya's delightful female scent through the door and could easily hear her typing away. Typing away? He burst through the door and saw Tanya sitting cross-legged on the bed, texting on her smartphone.

"What the hell are you doing?"

"Ummm, *texting*."

"I told you not to bring that."

"I had it in airplane mode while we flew over here, what's the big deal?"

With one quick motion, West snatched the phone out of her hand and held it up to her. "This is the problem." He closed his grip around it with such ferocity that pieces and parts popped and flew about the room, the powdered remnants falling from his now open fist. Tanya was both amazed and angered at the display. A touch of fear also crept in, as she would have sworn she saw his eyes flash red for an instant.

"Hey, that has all my contacts!"

"Had. And by bringing your phone after I told you to leave it in Tangier, you may now have a few new contacts just itching to make your acquaintance. A cellphone is the surest way to be tracked by anyone you don't want tracking you. Pack up. Plans have changed and we're leaving tonight."

Tanya glared at West, then stared at the pulverized remnants of her phone with a slight pout. As exciting as it may be, she was starting to think the world of espionage was not for her. Even though she thought West was a handsome man with an exciting life, in this little moment of losing a creature comfort, she realized what a paranoid and stressful life it really was. And as far as she knew, she was only scratching the surface.

Still, it was only her phone, and she was still willing to buck up and see this adventure through. She would get back at Burt, get a share of the treasure he had promised her, and show herself to be a real treasure hunter in the process. Until then, she was determined to stay the course. She thought she trusted West, but she was also realizing more and more that he was a dangerous man—a man who most likely killed people for a living. He did have his opportunity to kill her with her own gun in Tangier and he didn't. That would just have to be good enough for her.

They checked out of the hotel and West told her to wait at the Cardona Charters dock. West pulled in with the Cessna minutes later.

"Què! Cardona squawked as the seaplane floated in towards the pier. West craned his head through the open door and shouted to the annoyed Cardona. "Capità! Slight change of plans. I'll be going on to the mainland straight from our fishing trip and we'll need to tow the Cessna with us."

"Hòstia puta! I don't know that I like this, Senyor West."

"There's an extra coin if you can find it in your heart to warm up to the idea."

"Alright, alright," Cardona said and spat on the ground and set about tying the old seaplane to the stern of the *¿Qué pasa ahora?*. The night was still clear, but growing clouds were beginning to creep in. The moon was also growing and as West stared up at it, he could feel its effects on him, a primal, animal energy percolating inside. Not the intense feeling of when he first transformed during the last full moon, but a growing energy that would soon culminate when the moon was full again, and for the second time in October. A blue moon.

The *¿Qué pasa ahora?* trawled through the calm waters of the Balearic for hours without incident. The moon came out occasionally from behind the clouds, giving the sea a diamond-like shimmer. While Tanya and Cardona chatted away, West scanned through his night vison binoculars, hoping for a sign of *The Bootylicious,* or any lead he could follow. He felt the boat turn and went to the helm to ask Cardona what he was doing.

"Senyor, we not going any further that way."

"Why not? West asked.

"Because that get into dead zone, no good. There's volcanic shoal in these parts and some rocks sticking up that no one wants to hit, especially at night when difficult to see. This area is a no-go for vessels. On top of that, we're getting too close to where that ship's been anchored.

"Well, suffice to say, this spot intrigues me now. Can you get us closer?"

Cardona shook his head and muttered some expletives in Catalanese before answering. West could see the fear in his eyes building like the sweat on his brow. "You know I'd like to help you, but the Corsicans…"

"I understand Capità," West replied. "Just take us in a bit closer to the shoals and then we'll anchor the Cessna and go it ourselves."

Cardona accepted with hesitation and slowly turned the *¿Qué pasa ahora?* back toward the dead zone. West would have to confirm their present coordinates, but he figured they were somewhere halfway between Alcúdia and the French Riviera, with Corsica directly east.

They stopped a few hundred yards away from a small rock outcropping sticking up through the surface. Beyond that, there were more, according to Cardona, and some were just barely below the surface and some only partially above, depending on the tide and sea level. West would anchor the Cessna here and they would have to swim the rest of the way in. He knew he wouldn't be able to convince Tanya to stay in the plane, so he figured at least he was swimming with the buddy system, if nothing else.

They said their goodbyes to Cardona, West tipped him with the promised extra gold coin, and they were on their own. He explained to her there was a homing device he had placed in the plane and one for each of them in their diving gear to help them find their way back to the Cessna.

West was relieved to find out Tanya had scuba diving experience. Once they were geared up, he took the two submersible aquajets he had bought in Tangier and showed Tanya how to operate it. With the aquajets, they would be able to move with speed and stealth underwater until reaching the rock shoals, where they would plan out the next route. Moving just below the surface of the sea, they swam past the inhabitants of the nocturnal aquatic world, visible under the silvery glow of the moon.

They came up to the rock, and upon closer inspection the outcropping's top was approximately twenty feet in length and some ten to twelve feet in width. It rose up about five feet out of the water and was just big enough for West and Tanya to grab a hold and get their bearings. West climbed up on the still sun-warmed rock surface and took his night vision binoculars from his belt bag. He scanned around the periphery, and something caught his eye. He could see a form— possibly a craft, possibly *The Bootylicious*—another thousand yards or so beyond.

West explained to Tanya how the scrambled-channel earpiece comlinks he brought with worked, so they could communicate in an emergency while he did reconnaissance closer to the craft. She reluctantly agreed to stay at the rock and wait for West to return.

He swam for what seemed about five hundred yards and then surfaced to check his surroundings. He could now clearly see the craft, which was now approximately three hundred yards away. To his surprise, as the moon grew closer to full, his animal nocturnal vision improved, and he didn't need to use the night vision on his binoculars. The ship looked to be about a 150-foot motor yacht, outfitted as a marine research vessel, which fit the description of *The Bootylicious*.

Diving down, he made sure to descend to a level that would not produce any surface rippling and cautiously made his way closer to the ship. He took extra care to look for limpet mines or any other deterrents put in place to keep out potential intruders. With his enhanced night vision, the view of the sea life inhabiting the reef was unlike any he had ever experienced. He had swum underwater at night many times, but even with artificial night vision, it had never been this vibrant and alive, with every nook and cranny of the reef rocks teeming with life.

Swimming through the sharp, cavernous reef up ahead the ship's hull came into view. He floated up to the hull and carefully placed a small tracking device on the underside, muffling the sound with his hand to prevent underwater echo as the magnet attached. With deliberate slowness, he moved over to the anchor line and glided up alongside it.

Upon surfacing, he paused to observe. The yacht seemed very quiet, and he wondered where all of the crew could possibly be. He shimmied up the anchor line to the edge of the stern. Before pulling himself up, he heard footsteps coming from around port side. The footsteps drew nearer, and he pulled himself as close to the hull as he could. The footsteps soon faded into the distance. It looked like it was just one guard, and it would be a minute or two before he made his way back again.

Removing his flippers and attaching them to his tactical belt, he moved in silence over the side, narrowly missing a second guard coming around the corner on his watch rotation. Leaping quickly into the shadows, West flattened himself to the wall as the oblivious crewman walked around the deck.

Once inside *The Bootylicious*, West found the vessel nearly empty, save the two crewmen keeping watch on deck. Peering through a porthole, he saw two speedboats moored near the ship. He wasn't sure if the crew had gone onshore for the night, but he was almost certain they weren't aboard. The interior of the old and well-worn vessel was dark, but he could see the scuffed woodwork and exposed wiring of the patched-together ship, with some recent hastily added upgrades. He crept along the corridor, checking the cabins until he found what he was looking for: the office cabin.

In the center of the room there was a large wooden desk covered in clutter. On it was what he hoped would give a clearer picture of what Digby and the scar-faced man were up to: a battered laptop computer he assumed belonged to Burt Digby. West paused to listen for any guards, then resumed by opening his waterproof belt pouch to remove a standard-issue, yet specialized, hard drive scanner. He attached the scanner to the back of the open laptop and began copying the computer's files. Tacked to the wall near the desk were some maps that caught West's eye.

Looking closer, he saw the maps were not oceanographic and not actual maps at all, but hand drawn diagrams. The only markings were what looked to be routes, except one locator labelled 'Waldenburg.' The scanner was still working away when West heard a noise along the cabin corridor. The sound of footsteps and voices followed quickly. He saw the shadows as they approached the office door. With no other option, he grabbed the laptop scanner and ducked under the desk.

The sound of a voice speaking in a thick Australian accent was heard conversing with another crew member. The owner of the voice then entered the office and turned on the lights. West tightened up as compactly as he could get. He peered through the small crack where the desk joined and saw the voice belonged to a scrawny curly-haired man with a bulbous nose: Burt Digby. Digby held a walkie-talkie and began speaking into it loudly.

"Nah yeah, the Corsicans are all set now," Digby said.

"Then we should plan to move," the gravelly voice on the other end replied. "Ferenc and his men need to be in position."

Digby dropped the pen he was twirling and reached down to get it. West kept as still as he could. "We can keep the Corsican crew on the payroll a little longer and keep going for the next couple of days. No one's on to us yet." Digby continued his conversation while his hand fumbled under the desk for the pen. West saw Digby moving his body so he could look under the desk. He saw the pen had rolled near his foot and nudged it toward Digby's groping hand. Digby sat back upright with pen in hand.

"We can still get the rest out, we got time," Digby protested.

"Nein. We are already behind schedule," the man barked, "but Ferenc cannot be. Confirm with him that his team will be ready for Dittersbach."

Digby sighed and responded with, "Yes, sir. Roger that. It'll be right. I'll get ahold of him as soon as we have proper signal."

West heard Digby curse under his breath and get up from the desk. Even from his current position, he knew he could smash Digby and by extension, this whole operation. He might have done that at one time, but there was more at stake now. He had to know what they were doing. It was clear they were smuggling the Nazi Wolfsangel gold bars with help of Corsican gangsters, but why the sudden hurry? What did the hand-drawn maps mean and who was Dittersbach?

Digby fiddled with an old Transylvanian Navy field phone and after failing to get the reception needed to call Ferenc, cursed a little more. He put the phone down and started walking out of the room. At that moment, Tanya decided to contact West and his comlink let out a burst of static. West twisted his hand up to his earpiece and muffled the sound as best he could.

Pausing in midstride, Digby slowly walked back to the desk. He picked up the field phone and put it up to his ear. He gave a couple "Allo, allo's" and then set it back in its charging receiver. He blurted out, "Transylvanian f---king rubbish," to no one in particular, especially to the audience he didn't even realize he had, and then walked out of the office, shutting off the light. West allowed himself to breathe, before unknotting himself from his cramped spot under the desk. He clicked on the comlink.

"Tanya, what is it?"

"I don't know exactly but come back as soon as you can. You gotta see this."

11: IN THE GROTTO

After making sure all was clear, Val West took out his miniature camera and quickly snapped photos of the route plans pinned on the office wall while he finished the laptop scan. He moved over to the office door and heard Digby talking loudly from somewhere above deck. West had all he needed and decided to take the opportunity to leave while everyone was focused on what Digby was saying. From what he could discern, they were near port side, so he made his way along the starboard decking.

As it was too close to port, climbing back down the mooring line was out. West slowly lowered himself over the edge, straightened himself and dropped down into the water. He soon found his way back to the rocky outcropping and surfaced a few feet away.

Tanya called to him from atop the rock. "Val, come over here quickly. Climb up and check this out."

He followed her up the rock to a narrow, jagged crack running along a section on its top peak. "Listen," she said, and motioned for him to put his ear next to the fissure. He listened and could hear sounds below. Unnatural sounds, like those of mechanical equipment, along with muffled voices. To him it sounded like a construction site, coming from somewhere inside the rock. "Let's dive down and see where this sound is coming from, shall we?"

They held themselves against the surface of the shoal and moved downward. The brilliant moonlight was shining without cloud cover, and they could see the small, rocky outcropping was part of a much larger rock formation underneath. Diving deeper, they reached a depth of nearly eighteen meters to the ocean floor and found a large opening in the base of the rock.

The piles of rock rubble around the edges of the opening showed it had been recently excavated. West swam into the open mouth of what opened into a cave tunnel. He quickly pushed Tanya backwards and pulled her behind the rocks and debris. She was about to ask him what he was doing, when light beams pierced the darkness of the cave mouth. It was the headlights of an underwater sled, accompanied by divers. The sled moved by and attached to it was another sled with lifting balloons attached. Even in the dark of night and viewed in the murkiness of the depths, the moonlight bounced off the cargo in a shiny light... a shiny, gold-colored light.

So that was the game, West thought to himself. The gold was some-where in this cave, and it had been painstakingly removed through this tunnel, moving it underwater to *The Bootylicious's* mooring point and then distributing it to the Corsicans and whoever else was involved in this operation. Moved in small amounts at a time, they wouldn't draw the attention they would bringing it up to the surface. Depending on how much gold was in there, it made sense that they would have been working at it for the last two months.

Once the sled was out of sight, they swam back into the opening of the tunnel. West shined the flashlight carefully, hoping not to be seen by any others still inside. They moved through the twisting reef and rock of the tunnel, swarmed by thousands of small fish. Following the tunnel's snaking route, West examined the walls and could see that pieces had collapsed, and that it was once much wider.

West and Tanya wove through stalactites and stalagmites poking out from above and below, and then the tunnel became wider. It angled downward and they continued following its path. Up ahead, a faint light shined down into the water. They followed it up to the surface, where the tunnel led into a grotto pool. The inner surface of the hollow volcanic rock formation angled upward, creating a small beach. On the edge farthest from them, illuminated by a series of work lights, were men clad in wetsuits. West was trying to get a glimpse of what they were doing but couldn't from his present position. He looked over at Tanya and hoped she could handle what he was about to ask. "I'm going to need to get closer. At the speed they were going, the sled won't be coming back for at least another twenty minutes or so. You go back up to the surface and wait for me next to the shoal."

Tanya shivered. It was either from the cool water, the idea of going back up by herself and most likely a combination of both. "But..." She had started to speak but saw the look in West's eyes meant there was no room for argument.

"Go now. If I'm not back in ten minutes, get to the Cessna and get the hell out of here." She reluctantly replaced the regulator of her scuba mouthpiece and swam away toward the tunnel.

West moved along the edge of the cave wall until he found a partially submerged rock formation to hide behind. From there, he had a full view of the shore and the workers. To his surprise, he saw the salt-encrusted rusty remains of a World War II German U-Boat, peeled open like a sardine can gone wrong.

The workers were carrying out gold bars and placing them on to another sled. The large XB series U-Boat could have carried at least twenty tons of Wolfsangel mark Nazi gold bars worth billions. There were only a few stacks of bars left to be loaded, but he could see from the amount of movement and tracks on the grotto's beach, they must have made dozens of hauls over the last month or so, confirming the time-consuming nature of this operation.

And there among the workers, clad in a black diving suit, was the scar-faced man.

West half expected to see him, and when he did, he felt his pulse rise unexpectedly. Next to scar-face was another figure also clad in a black wetsuit... but with the head of a wolf. He strained his eyes to verify, but there was no doubt. This had to be the werewolf that killed Wildebeest and bit him in Transylvania, and this scar-faced man had it under his control. West was also puzzled how this werewolf could be in werewolf form, with so little WLF rays from the scant moonlight shining into the grotto. Could it be that lycanthropy was able to be induced by command? His thoughts were interrupted when he noticed the werewolf sniffing the air and making whining noises.

"You smell something, Húnd?" asked the scar-faced man. The werewolf stood there with its tongue hanging out, breathing rapidly and continuing to whimper. The man put a pair of goggles and respirator on the werewolf, then patted it on the head. "Follow." The werewolf tilted its head, listening. "And bring him back to me."

West couldn't make out the conversation between the man and beast but thought about the possibilities of what he had discovered. Outnumbered as he was, he could try to stop the entire operation at this moment and contain it to the grotto. He could then bring the werewolf back to Borge to generate a cure. It was a big chance to take, and one that could easily end up in failure.

It was also possible that this "henchwolf" might be able to detect him due to the heightened lycanthropic night vision and scenting ability. He was also outgunned. The only weapon he was carrying was his brand-new H&K MK23 .45 caliber semi-automatic handgun with silencer, issued to him by Dr. Borge and good for firing both in and out of water. But it didn't have silver bullets and the henchwolf wouldn't be incapacitated by lead alone. He knew the better option was to get out while he was still undetected and make plans with Commander 7 on the next move. This discovery, along with the data obtained from

The Bootylicious may point to where they were going next. He decided patience would be the better virtue and swam back into the tunnel.

The scar-faced man watched the werewolf slide into the waters of the grotto and paddle towards the tunnel. He switched on his walkie-talkie and ordered Digby to get the speedboat ready on standby.

West swam quickly through the cave tunnel with only the silver moonlight pouring in from the mouth for illumination. He powered his way up and grasped the rocky ledge of the outcropping, relieved to find only Tanya waiting for him. He shushed her before she could speak and looked around for a sign of the henchwolf but saw nothing.

Satisfied they had not been seen, they dropped back into the water, using the aquajets to quickly get back to the Cessna. West hurriedly pulled up anchor and started the plane, keeping the landing lights doused. As the plane started, he heard a thumping noise and the plane lurched slightly. He wasn't sure what it was, but it wasn't a bullet hit—possibly some wave chop? No matter what it was, he wasn't staying to find out and sped along the sea for as long as he could before taking off into the air and even then, holding off on turning on the lights until they were a good distance away.

Now, with some information to work with, he decided to contact ParaCommand. Tanya took over the controls and West flipped open a hidden dash panel containing a telegraph key. He powered it up and began tapping out a coded message through the pulses of radio waves to Dr. Borge and Cedric. After a few moments it was received and rather than try to describe everything in coded messaging, West asked Borge to call in via his implanted NeuraComlink.

The sounds of tuning frequencies and static filled his ear and in moments, Borge was speaking directly into his head. "We shouldn't use this method unless necessary. The neural connection could weaken over time," Borge said.

"The last time you used this connection, you contacted me over a raised heart rate. And I did say, 'Don't call me, I'll call you. Are Commander 7 and Cedric able to listen in?'"

Borge ignored the jibes and went to work with the control system that was causing him a bit of trouble. "I'm patching the Commander in right now, although my systems here have a few bugs to work out. We're set up at the base in Cimetière du Château, in Nice, and Cedric is in Monte Carlo at the moment.

"He has a suite reserved for you at Hotel de Paris Monte-Carlo. You're to meet him at the Casino de Monte-Carlo, where he'll be playing a little Chemin de fer. I'll be staying here. Isn't that fun? Cedric also said to let you know evening dress has been sent to the hotel for both you and the girl. He hopes she will like the selections and that he's never guessed wrong on a lady's size. He says it's a psychic power of sorts."

West smiled at Cedric's efficiency in obtaining the mostly underappreciated, though necessary, equipment needed to be convincing in a spy operation: style and fashion. "Splendid. We'll be landing at the Port Hercule Marina shortly and will check in with him at the casino as soon as we can."

West relayed the rest of what he had found, including the references to "Waldenburg" and "Dittersbach." The names did not mean anything to Borge or Commander 7 at mention. They would have to see what they could turn up in the ParaCommand files. If the intelligence he had just gathered yielded no clues as to where scar-face and Digby would be going next, he suggested perhaps the Corsican underworld could provide some answers. Commander 7 replied that Cedric was already on top of it, and would no doubt have some leads by the time they met in Monte Carlo.

West signed off and wondered about the drag on the plane. It seemed off, but it was an old plane and at this point he just hoped it would hold together long enough to get to Monaco. They were flying at top speed and would be landing at Port Hercule in another twenty minutes or so. With Tanya at the controls and with the satisfaction of successfully getting away from an intense spying operation unseen, he allowed himself to momentarily drift off to the steady sound of the old Cessna 172. As he dozed, the image of the hench-werewolf filled his dreams, ensuring his short break was restless.

West awoke as Tanya started the descent. They were just touching down on the water when he heard another loud thump and the plane rattled, jarring him further awake. He looked over at Tanya. She was fine and so were the controls. Strange bit of turbulence, he thought as they coasted into the piers at Port Hercule Marina.

He took the controls, piloting the Cessna into a pier opening, where an attendant came out to moor the plane for them. On the pier, Tanya marveled at the beauty of the lights of Monaco and Monte Carlo beaming from up in the hills and repeated in reflections on the bay. The attendant explained that he had been sent by one Sir Cedric Kenton and took their luggage, gesturing toward a car waiting to bring them to the Hotel de Paris Monte-Carlo. As they left the pier, West looked back at the plane, noticing what looked like long scratches running along the side of the plane. They weren't there before.

Following the attendant, both West and Tanya were looking forward to a hot shower and clean clothes. It was already late at night, by the time they sped off in the car, but time didn't exist at the Casino de Monte-Carlo. West needed a plan and knew he was stuck for one. Even though he generally despised casinos, he knew it was the best place to be if he and Cedric were to connect some dots and decide on a strategy.

At the pier where the Cessna was docked, a black wet-suited figure arose from the water and leaped up onto the shore. Shaking violently, water flew off of what was a larger-than-human-sized wolf's head, eyes blazing, drool dripping from its gleaming fangs.

12: CASINO BATTLE ROYALE

Tanya could hardly believe the grandeur surrounding her in the luxurious suite Cedric booked for at the Hotel de Paris Monte-Carlo. A traditional grand hotel built in 1864, the Hotel de Paris Monte-Carlo, with its perfectly planted palm trees, fountains, and classic Belle Epoque architecture seemed like a something out of a storybook fantasy to her. Adding to the opulence, she and Val West enjoyed a gourmet meal delivered by room service. At least hers was, with filet mignon as the main course. West had only wanted a raw steak, which he wolfed down, displaying less gentlemanly manners than he had to date.

Sir Cedric had been dead-on in his sizing and had generously provided numerous choices for her evening wear. She was now in a very expensive and elegant black evening gown with gold sequin flourishes. Prior to this, the fanciest she had ever dressed was for her high school prom back in Cleveland. Now she was feeling how far away from that life she actually was.

While West was in the shower, she thought of all that had transpired in such a short amount of time. The thrill of adventure she could feel coursing through her was the thrill she had hoped to find with treasure hunting... with Burt. Still, there was an unsettling air of danger running through it all like a chill breeze interrupting a comfortably warm afternoon. She poured herself another glass of the complimentary champagne and tried to take her mind off it. West appeared from the adjoining bedroom, looking resplendent in a white tuxedo jacket with black trousers.

He was finishing tying his bowtie (he didn't even need to use a mirror, Tanya gushed to herself) and she couldn't help thinking how well he cleaned up. Perhaps it was the champagne doing the thinking, perhaps not. West was thinking the blasted spysuit he had to wear was a bit ill-fitting underneath the tuxedo, and again proving to not be the second skin that Dr. Borge had advertised it as.

"Miss Nimble," West said, looking her over, "you look quite fetching this evening."

"You look almost respectable yourself this evening, Mr. West... it also happens to be nearly 1:00 a.m."

"The night is still young and so are we."

She paused and narrowed her eyes at him. "Just how old are you anyway?"

"How old do you think I am?"

Tanya thought for a moment. "I'm going with thirty-two."

West was amused, especially with his forty-fifth birthday coming up. "Very close, darling. In fact, I don't feel a day over twenty-nine." He turned and looked her in the eyes. "And you're twenty-seven as of last month. Happy belated birthday."

"How did you know that?" Tanya asked him, curious as to what else he knew of her.

"Part deduction from what you had already told me, part reliable sources. Now, while the night is still as reasonably young as we are, shall we make our way to the casino?"

Tanya took hold of his arm, and they walked through the grand lobby of the hotel, past its marble colonnades and crystal chandeliers to the stairway, which in just a few steps, brought them to the legendary Casino de Monte-Carlo.

Even at this hour, the casino was still busy. The patrons never worried about running out of time, just money. The true high society, high style, high rollers never ran out of either and somewhere in this mix of jetsetters of all nationalities, all dressed in their best formal evening wear, was Sir Cedric Kenton. He was one of them, born into it as a true aristocrat… yet he was not, with his double-life in the espionage game.

The Casino de Monte-Carlo is perhaps the most famous casino in the world. West had little use for gambling in his personal life, but he had been here many times in a professional capacity and knew if information was needed, some of the most powerful and connected people could always be found here. Not that they were all criminals—although some certainly were—but the scent of crime would always be lingering nearby.

Tanya took in the atmosphere of grand décor, feeling quite glamorous and a little less self-conscious with each sip of champagne. She gazed at the marble-and-gold interiors with their ornate engravings and up at the exquisite stained-glass skylights throughout. "Try not to look like a tourist," she continually reminded herself.

They wound their way through the exclusive rooms of the casino and found Sir Cedric standing near a baccarat table. He looked to be having quite a night, looking even more elegant than usual, wearing a very fashionable red velvet Bottega Veneta tuxedo jacket with jet black pants, festooned with two ladies draped over each arm, and topped off with a dignified silver-headed cane.

"Val!" Cedric said, a touch too loud, "Come over and meet my special ladies."

The two women gave a reserved giggle, which would have been more forceful if not for the years of etiquette which was second nature in their level of breeding. "May I present Dame Hancock and Lady

Birnamwood. Dame Hancock's mother was a teacher of mine back at Eton."

"She was a classmate, you cad," Dame Hancock zinged back at Cedric. West formally kissed each of their hands in introduction as both eyed him up like cats waiting for treats. Tanya eyed them up like a cat looking for a fight. By his estimation, Dame Hancock was about fifty years old, but was aging well. Lady Birnamwood looked even younger—perhaps late thirties. Definitely two feathers in the cap of Cedric, who was certainly not slowing down even in his mid-seventies.

"Dearest Tanya," Cedric said, clasping her hand and giving it a delicate kiss. "I do hope you found the selections for this evening to your liking." Tanya blushed a little and answered that everything had been impeccable. "My dear ladies," Cedric continued, "Please excuse Mr. West and me for a few moments... distinguished gentleman talk." The two women eyed up Tanya with more ice than they had in their drink glasses.

"My dear boy," Cedric said as they walked over to the bar. "It seems Her Ladyship has received a very interesting proposition, and not even from me. A true rotter and scalawag has made an offer to her on some gold bars it would seem. Quite collectible, these are, and with a most peculiar mark."

"And who is the seller with this remarkable opportunity?"

"Do you see the rather portly bald gentleman over at the baccarat table? The one with the divot in his forehead, who thinks he needs to wear his sunglasses inside, and at night, and smokes rather rank Albanian cigars?" West took a drink and casually turned his head toward the baccarat table. "That's Antoine, pronounced 'An-Twine' Lavu, a Corsican 'businessman,' shall we say, and little brother to the Corsican capo, Petru 'Big Ass' Lavu. In less formal circumstances, he is known as 'Twiney the Bitch.' I assume that's how the scarred divot came to be on his forehead. Snitches and bitches and stitches and all that. Despite being fairly low-level, due to his brother, he is still very well-connected, and the lack of skill he displays at Chemin de fer would also explain why he needs to raise some capital." He held up a lock pick. "I took the liberty of reserving a private room for 'negotiations.'"

"Splendid. You get him to the room, and we'll have a little talk with Twiney. This would be a good time to find out if he's still a bitch or if he just looks like one."

"Quite. In the meantime, what are your plans with Miss Nimble?"

"Once we're done here," West said, "I'll get her back to the hotel where she'll be safe… from you as well."

"Oh, come now, old cock. But yes, business first. You know, I haven't been here in quite some time, but it didn't take long to find some ladies with loose lips."

West slapped Cedric on the back. "Your reputation precedes itself, Cedric. Shall we invite Mr. Lavu for a private game of chance?"

***

Antoine "Twiney the Bitch" Lavu was busted. Flat broke. Being he would not be able to get back in for the next round of play, Cedric's invitation to a private baccarat game was rather timely. He did not have the funds yet, but these private game suckers didn't know that, and he was planning to leave with their money whether he won or not. Lavu followed Cedric to a private gaming room in the exclusive area of the casino. They entered the room to find Val West seated behind a game table. Lavu's ever-present paranoia set in when he looked around the room, and noticed there was no dealer present. Sweat began trickling down his round cheeks.

"Good evening, Twiney," West said with a welcoming grin. "We're so glad you could join us. After all, it isn't often we get to play with a man of your stature and distinction."

"Yeah?" Lavu asked, unsure if this was a put on or not. "Depends on what the game is. Enough of the small talk. We gonna gamble or you just gonna play with yourselves?"

"The gamble is yours," West replied, "However; we are playing a different game, one that involves gold bars. The kind with little Nazi symbols on them."

"I don't know nuthin' about that." Lavu turned to leave the room. Cedric moved toward the door, while West called him back over to the table and gestured to take a chair, which Lavu took with hesitation.

"We're just looking for some information," said West. "And we are willing to pay for it. How does that sound?"

"It sounds like bullshit. Why should I tell you anything? Go f---"

"Tsk tsk, Twiney," West said, leaning closer, "It's been a very long day and I'd rather not be at this the rest of the night." He sent a straight-knuckled jab into Lavu's face striking him hard right above the eyes. The scar tissue on his forehead divot broke open and blood began running into his eyes. The force of the punch sent Lavu falling backwards in his chair to the floor, where Cedric quickly grabbed the handgun out of Lavu's shoulder holster. Lavu grabbed at his arm, in a vain attempt to retrieve his gun. Cedric calmly took his cane and held its tip above Lavu's face.

"Now, now," Cedric admonished. "This cane would be enough to create another dent or two in your face. But, my dear bitch-man, we don't need to resort to that, for it has some special customized features." A shining sword blade flashed out from the end of the cane, stopping with its point pushing into Lavu's nose.

A wild impatience came over West. With a sudden fury, he leaped over the table and crouched over Lavu. With fangs bared, West glowered at him, his eyes flickering with a red animal glow. Lavu couldn't tell if this man's eyes were glowing red or if it was the blood trickling into his eyes that made it seem that way. No matter what the answer was, he felt the pure terror of being in the presence of a dangerous animal. West let out an inhuman growl and the smell of urine soon followed. Cedric stepped back, to avoid the growing puddle pooling under Lavu.

"You shouldn't try to piss on my friend, it brings out his bad side," Cedric said to Lavu. "By the way, does your brother, the big Don, know you're out trying to sell his gold at the casino? I shan't imagine he'd be too happy with you should he find out. He might even give you a new divot somewhere else on your face."

Lavu looked over at Cedric, his face white with fear. "Va bè! Va bè! Okay, okay! I'll tell you what you want to know, for Christ's sake!"

"That's the spirit, old chap," Cedric said. "Tell us about this scar-faced bloke, the one excavating the gold out of the Balearic."

"I can't tell you that."

West snarled at him.

"Okay, I can tell you that!" He cautiously reached up to wipe some of the cold sweat off his bloodied face. "I don't know who he is, only that he was waving around a lot of gold and didn't like questions. We did some work for him, gave him protection around the site and we made a deal to handle the gold for him."

"What kind of deal?" West asked.

"He wanted cash. He's financing something and he made us a deal. We got official permits, moved the gold, helped with the salvage, made sure no one snooped around. He paid in gold, plus I–well mostly my brother–and some of the others bought gold bars for fifty cents on the American dollar."

"What are his plans?" West asked. Lavu let out a childish whimper. "Come on now, don't be shy."

"He… he has a connection in the Transylvanian military, a general, I think. Some gold went directly to the Transylvanians and the rest to the different smelting locations. We're taking care of his boat and bringing him and his buddy, the Australian, up to somewhere near the Czech Republic, I think. That's all I know, I swear."

"What about his pet?"

"What? Um, I dunno… there was some guy he had with him, a big goon with a wolf mask, if that's what ya mean. Didn't ever say nothin', always kept the stupid mask on." His breathing increased to the point of hyperventilation, and he began sobbing.

"Twiney, you really are a bitch," West said as he gently patted Lavu's fat jowls. "Never change."

West leaned down and again growled deeply at Lavu, who let out a high-pitched squeal, then promptly fainted. Stepping over the prone body, Cedric flipped a handful of casino plaques into the air on his way out, the plaques bouncing off Twiney the Bitch's blood-soaked chins.

***

Out on the casino's main floor, the ladies, Dame Hancock and Lady Birnamwood, had not warmed up to Tanya and Tanya felt the same. She wandered about alone, taking in the atmosphere, wondering if she would ever come here again under different and less dangerous circumstances. She was also nervous about being left behind and wondered if maybe she had just been ditched. Tanya looked up with a sigh of relief to see Val West and Sir Cedric amble back in casually, as if they hadn't just thoroughly thrashed someone.

"Tanya, it's late and time we be going," West said.

"Val, let's play one round of baccarat. I've never done it. Can we please just play one round and then we can go?"

He was a feeling slightly tired, but once he thought about it, he was going by what would have only recently been past his bedtime. He should take advantage of this boundless energy, which seemed to grow as the moon became fuller, while he still had it. No, he wasn't tired after all. He decided to show her a round or two of Chemin de fer and then they'd retire to the suite.

He figured they had at least a half hour before Twiney the Bitch stirred and started making a racket trying to get out of the private room. When they left, he had pulled the door shut with a force that splintered the door into the jam, giving them another few minutes before it could be opened. Even then, would he dare start anything with him and Cedric? Most likely not, he surmised, and went off to the tables with Tanya.

They chose one of the baccarat tables in the middle of the casino's salons, The La Salle Europe Room. The waxing moon was shining high through the marvelous stained-glass skylight above, crowned by its eight enormous chandeliers. West instructed Tanya on how to play and she showed a little beginner's luck. Soon, they found themselves enjoying the very late evening. The one round had become two and they were about to play a third round, this time as partners.

Tanya excused herself to powder her nose and West took the moment to center himself. He had a job to do, and this had more at stake for him personally than any mission had ever had. This was a pleasant break, but he didn't have time for it. It was past time to leave, and once Tanya returned, he would have to break it to her just when she was having so much fun. He looked up at the huge, decorated skylight, with its intricate metal patterns supporting the stained glass, glowing blue from the moonlight directly overhead. A shadow cast across the skylight, one not simply a cloud moving in front of the moon.

The shadow exploded through the skylight, the force shattering the surrounding clusters of chandeliers. The dark form leaped down onto the casino floor among the throng of shocked casino-goers screaming and running, thinking a bomb had just gone off. One just had, in the form of the explosive power of the henchwolf, crouched on its haunches, looking for its quarry.

It let out a long howl under the shafts of moonlight spilling into the open hole of the casino ceiling. West quickly registered what was happening and decided to push his spysuit's WLF ray injection button, putting the situation in Borge's hands. He heard the tone in his ear as Borge took control and he leaned back, losing himself... losing control... as he became LoneWolf.

The eyepiece sprang up and into position over LoneWolf's left eye and Borge was in command. Viewing through the eyepiece camera, Borge scanned the area and stopped once he saw the drooling henchwolf glaring at him. The red eyes blazed, and it launched itself at Lone-Wolf. Borge moved his joystick controller to dodge the attack and was pleased to see it work smoothly as the first actual field combat test. He had a full view of LoneWolf's position from the eye-camera displayed on the large monitor in front of him. It was just like when he played his video games and as a proud master gamer, he knew this was a real opportunity to use those skills now in a game with much greater stakes.

Cedric heard the commotion and ran out of the bar. He saw the expected chaos of an onrushing crowd and the unexpected sight of two werewolves—one in a diving suit and one in a torn white tuxedo jacket—circling each other. This wasn't the type of situation they had intended to use LoneWolf for and he hoped Borge would be able to keep him under control. His eyes darted around the large area of the casino floor until he spotted Tanya hiding behind a railing. Pushing through the crowd in front of him, he ran over to her and led her to the closest safe place, behind a large marble column.

"What the hell is going on?" Tanya shouted. "Where's Val?"

"He went to get help," Cedric responded with the first, most plausible excuse he could think of.

Tanya was looking at the two monsters growling at each other with increasing intensity. She turned to Cedric with a look of disbelief that West had just gone off without them. "But what about us?"

"We'll be fine. You've still got me," Cedric said, trying his best to be convincing in his conviction.

Cedric and Tanya peered out from the column to see the circling werewolves attacking each other simultaneously. Once they became locked in combat, they left a trail of destruction in their wake as they battled throughout the casino, flinging each other into walls and leaping off the giant chandeliers, crashing to the ground after them. Lone-Wolf was struggling to free himself from the large marble column that the henchwolf had toppled onto him. Staggering over near the column behind which Cedric and Tanya were taking cover, the henchwolf caught sight of them and licked its sharp canine fangs.

Cedric did not hesitate and drew his cane, pushing the button to pop out the silver sword blade, and struck a defensive position. Lone-Wolf had freed himself and was moving across the room in pursuit of the henchwolf. When it saw LoneWolf, it turned its attack to Tanya and Cedric, swinging its claws at them. Cedric slashed back with his cane sword and missed. Enraged, the beast went in for the kill, slashing toward Cedric. This time, the blade hit its mark, striking the paw clean off, sending it flying into the air and landing on a nearby roulette table.

The henchwolf let out a deafening screech of howling pain. Lone-Wolf grabbed the distracted henchwolf and sent it crashing into the next closest massive marble column. It leaped up and lunged at Lone-Wolf, spearing both of them through a row of gaming tables. Dazed, the two monsters were still for the moment, lying in the rubble of green baize and broken wood. Borge furiously worked his controls, button mashing to get LoneWolf back up. The injured and bleeding hench-wolf rose first. It climbed on top of the still-prone LoneWolf with jaws wide open, prepared to take a fatal bite out of LoneWolf's neck.

Cedric came to LoneWolf's defense with his cane at the ready. As he approached, the henchwolf got up, turned around and leaped toward him. Not wanting to press his luck by trying another one in a million slice, he instantly reacted by pushing two buttons together on each side of the sword cane hilt. He aimed it toward the rapidly advancing henchwolf and sent a blast of highly concentrated bear spray into its face. The henchwolf cried out as the spray made contact and used its remaining paw to cover the searing pain in its eyes.

LoneWolf was up and moving toward henchwolf. Instead of at-tacking, the henchwolf turned and fled into the adjoining bar area. LoneWolf followed at its heels. They crashed into the bar and over onto the floor behind it. Borge saw the rows of expensive bottles and had LoneWolf begin picking them up, throwing them at the henchwolf one after the other. The henchwolf—eyes burning, hand lopped off—finally felt the need to retreat. It let out a ghastly scream and jumped through the window of the bar to the outside.

Borge sent LoneWolf after, jumping down to ground level. Gone. Borge adjusted the controls to enhance scent receptors and night vi-sion, but found nothing, the scent obscured by the bear spray and the alcohol the beast was drenched in. Lurking in the shadows, he had LoneWolf search as long as he could, but within minutes, police and emergency services were all over the scene. Forced to give up for the time being, he activated the colloidal silver solution, and within sec-onds he turned back into a now disheveled Val West.

West staggered around trying to get his bearings while being quickly filled in by Borge through the NeuraComlink. Wearing what remained of his tuxedo, he climbed up the side of the casino wall, en-tering back in through a second-floor balcony. Making his way back down to the gaming rooms, he snuck into The La Salle Europe Room and found Cedric and Tanya. They were purposely off to the side to avoid having to make a statement to the police, but still able to be found by West when he returned. Tanya saw him approach and looked over his torn tuxedo jacket.

"What happened to you? Where have you been?" she demanded.

"I was at the baccarat table when this dreadful creature crashed down through the skylight. The damn thing nearly fell right on top of me, and I ran to get help."

"Some help. Besides, I thought you carried a gun." She eyed him with suspicion. "Anyway, there were two of them… and Cedric had no problem taking them on."

"Cedric has always been a go-getter. Anyway, now that that's over, let's have a drink and call it a night, shall we?"

On their way out of the room, Cedric walked over to a still spinning roulette wheel and took the now-human hand spinning around it. "Looks like he had a losing hand," he said to a still-in-shock roulette dealer. With sleight-of-hand precision he took out his handkerchief and wrapped it inside before anyone could catch a glimpse of what he was doing.

He walked back over to West and Tanya and the three of them left the casino. They paused to relax in the warm late-night air of the Riviera. Cedric raised his cane, twisted off the top and took a good long drink. "This was my customization," Cedric said, wincing from the strong whiskey. "Don't tell Borge." He passed the cane to both Tanya and West and they each had a long drink. Cedric reached inside his coat and gestured to West to look at what he had wrapped in the silken monogrammed handkerchief. "You may have lost track of this gruesome beast, but we do have him fingered," he said with a wink.

West studied the human hand under the cloth and his mind raced with possibilities. This hand had the henchwolf's DNA. This could be enough to generate a cure.

"Yes," West said with optimism. "This could come in quite handy, indeed."

13: CEMETERIA RIVIERA

Seven miles down the M6007 along the Riviera, in Nice, was the French base of ParaCommand, located in the scenic cemetery known locally as the Cimetière du Château. Dr. Hector Borge sat down at his control console office with a nice warm cup of his favorite carrot juice. He looked around at the sparse construction and knew it needed a lot of work—work he never had time to get done.

While he was stationed here in the musty old crypt chosen as the ParaCommand French base of operations, Borge would have time to improve the security systems and other operational systems. He still missed the comforts of the more spacious and state-of-the-art facilities at the Highgate Cemetery base in London, a place he had come to call home. A pinging noise began chiming from his computer with a news item alert. The headline read:

TERRORISTS IN MONKEY MASKS SOUGHT
IN MONTE CARLO MACING MELEE

Borge was pleased the specially built cane he made for Cedric had done its job. He was even more pleased that the headline was suitably inaccurate and wouldn't need any further cover-up efforts by Para-Command.

***

Before leaving with Sir Cedric Kenton to the Cimetière du Château, West thought it was well past time to get Tanya safely tucked away in the hotel suite. As Cedric bid Tanya goodnight, coded tones began chirping from his wristwatch. Cedric motioned for them to stay. He began twiddling a knob on the side of the watch and an antenna rose out of the top. His fingers tapped a musical code along the watch face and within seconds, the sound of a decrypted analog audio transmission tuned in. It was Commander 7.

"I trust agent LoneWolf is with you now. It appears you gentlemen have had some unwelcome company tonight. It also looks like our target will soon be on the move. LoneWolf—I want you to keep tracking *The Bootylicious*'s movements. With the murky international waters situation in that area along with their Corsican protection, we can't move in while they're at sea. They'll have to bring her ashore eventually and likely soon."

"Sir," Cedric replied, "We've just received information tonight that the Corsicans Digby and this scar-faced man hired will be bringing them into Europe. Somewhere near Czechia is all we have to go on for the moment."

"Most likely a rendezvous point. My guess is this is where General Ferenc comes in and I want to know what his dealings are with these two."

"Indeed." Cedric continued. "Also, the informed source we consulted said scar-face was selling gold to the Corsicans for fifty cents on the American dollar. Strange, that. To spend so much time and effort excavating it in secret and then sell it for so low."

"Sounds like someone needs money and is in a hurry. Still made quite a sizable amount though, I would imagine. I have no doubt this is how Ferenc became so interested. LoneWolf, we'll need to look at the computer scan and photos you took aboard *The Bootylicious* straight away."

"I'll be on my way with Cedric to the base directly, sir."

"Good. And watch out for loose wolves that may bite."

The transmission went to static and Cedric's watch converted itself back into its regular appearance of an expensive vintage Enicar Ultrasonic wristwatch.

"How do you get one of those?" West asked. Cedric smiled. "Yes, well...good luck getting Borge to construct another one. I'll leave it to you in my will."

West turned back to Tanya, who had been pretending not to listen to the conversation with Commander 7. Cedric's car arrived and he waited with the driver while West and Tanya went up to their suite at the Hotel de Paris Monte-Carlo.

Tanya stopped in the hallway. "Val, I want to come with you."

"I'm sorry, Tanya." West gently took her by the arm and continued walking. "Where I'm going is classified and I can't take you there. You'll be safe here, and locked in. I'll only be gone for about a half hour or so. I promise."

Entering the suite, the tipsy Tanya found herself tripping on her heels, sending West on to the bed and her on top of him.

"Now this is a nice switch of position," West said, their faces dangerously close to one another. "We should fall on top of each other more often."

"We are getting good at it," Tanya said, her lips trembling. "And there's still time for more practice."

As much as West hated to do it, he ignored her fantastic scent, along with everything else he was finding fantastic about her and rolled her on to the bed.

It took an extreme act of self-discipline that he immediately resented. He now had the body of a twenty-five-year-old and the sex drive of a seventeen-year-old, combined with the prowess and experience of a forty-five-year-old. Not surrendering to the literal animal passion coursing through him was the most difficult part of this mission thus far. He also wondered if he might rip her throat out in the heat of passion. Regretfully, he removed her arms from around his neck and stood up. "I'm sorry, but there isn't time. At least… not right now."

Tanya gave a pout of disappointment but understood. "Before you go… the next site Burt and scar-face could be going to could be the Nazi Gold Train." West looked at her with curiosity. "Just a few years ago," she continued, "there were some digs near Wroclaw, in Poland."

West was indeed curious about this. The location wasn't too far out of line with the rendezvous point planned near Czechia. "What did they find?"

"Nothing. But maybe this scar-faced man knows something the treasure hunters didn't. He knew where this U-Boat filled with gold was, after all."

West thought for a moment. "So… maybe the treasure hunter's information was close, but they were digging in the wrong spot."

"Exactly. Oh, please let me go with you. You tell me what you find out from on board *The Bootylicious* and I can help you pinpoint the location."

West gave a slight frown. "We'll talk about that later and you can tell me more. We'll have to wait now for *The Bootylicious* to move and see if our friend with the 'wolf mask' shows up again. I'll be back soon."

"Val," Tanya called out to him as he walked out the door. "Be back soon."

***

Sir Cedric's driver pulled up to the gates of the Cimetière du Châ-teau. The necropolis, built on the ruins of an ancient citadel, stood on a lonely hilltop. Looking down toward the sea, it afforded quite a view, the lights of the Riviera twinkling in the distance.

Cedric thanked his driver and asked him to park and wait down the street. The driver nodded. He was more-than-generously paid by Cedric and immune to eccentric behavior, having spent years dealing with the Monaco jet set.

They walked for a short distance down the darkened road running alongside the cemetery. With a quick motion, Cedric hopped over the small fence surrounding it and West followed. The moon was in de-scent, but still shining enough to see the rows of white tombs looming over the city below. The light warm breeze was soothing after such an eventful evening, and a welcome contrast from the seemingly always chilly Highgate Cemetery headquarters.

The two men wound their way up the walkway to a row of mauso-leums topped by pointed spires. West noticed the one incongruous thing, but one only a keen observer would pick up. Mounted atop the mausoleum roof was a small, retractable satellite dish, whirring away in continuous rotation. "Ah, yes. Our communications system," Cedric explained. "It's used to contact the satellite that connects to your NeuraComlink. Still can't pick up any cable channels, though I've tried." Cedric walked up the steps, past weathered stone columns to the door of the decaying mausoleum, opening it with a skeleton key. "Secret entrance not up and running yet, I'm afraid," Cedric said apol-ogetically. "We just finally got a few security measures in place. It's all a bit of a work-in-progress."

Once inside, they walked across the granite floor, past two stone coffin-tombs to the back wall. There were three arches, each with a memorial plaque attached. He went over to the plaque on the left side, flipped it open and punched in a code. The concrete wall slid up, revealing a staircase to a lower level. The torch lights of the stone stairway led to the brightly lit secret lab where Dr. Borge was seated, enjoying a late-night sandwich. "What've you got?" Borge said through a mouthful of food.

"Fingerprints," West said, dropping the severed hand in front of Borge, which caused him to spray the half-chewed food out of his mouth.

"For Heaven's Sake, West! What's all this then?"

"This," Cedric said, pointing at the hand sprawled out on the table, "is our furry friend's hand in humanoid form, lopped off courtesy of the silver sword cane you so kindly provided me with."

"I'd like you to analyze it," West said. "Find out the identity, and then, according to what you said, a cure could be generated from its DNA, yes?"

Borge put down the sandwich and picked up the severed hand. "I think it's a possibility, but that will have to wait until I'm back in London. I simply don't have the equipment here for that, but I will get some samples preserved right away. Fingerprints, we can do. As a field location this lab still needs a lot of work, but still, we were really lucky to get a spot here. Do you know how hard it is to get in this place?"

"Not as hard as it is to get out," West replied. Borge ignored the comment and went back to his sandwich.

Cedric looked over the base and gave an unsatisfied harrumph. "Thank God I booked a suite for me as well," he said. "This place is still in dreadful shape. There's not even a single bedroom suite constructed yet. Borge, you can stay here if you want, but I wouldn't be caught dead here."

"That suits me fine," said Borge. "I won't have to put up with your snoring, which can shake the concrete walls back at Highgate."

"Oh, Balderdash," Cedric sniffed.

"I'd love to hear more of this riveting conversation," West said, looking at his watch. "But we really must be getting back to the hotel."

"You go on ahead," Cedric said. "Late as it is, I'm going to be staying on a while longer. Tell the driver to wait at the hotel until I call him to come back for me."

The short drive gave West a chance to think for a moment. There was still a wounded and dangerous monster prowling the Riviera. Where was it now? When would it attack next? He still had to stop it. LoneWolf had given it a beating, Cedric had taken its hand and bear-sprayed its eyes, but it was still a deadly threat and still on the loose. And how was it being controlled by the scar-faced man? Did he have a similar control method to the one Borge used to control LoneWolf? So many questions still remained about this man. Who was he? How did he find this creature, his henchwolf?

Then there was the hand. The thought of this gave West some hope. Could Borge generate a cure from the DNA taken from the hand? After the mission was completed, he could be 100% human again, and he would put all of this paranormal business behind him.

The car was pulling up to the hotel. In a few minutes, he would be back in the suite with Tanya. She would be fast asleep by now. He was still curious about what she had said about the treasure hunts in Poland. Maybe he should bring her along, after all. It would be dangerous, and he always hesitated over involving a civilian in a potentially life-threatening situation. However, from what he had come to know of her, if she wanted to come, there may be no stopping her.

***

Tanya Nimble was pacing throughout the hotel suite. After what she had seen that night, she was terrified and despite her attempts to be strong about it, she was relying on Val West to keep her safe. She

126

was reasonably certain he was in some secret service—perhaps the Canadian Secret Service. Was there even such a thing?* He was only to be gone about a half hour, but time was crawling. She gave in to her anxiety and went down to the lobby to wait for him.

At this late hour, the only person in the lobby was the concierge. Still, at least there was someone nearby and she would be able to meet West as soon as he came back. The police were still on the scene at the casino, and after a brief lockdown, the hotel was open as normal. She stood waiting impatiently, watching through the large windows set in the ivory walls alongside the entryway of the Hôtel de Paris Monte-Carlo. Headlights heralded an arrival. At this hour it had to be West, and she felt a sense of relief wash over her. She moved to the door to meet him and much to her stunned surprise, it was not Val West entering.

"Tanya!" the dumbfounded voice of Burt Digby exclaimed. "Bugger me, what the flamin' hell are you doing here?" The scar-faced man was right behind him, followed by two large Corsican thugs.

Tanya was too shocked to respond. The concierge walked over and asked if everything was all right. The scar-faced man looked at the concierge and said to him in a thick German accent, "Everything is quite fine. We are with her. We are all just so happy to be reunited that she is practically speechless."

She tried to stop shaking, but the introduction of a gun barrel being pressed into her back by one of the Corsicans made it impossible. The gun was jabbed a little harder into her spine and she slowly nodded to the concierge. The concierge smiled and nodded back and went back to his post. "We were expecting someone else," the scar-faced man

---

* There is. The Canadian Security Intelligence Service (CSIS)-- *Editor.*

said to her. "I expect you were also expecting someone else, Fräulein. Now, let's go up to your room and prepare for a warm willkommen."

Minutes later, West entered the lobby. Dawn was not far off, and he was now looking forward to getting at least a few winks of sleep before what would be another hectic day. He bounded up the staircase and down the hall to the suite. He opened the door quietly, assuming Tanya to be sound asleep. The spacious suite was dark, save for a lone lamp in the center of the main room. Tanya was not asleep. She was standing in the lamplight, facing the balcony window.

West's senses went wild... something wasn't right. Before he could react, he felt a steel fist smash into his face and a knife-edge chop crash into his back, buckling his knees and dropping him to the floor. Dazed by the surprise attack, he tried to get up, but could only lie there looking at the two ugly Corsicans pointing their guns at him. He looked around the room and off to one side was a fidgeting Burt Digby. The other side held a figure, seated in the shadows. The chair turned toward West, and he met the gaze of the scar-faced man.

"Alles klar, Herr Kommissar?" the scar-faced man said with a severe hiss and a mocking grin. His red eyes glistened with menace. "I do believe you have something that belongs to my pet Húnd. He was quite attached to it." He turned to one of the Corsicans and barked, "You! Get his gun." The Corsican leaned over to take West's gun from his shoulder holster. He decided to make a move but was stopped by the violent force of a jackboot smashing into his mouth.

The scar-faced man stood over him and drew his lips back in a gruesome grin as he watched blood trickle from West's mouth. The Corsican handed the gun to scar-face. "Was ist das?" he asked while curiously examining West's H&K MK23 handgun. "Is this a toy? That is not a gun. This is a gun." He took out a vintage Mauser HSc pistol and pointed it down at West. "Now, mein Freund. Húnd has been following you with his Schnauzen. You are here, but where is das Biest?"

128

A frightening howl echoed through large open windows of the balcony. "Ah, Húnd has come back and with that kind of racket, he'll wake up the whole neighborhood. It is time to depart. That is, for us to depart, not you. My Corsicans and their friend will keep you company. West turned to see the rumpled figure of Antoine 'Twiney the Bitch' Lavu wobble through the doorway. Digby and the scar-faced man made their exit, dragging the struggling Tanya out with them. Lavu leered at West and closed the door.

West gave him a wink. Lavu gave an order in French to the Corsicans, and the muscled one in red punched West straight in the gut, then got him up to his feet so the fat one in black could take his turn. Lavu then decided to take his turn, while the Corsicans pinned back West's arms. Lavu snorted through his nostrils and gargled in his throat, conjuring a mass of snot-filled spittle. He leaned in to aim his spit directly into West's face. West reared back and kicked Lavu hard in the stomach. Lavu tumbled over backwards, his spit spattering his own face and clothing.

The two thugs slapped West around while Lavu attempted to compose himself. He rose up from the floor and produced a stiletto switchblade from his pocket. He again walked up to West and this time, he stuck the knife's hilt under West's chin. "One flick and this blade slices up through your neck, needlessly soiling this nice white carpet."

"Well, we certainly don't want that," West replied. "I guess I have no choice but to have a conversation with you."

"Sensible. We might not even kill you." Lavu moved the knife away from West's throat and took a step back. "Depending on what you say and how much value your life has to you, I'm sure a deal can be made that will be satisfactory to all of us."

"So, it's a matter of money then?"

"Of course. What do you think I am, some kind of savage?"

West paused without answering. "If it's cash then, let me get my pocketbook." He moved to reach toward his inside jacket pocket. The two thugs tensed their grip on his shoulders. "Your boss already took my gun. I'm harmless." Lavu nodded to the two hoods to ease up on West and allow him to proceed. His hand moved across his chest and slipped his thumb between his shirt buttons, his thumbprint finding the LoneWolf activator. He heard the NeuraComlink power on in his ear and knew Borge would be at the ready.

"Now, Borge!" West shouted and nothing happened. No light emanated from the LoneWolf activator chest piece, no rush of endorphins as the WLF photons triggered his metamorphosis into a werewolf. Lavu and the two Corsicans looked at him oddly.

"Who are you calling Borge?" Lavu asked, confused.

West pushed the button again and said, "Activate, now!" The Corsican in red turned to Lavu and told him in Corsican, 'This man is crazy.' West didn't know why Borge wasn't responding to activate the suit, so he instead gave a frustrated pained half-smile, shrugged and said, "Guess we'll just have to do this the old-fashioned way."

He feigned seeing something on the other side of the room. It was enough to distract the thug in black. West jerked his leg out and kicked the gun out of his hand, the pistol landing somewhere across the suite. The Corsican in red moved to shoot. West knew it was coming and sidestepped as the bullet missed and went into the wall.

Lavu looked on, unable to process what he should do. West jumped on top of the sofa, while the man in red was attempting to shoot again. West did a flip off of the sofa toward him, grabbing his neck in midair and smashing the back of the man's head into the floor with all of his force and bodyweight.

In the confusion, the Corsican in black scrambled to find his gun. Lavu decided to throw his switchblade at West. He missed, the knife sticking into the wall near West's head. West reached back and grabbed the knife, pulled it from the wall and sent it straight between the eyes of the thug in black as he was about to fire the gun he had just recovered.

Antoine 'Twiney the Bitch' Lavu was without a weapon and cowered before West. Enraged and filled with adrenaline, as well as feeling the effects of the waxing moon, West grabbed Lavu by the throat and picked up his rotund body with one arm. If his throat hadn't been so tightly gripped by West, Lavu would have screamed as he looked into the glowing red eyes and clenched fangs staring back at him. Instead, he exercised his only available option and emptied his bowls onto the hotel suite floor.

"You're soiling the carpet," West rasped through gritted teeth, "You bitch." West had to catch up to Tanya and had already wasted minutes with these three hoodlums and would waste no more. He tossed the terrified Lavu through the door of the hotel suite, the door disintegrating on impact. West ran through the open door, trampling the groaning Lavu.

Racing out of the hotel, West bounded through the parking lot and over hedges and barriers. He wasn't sure where they had taken Tanya, but knew they had to be leaving by water if returning to *The Bootylicious*. He sniffed the air and caught a whiff of Tanya's scent, and it was tinged with fear.

He ran along the brick surface, looking over the railing as he went. Running over the top of a parking garage, he found himself at a railing just above the concrete support pillars alongside the Jetée Lucciana pier. West looked down and saw a speedboat tied off, motor running. He ran along the top of the concrete barrier and jumped down to the top of the white cement column directly above it.

Digby and the scar-faced man were pushing Tanya into the waiting speedboat. West stood on the edge of the column, ready to pounce. The scar-faced man stopped and looked up at him. He raised his

Mauser and pointed it at West. "Halt!" the scar-faced man shouted up to him. West intended to ignore the man, until he flashed a wicked smile and turned the gun pointed at West to Tanya's head.

He shouted at Digby, "Move, schnell." Digby untied the rope from the moor. With the tip of the gun pressed into Tanya's temple, the boat sped off over the dark sea. West stood atop the concrete column and could only watch as they disappeared into the last whispers of the night.

There was no choice. This man would surely kill Tanya and probably still would once her usefulness was over. He owed it to her to get her out of this mess and his only consolation was the tracking device placed on the hull of *The Bootylicious*. The last sounds of the speedboat echoed away, leaving only the quiet lapping of the waves. A static sound broke into West's ear, followed by the modulation of a frequency signal. The signal tuned in and Commander 7's voice came through.

"LoneWolf. You need to get back to the base right away."

14: DEAD MAN'S HAND

A pleasant breeze wafted down into the lab through the small open window in the mausoleum above. Just moments earlier, Val West had left the Cimetière du Château for the hotel and now Cedric sat down with a whiskey and water to relax and to contemplate the night's bizarre events.

Even though they didn't have the usual amenities and equipment they had at the main base at Highgate Cemetery in London, Dr. Borge and Sir Cedric had come to enjoy their time at the idyllic French coast location as 'Cemeteria Riviera.' It had been a long night, even by Cedric's standards. Even now, in his seventies, Cedric could still live the nightlife until the wee small hours, but he had exceeded his limits and it was time to head back to his suite at the Hôtel de Paris Monte-Carlo. He leaned back in his seat and was just getting comfortable when a loud thumping sound came from outside the walls above.

Borge stopped his work and turned to Cedric. "Did you hear that?"

"I did," Cedric said as he swirled the ice around in his glass. "Better not be those damn ghost hunting kids traipsing about the cemetery again." Borge looked at him with concern. Cedric downed his glass and stood up. "All-bloody-right, I'll check it out."

He picked up his cane and started up the steps to the mausoleum above. He crept over to the outer door. The heavy old stone door opened with a creaking, aching moan. He peered out and let the pleasant current flow over his tired face. In the darkness of the end of night, there was nothing to see or hear but the quiet lapping of the Mediterranean Sea from down below the hill. After taking a moment to make sure all was clear to his satisfaction, he heaved the door shut.

At his control console, Borge was fiddling with the communications dish. He couldn't get a signal. There was a security camera mounted on the mausoleum roof, and if he could get it to turn, he could see the dish and get a better idea of what was causing the technical difficulties. With some further fiddling, he was able to get the camera activated and it began to turn on its rotor. The camera panned and stopped. The dish was broken off the mount.

Then two fierce, piercing red eyes filled the view screen.

Cedric heard Borge shouting at him through the open door to the lab entrance below. Another mouse, he assumed to himself, and started back for the lower level. A crunching sound gave him pause. He turned back again toward the outer door and was hit by a force which blasted him over a coffin crypt, knocking him against the back wall.

The henchwolf had burst through the mausoleum door and was standing in front of Cedric, slime dripping off its jutting fangs. Cedric instantly reached up and hit the lockdown button, the rock wall security barrier shaking the mausoleum as it slammed down, sealing off the only entrance to the lab below. The beast let out a hideous and mournful howl that rattled the stained glass of the small windows.

A trickle of sweat ran down Cedric's face as he leaned on the wall, trying to get his wind back and plan his next move. The werewolf snarled, and as if pointing at Cedric, raised the bloody stump where its left hand once was. His cane had fallen next to him, and he moved his hand toward the cane, keeping his eyes locked with the great beast standing before him. He knew he had one shot at this and was damn well going to take it. With cane in hand, he simultaneously forced himself up and drew the sword from the cane. He held the sword before him, the crouched henchwolf snarling and licking its chops. Cedric steadied himself. The beast launched forward, slicing with its massive, sharpened claws.

Cedric had bled out even before all of the pieces of him fell to the ground in a crimson puddle. The blood-spattered silver blade clattered to the ground beside him.

Borge cried out in anguish as he watched this happen before him on the mausoleum security camera. The werewolf leapt and clawed at the wall, trying to break through the barrier. Borge was trapped in this underground tomb and with the communications link down, he had no way to contact West and activate LoneWolf. Dust and rubble began to fall, and cracks began spidering the wall as the monster tried to force its way through. Borge had to stop it from getting in, but how? The security wall was supposed to stop an attack, and so were the other usual security measures which weren't installed yet.

Scrambling, he looked for something to stop this creature once it finally broke through and mauled him to pieces, and it looked as though it was just a very short matter of time. He ran to his equipment storage room and grabbed a frequency generator. He had tested this on West during their training period and he hoped like hell it would work now. His trembling fingers could barely make the connections he needed to make as he pulled out the wires and frantically worked to connect them to a large amplifier speaker. A clawed hand pushed its way through the fissure it had made in the wall. Ignoring the imminent danger, he focused only on connecting the frequency generator. Got it! He didn't have anything else to fall back on, and like Cedric, he had nowhere to run.

He powered on the generator and tuned it to the range of 23 to 54 kHz, the frequency range used for dog whistles. It had worked on LoneWolf, but he had only tested to see if it produced a response. It was just a quick test, but LoneWolf had not liked it. He had to hope this werewolf would like it even less.

Borge placed both hands on the large, heavy amplifier and pushed it as much as he could with his limited mobility. He moved it to the wall, where two glowing evil eyes stared at him through the large open crack. With the generator on and tuned in, he turned the volume of the amplifier as loud as it could go. This amplifier had enough decibel strength to blow out windows. As long as the frequency generator was properly connected it would hopefully be enough to at least slow down the beast.

With a quick prayer, Borge switched the amplifier on. Nothing. Borge felt his stomach sink. The head of the snarling, snapping creature was now through the hole and the rest would follow in a matter of seconds. Borge prepared for his demise and took a last look at the amplifier, the one he had pinned his hopes on. He wanted to curse God for mocking his prayer.

In this last look, he noticed that in his haste, it was still unplugged. The werewolf plunged through the wall in a burst of rubble. Borge dove to the floor and grabbed the electrical cord. The beast gave a terrible roar, grabbing Borge's leg, yanking him up towards its frothing jaws. With one last thrust, Borge pushed the plug into the outlet with all of his force. The amplifier speaker came to life with a loud hum and blasted out a screeching frequency Borge could not hear, but the beast could. Yowling in pain, it dropped Borge to the floor, desperately trying to cover its ears from the sonic assault with its one remaining paw.

The beast retreated, then tried lunging again at Borge, while alternately backing away in pain as the amplified frequency tore at its eardrums, beating a sharp pounding pain into its brain. Borge crawled over to the amplifier cabinet and hid behind it as a shield. Another few seconds passed, and the creature could take no more and ran out of the lab up into the mausoleum.

Borge, feeling braver and with a stronger sense of faith than he ever felt in his life, went to his control console and patched in the frequency and blasted it through the intercom speaker wired to the outer door of the mausoleum. This extra blast pushed the already reeling henchwolf further back into the cemetery. Borge moved through the broken security wall with a handheld frequency generator he had just connected to a wireless speaker and moved up the steps to see the beast fleeing down the road out of the cemetery. He breathed a sigh of relief, crossed himself, and went back down to the lab, leaving the amplifier on at full volume.

***

Dawn was breaking over the Cimetière du Château. Normally, it would be a spectacularly beautiful scene with the sun about to rise over the sea, the birds singing, the fresh smell of dew and the sound of rolling waves just beyond. This morning, however, had a feeling of tense dread hanging over this tranquil scene and this feeling filled Val West as he hopped over the cemetery gate.

The call from Commander 7 through his NeuraComlink didn't offer any information, but the fact that the call came directly from the Commander was enough for him to expect the worst. The worst greeted him as he walked up to the crumbling mausoleum, now in a state of destruction.

Dr. Borge poked his head through the large hole made in the broken wreckage of what used to be the doorway. He was pointing his handheld loudspeaker like a weapon. Recognizing West, he dropped it and hobbled over to him. "West, thank God you're back!"

"What in the hell is going on? Where's Cedric?"

An ashen look came over Borge's face as his head dropped down. "Come inside. We need your help. The Commander will be calling to speak with you."

West swallowed hard as he steeled himself knowing something terrible lay ahead. He walked with Borge up the stone steps, the ruins of the mausoleum looking like a bomb had dropped on it. They entered to the destruction awaiting inside: the upended stone coffin crypts, the blood spattering the walls, the rubble of what was the stone security barrier protecting the secret lab, and most strikingly, the remains on the floor, covered by a sheet.

West walked over to the body and slowly pulled back the sheet to see Cedric's face, drained of all color, most of his blood having been spilled on the ground beneath him. The claw and teeth marks told the entire story West needed to know, and he went cold as he gently replaced the cover over Cedric's face.

Borge began speaking but stopped to clear his throat. "That monster we fought at the casino... it came back after you had left. Cedric activated the security barrier and tried to fight it off. He saved my life. It almost got me, except I remembered when I tried the dog whistle frequency on you as LoneWolf, and I was able to blast it with the amplifier."

West grimaced as he pictured what had gone on just a short time earlier. "Why the hell didn't you call me?"

Borge lifted his head up from his hands. "I tried. The bastard was up on the mausoleum roof when I saw it through the security camera, and it had mangled the communications satellite. I couldn't call anyone. When Commander 7 saw the signal was down, he patched in directly to your NeuraComlink."

West gritted his teeth. "That's two of my best friends now that this son of a bitch has taken." He had seen death many times in his career as an agent. Many times, it was people he knew and worked with, the only people he could call close in his lonely profession. Even though it was human nature to grieve, this business didn't allow time for it. He had to get this creature, not just for himself, but also for Wildebeest, and now, Cedric. He would bring it in alive and it would pay for the death and destruction it had caused, beast or not.

The adrenaline propelling Borge had finally worn off. A listlessness came over him as the harsh reality sunk in. "Commander 7 is handling the cleanup," he said. "Cedric... he was my friend, and—"

West placed a reassuring hand on Borge's shoulder. "I know. He was my friend too, and a good man. And we will grieve for him. But as you know, we can't do it now." Borge nodded in understanding to West and took a few deep breaths to compose himself. "Help me bring Cedric down into the lab. The Commander will be calling soon."

The two of them acted as grisly pallbearers, gently carrying down the remains of their fallen comrade. They worked together to repair the satellite and patched up the underground entrance to the lab as best they could. After a time, Borge was able to restore all systems and the blinking lights and whirring sounds of the mainframe computer console came back to life.

Borge summoned West over to the main computer screen. "The data has come in on the fingerprint scan we did on the werewolf's hand." West eagerly looked at the computer screen as the file information marked "Top Secret" appeared.

This situation had already gone past bad into several shades of worse. Now it was to go one step beyond. He knew the face in the photo, but still looked at the name anyway as a sickening feeling washed over him.

SUBJECT IDENTIFICATION CONFIRMED:

HEDISON, THOMAS
International Command Agent
Codename: Wildebeest

***

After a choppy ride in the speedboat, Burt Digby, Tanya Nimble, and the scar-faced man boarded *The Bootylicious*. Despite Digby's protestations, scar-face had kept his pistol aimed at Tanya the entire time. Once aboard, she was taken to the hold and locked in a cabin.

It had been made clear they were to prepare to pull out and move on to the next location, but Digby was more interested in talking to Tanya. How she went from minding the desk at his office in Tangier to wearing an evening gown and accompanying a spy in Monaco was something he couldn't quite fathom.

Now she was nothing but a quick insurance policy to the scar-faced man. He would probably demand she be killed before long. But to Digby, she was a woman he still had real feelings for, and he wanted answers. If they were the wrong answers, then in spite of any feelings, he thought it was possible he could find himself agreeing with his employer on her future. He found a moment to slip away from the preparations going on aboard *The Bootylicious* to enter Tanya's cabin.

"Tanya," Digby said, (it always sounded like Tonn-ee with his thick Australian accent) "We need to talk."

"I'll say!" Tanya started throwing every nearby object she could get her hands on at him. "Who the hell do you think you are?"

Digby dodged the barrage of harmless items being thrown his way. "I was just about to ask you the same thing," he retorted. "Are you

140

working for the secret service now? For how long? The whole time we've been together? Wot?"

"Not hardly! You're the one who ditched me in Tangier, leaving me to the wolves!"

Burt chafed at her choice of words. "Don't say that."

She glared at him. "It's true. I haven't heard from you in over three weeks. What was I supposed to think?"

"You weren't supposed to think," he said with a sneer. "I asked you to mind the office, a fairly simple thing."

"Yeah, and I'm not your office manager. We were supposed to be partners. And unlike you, I have a legitimate archaeology degree."

Digby did his best to ignore the sting. He kept himself in check, pushing for answers. "That's a, uh, fair point. Ya know... I'm thinking we can maybe still be partners. But I need to know what in the bloody blue hell you're doing travelling around with this secret agent or treasury man, whatever he is."

"I'll tell you why. I was afraid for my life. People were coming for you in Tangier... more were on their way. And I had no choice. I had to go with him. Even though he's a dangerous man with the Canadian Secret Service, at least he was concerned for my safety."

Digby paused for a moment. "There's a Canadian Secret Service?" He looked at her and saw her fiery temper continue to rise. With the conversation not going well, he walked over to the cabin door and brought in a small tray of food left outside. "We'll talk again soon. Just hang tight. We'll be on the move soon, so for now have some grub and tea." He left her, the door locking behind him.

Tanya was hungry, so instead of throwing it all at Digby the next time he came to talk, she ate the food. She was grateful for the tea, for she wanted the caffeine boost to stay awake and alert. She gulped it down and found it as disgusting as the sandwich given her. It had a strange bitter taste and within a few moments, she felt even more tired

141

as the room started spinning. *Goddamn you, Burt Digby* was the last thought she had before darkness overtook her.

***

Val West opened his eyes, not sure where he was. He had hoped the events of late had been just a nightmare, but as he looked around, he saw he was still in the ramshackle remains of the base at Cimetière du Château. It was all a nightmare, and all too real: Cedric was dead, and killed by, of all people, Tom Hedison—Wildebeest—one of his best friends from the service, now a werewolf henchman under the command of the scar-faced man. His hopes for a cure were also once again up in the air. The clock above the computer console, where Borge was working away, showed he had been asleep for over twelve hours. He may have needed it, but he damn sure didn't have the time for it.

"Borge! Why did you let me sleep so long?"

"I didn't. Commander 7 ordered it."

"Maybe so, but now is not the time. I need to get back to *The Bootylicious*. Forget waiting for them to come ashore."

"I'm afraid *The Bootylicious* is out of the question. The tracking device showed it on the move several hours ago. It moved out into deeper waters, and then stopped. After a time, the signal itself went dead. I couldn't get a visual from any of the sources in the area. We have to assume the ship has been scuttled."

"That explains what Twiney the Bitch meant when he said they'd 'take care of the boat.' Well, that settles that. We have to figure out where they've gone next. Twiney did say the Corsicans had arranged to bring Digby and scar-face at least as far as the Czech border. What did we get from the data I brought back from *The Bootylicious*?"

"Not much, I'm afraid," Borge said with a look of disappointment. "The scan of Digby's laptop contained 5,278 photos of nude or partially nude women. Quite a collection, but not much help to us."

West sighed with irritation. "We do have the photos I took. What do you make of the sketches?"

"I do concur that it looks like it could be a rail line. The location marks don't match up, however. The names you heard—Waldenburg and Dittersbach—came up as two separate locations in Germany, but they are also over five hundred kilometers apart. The railway sketch doesn't match with either of them. Quite puzzling."

West thought for a moment. "There is something else. Back at the hotel, Tanya told me about a treasure hunt a few years ago for a buried Nazi gold train. Fits the profile of their M.O. and the sketch does appear to be a railway. What can you dig up on that?"

Borge went to work at his computer, accessing both the public files and the classified files on the legend of the Nazi gold train. "Here's what turned up: there were attempts by numerous treasure hunting groups within the last five years to locate and recover a Nazi gold train. One of these treasure hunters allegedly had a 'deathbed confession' of the location of the gold train, located underground in Wroclaw, Poland."

"Yes, that's the one she was telling me about."

Borge read further into the file. "Sorry to disappoint, but after several attempts at excavation, as well as a sonar scan, no train or treasure was found."

"Perhaps Digby and this scar-faced man have more accurate information. They did locate a Nazi U-Boat filled with gold in an underwater cave, after all." West considered the information they had while Borge continued to look through the files, displaying the text and images on the large screen of the computer console. An image came up on the screen and before Borge could move to the next, West shouted at him to wait.

"That's him!" West said, both agitated and excited.

"Who?"

"That's him," West exclaimed again as he pointed at the photo displayed on the screen. "The scar-faced man."

"What? Are you sure?"

"Yes, I'm positive," West said, locking eyes with the image on the screen staring back at him. "Now we've got you, you bastard."

Borge furrowed his brow. He looked at the screen again. He looked over at West, his eyes still locked in on the photo. He didn't want to have to give him the information he knew but knew he couldn't withhold it.

"West," Borge said with reluctance. "I'm afraid that's impossible."

15: OPERATION WERWOLF

Burt Digby looked over the angelic form of Tanya Nimble lying in a state of stillness. He was sorry it had to be this way. He gently placed his hand upon her and thought about all she had meant to him. He moved his hand down to the lips he had once kissed passionately. He then felt the sudden sharp bite of teeth clamping down hard on his finger.

Digby yelped, pulling his hand away. Tanya had awoken with a fury, screaming at him while he tried to shake off the pain. "Do you normally drug your girlfriends?" She lunged at him until coming to an abrupt stop from the handcuff chain binding her arm to a rusting metal pipe.

"Easy now, you wildcat," Digby said, examining his finger for blood in the bite mark. "If it wasn't for me, you'd be floating face down in the Balearic right now."

"Yeah, you're quite a hero." She shifted on the long wooden crate she was seated on and craned her neck to look around. She couldn't see anything beyond the large room they were in, which was lit by a lone swinging light bulb. The room was grimy and filled with dirt, dust and the smell of damp earth and decay. In the near distance were the sounds of banging and hammering, along with the loud sounds of machinery.

"I'll have you know," Digby retorted, "That I had to fight to have you brought here, and we are now at the site of a very large and legendary gold cache. Where, I can't tell you… yet. But what I can tell you is this is a very exciting find and hopefully the end of this nightmare."

"Nightmare? It seems to me you've had quite a time, gallivanting all over and keeping this all to yourself."

Digby frowned and began pacing. "That's where you're wrong. I thought it was going to be the big break I was always looking for. If you knew what I've been through, you would maybe be a little more understanding."

"Then tell me." She pulled at the chain and found it was securely fastened. "It's not like I'm going anywhere." Burt turned away from her and breathed in deeply. She could see his hesitancy and wondered what could be so bad he wouldn't want to explain it. Sure, he was involved with thugs, thieves, and killers, but she already knew that.

"Alright, Tanya." He let out a long breath and looked up at the ceiling. "I'm going to tell you everything. And know that it is all true. As crazy as this is all going to sound, I assure you it's not just a big load of bull dust."

"That will be a first for you. But I promise to listen, as long as you promise to tell the truth." He swore he would and had a look in his eyes she had never seen before. As untrustworthy as Burt's reputation was, she knew what he was about to say would be the truth. Suddenly, an unexplainable feeling of fear washed over her.

Burt Digby walked over and sat alongside her on the crate. He took a few more deep breaths and finally started to speak. His voice was quavering. "Remember a few months back when I told you that I had a lead on something big, but couldn't say?" Tanya nodded to him. "Well, it's like this: Stinky Spielsdorf's uncle knew a bloke whose dad was a Nazi officer in the SS in World War II. This fellow was on his deathbed and told him about a diary passed down from his dad that supposedly had the location of Himmler's silver rings. Don't ask, but Stinky managed to get his hands on this diary.

"Now, if you haven't heard about this bit of Nazi lore, Heinrich Himmler used to give a special award to his SS men. It was a silver ring, known as the SS-Ehrennring, an 'honor ring,' engraved with occult symbols and at the head of the ring, a skull. Some called it the 'Death's Head Ring.'

"In '38, Himmler sent an order that all of the rings belonging to dead SS officers be returned to him and put into a treasure chest he kept at the Nazi's occult centre at Wewelsburg Castle, in Germany. Then, in 1944, he ordered no more rings were to be produced. There were some 11,500 of these rings and Himmler gave orders to have the chest with all of them hidden. There were always rumors as to the location, but one was that they were hidden in the mountains near the castle, in a cave where the Nazis blasted the entrance shut. That didn't narrow it down too much, but the guy Stinky's grandad knew had a first-hand account in this diary, with the location marked.

"Now, as a load of silver, this wouldn't bring a helluva heap, but as sought-after World War II collectibles, we knew we could make a good haul on this. Stinky knew I could get the equipment lined up, so I met him in Wewelsburg. We made plans to go to the site at night, during the full moon in August, when we could do this without having to worry about using big work lights. This was all totally illegal, and we had to get in and get back out as soon as we could.

"The light from the full moon was brilliant… couldn't have asked for better conditions. And we found it all right, just like the diary map said. We brought in a mini excavator off the truck and it didn't take too long to uncover the rubble to find the cave entrance. With the moonlight flooding into the mouth of the cave, we walked in, just the three of us—me, Stinky, and his mate, Gunther. Then we saw it shining as the moonlight struck it: a large box-shaped container, about eight feet long and tall, covered in silver.

"We put chains on it and dragged it out of the cave, so we could get a better look and open it under the light of the moon. It was in two pieces, the outer layer being a silver-plated lid that slid over a cover for an inner box and sealed with concrete on the bottom edges. Gunther got on the excavator, and we put the forks in the edge and used it to pry the lid up. Goddamn bloody heavy it was, too! That wasn't working so well, so we were able to hook the crane winch on to it, and she started to lift free. As the top lifted off, we could see a large spike inside, in the center of the cover layer, sticking downward. Finally, the silver lid was off and the under layer, made of lead, was just as tall as the outer layer."

"We took a break for a few minutes to make sure all was clear and no one was on the nearby road. The box was now open and all we had to do was get on something to get up the eight feet to look down inside. We moved the excavator alongside it and climbed up to get a better view, as the light of the full moon was shining down straight inside of the box.

"I thought we would be seeing the moonlight reflecting off all the silver rings inside, but instead all that was in there was a corpse, wearing a tattered Nazi uniform, with a big slice in its chest where the spike had impaled it. Stinky climbed down to look for the rings. Gunther and I shined a light down inside and then saw a red glow flash. I heard Stinky scream the most awful scream I ever heard and we saw the red glow was an animal glow, and it was coming from the corpse's eyes! They were open, and this wasn't no corpse.

"Next thing I saw was Stinky's head flying straight up at us, blood spraying out of his headless neck like a geyser. I ran and hid in the bushes… it was fight or flight and I panicked, what can I say? This… thing jumped out and tore poor Gunther to shreds. It… it was a huge wolf-like creature that walked on two legs and was looking around with these horrible glowing red eyes and snorting through its wolf snout. It started devouring him, blood spattering from its chomping fangs.

"I was frozen—couldn't move or even piss myself, which is what I wanted to do. The thing stood up and let out a howl that sounded more like a demon than a wolf. Sweet Suckin' Jesus, I was scared and knew I would be next, but was paralyzed with fear and couldn't move. The beast howled at the moon a few more times, and the sound chilled me straight to the bone.

"Then, watching from inside the bushes, I saw it turn its head and look straight at me. I knew it saw me as we locked eyes. And then, sure as shit, as I watched it before me, it held my gaze and slowly started changing its shape. The ears got smaller and moved down the head. The claws turned into human hands. The fur went in and the snout retreated back to the face of a man… the same face of the corpse that was inside the container.

"Now the man was naked. All of the rotting Nazi uniform had fallen away and he was standing there naked, wearing only a large belt. It was a big belt, like, you know, a wrestling championship belt or something, with fur on the leather strap and shiny gold side plates, and a larger gold front plate with a sculpted wolf's head.

"The face just stared, lit blue by the moon and the red eyes burning into me. I could see this gnarly scar across his face and then he smiled at me like he was the devil himself. He walked over to me and started speaking in this raspy hiss, in German. I struggled to speak and finally told him I didn't understand, that I didn't know much German. He then asked, 'Englander?' I told him, no… Australian. He then said, 'Ah, a dingo,' and began speaking to me in English, asking me what I was doing there.

"I was looking for treasure," I said to him. "The SS Ehrenrings of Himmler are supposed to be buried here."

"The man flew into a rage at the mention of Himmler and then spat on the ground with disgust. 'You are mistaken. But here is my ring.' He held up his left hand to show his gold ring, emblazoned with the Wolfsangel mark. 'You understand,' he said, 'I dislike silver. If it's gold you are seeking, little dingo, then I will show you where to find it. You work for me now. You work for der WolfFührer.'

"From there he began revealing his plans to retrieve the gold caches he hid during World War II. We couldn't recover any gold from the first site—a shopping mall had been built on top of it. I thought I should run at that moment, but then he said we would go back to Tangier and use *The Bootylicious* to go to his next site, and he guaranteed the gold would be there. That was in the Balearic Sea, where there was a U-Boat... God only knows how the Nazis ever got it in there, inside a hollow rock formation. And it was filled with gold! Gold bars, all with the Wolfsangel mark.

"It took forever, it seemed, to haul out the gold bars, but we finally finished when we ran into you. I didn't mean to get you involved in this. Everything he's got me into—murder, dealing with gangsters and these bloody werewolves... I just want to get my gold payoff and then we can get out of here and away from him forever. I know this all sounds flat out crazy, but it's all the Gospel truth, I swear it."

Tanya had been listening to his story in rapt attention. For a time, she had listened in disbelief, but the conviction with Burt told it and when he told of the U-Boat—he didn't know she had also been there, with Val West—she knew he was telling the truth, no matter how crazy it seemed. Digby was trembling and breathing heavily from the stress of recounting his experience. She moved closer to him and put her free hand on his shoulder.

"Oh my God, Burt." He leaned on her, and she didn't pull away. "What are we going to do?"

***

"Why is it impossible?" Val West asked Dr. Borge as they continued to look at the photo of the scar-faced man on the computer screen. "I would have said that about a lot of things until recently."

"Because," Borge replied, "That's Otto Skorzeny. He was a Nazi SS Commander known as 'Hitler's Favorite Commando,' among other things."

"And the leader of the Nazi project known as Operation Werwolf," said Commander 7's voice over the speaker as he joined them. "He was also a daring and outstanding soldier, no matter his allegiance. If LoneWolf says that's who he saw, then I am inclined to believe him. There's also enough unsubstantiated claims dating back to World War II to more than suggest this is not only a possibility, but now a reality, with LoneWolf's identification of him."

"Listen, I know of the name," West said. "I admit, I'm not overly-familiar with Nazi history and lore, so what is the story on Skorzeny?"

Commander 7 instructed Borge to bring up a detailed file on Otto Skorzeny on the view screen.

SKORZENY, OTTO
OPERATION: WERWOLF

SS Lieutenant-Colonel.
Born: June 12, 1908.
Height: 6' 4"

Austrian-born German SS-Obersturmbannführer (lieutenant colonel) in the Waffen-SS during World War II. A top leader of special forces known for his daring missions, Skorzeny was wounded by shrapnel from a Katyusha rocket attack in December 1942.

Awarded the Iron Cross for bravery after continuing to fight through his injuries. Upon recovering, Skorzeny was assigned a staff job with the SS in Berlin, where he developed new strategies for commando tactics and warfare. Due to his wounds, he could no longer be an effective soldier on the battlefield and began seeking experimental procedures to allow his return.

Via the lycanthropy experiments of Nazi scientist Dr. Josef Mengele, extracted lycanthrope venom was injected into Skorzeny, mutating his genetics into a werewolf. Mengele used venom produced by Skorzeny on other Nazi soldiers to create more werewolf super-soldiers. This group, led by Skorzeny as the Alpha Wolf, formed a new elite commando unit known as the SS Werwolf Wolf Pack.

Through the blitzkrieg tactics of the SS Werwolf unit, Skorzeny quickly became known as Adolf Hitler's favorite commando. Given Hitler's penchant for the occult, he began adopting the werewolves into his future plans, even designing strategically located secret bases called "Wolfsschanzes"—Wolf's Lairs.

Commander 7 paused the file recording. "Things do get murkier, believe it or not. There are rumors of SS Chief Heinrich Himmler and Dr. Mengele becoming concerned with Skorzeny's growing power and fearing he would overthrow them, as well as Hitler. History says Otto Skorzeny surrendered to the Allied Forces in 1945 and then escaped to Spain before he could be tried at Nuremberg. He went on to become known as 'The Most Dangerous Man in Europe' and was involved in international espionage and crime until his death in 1975. However, it would seem that is not necessarily as straightforward as it would seem.

"Otto Skorzeny's first cousin, Bluto Skorzeny, served under Himmler's SS Command. He resembled Otto well enough, apart from not having the distinctive facial scar that marked him. In 1945, Bluto was reported dead, but no grave was ever found. Around this same time, Otto, showing no signs of being a werewolf, surrendered and was arrested. Over the years a conspiracy alleged that due to slight inconsistencies in photos, it wasn't the real Otto who surrendered and was ultimately acquitted in 1947, but Bluto, who had facial surgery performed by Mengele to more closely resemble Otto.

"Most Operation Werwolf files, particularly those of Dr. Mengele, were destroyed in the war. Enough pieces and parts of them were recovered by Allied forces to put together what we know. Although off the record—and officially denied by them—many of the German scientists brought to the United States as part of Operation Paperclip told the Americans Mengele had found the crypt of a 19th century

153

vârcolac—a Master Werewolf—in Transylvania. He then removed the silver stake in the corpse's heart and used the reanimated werewolf to extract the werewolf venom used on Otto Skorzeny."

West considered all he had just taken in. This was not the usual garden-variety spies, traitors, or even megalomaniacs he was used to dealing with. He gave a sigh, thinking of what he was up against. "Well, at least I now know who the werewolf was that bit me, and also Wildebeest, so that's something. Getting him is going to be a whole other thing. But how did he lead a Nazi werewolf commando unit? He must be able to control his werewolf powers somehow."

Borge looked up from the files he was scrolling through. "This may be the answer." He pointed to a drawing. "This is known in folklore as *Der Wolfsgürtel*—a wolfskin belt. These files suggest the vârcolac corpse was still wearing the belt when he and Mengele unearthed the crypt in Transylvania, in 1944. The speculation is, after the experiment with the werewolf venom injection, Skorzeny took the belt and put it on himself. Finding he could be consciously aware while in werewolf form, he used this ability to command his Nazi werewolf squad. He was already the alpha werewolf, as the commandos were given injections derived from Skorzeny's werewolf venom glands."

"Very good find, Dr. Borge," said Commander 7. "Now, we just need to know what his next step is. Any more on the data retrieved from *The Bootylicious*?"

"Not exactly, sir," West said. "But we have two possibilities."

"That is good," Commander 7 replied. "But not good enough. We need to narrow these two possibilities down to one certainty."

***

Tanya was still stunned by what Burt had told her, possibly the most bizarre story she had ever heard. Beside his sincerity in his telling

154

of it, she also thought of the fight at Casino de Monte Carlo. At the time, she thought it was two maniacs in wolf masks, but now with what Digby had said, it seemed to her to add up, even if the numbers didn't appear to make sense as accepted reality.

Digby had kept his head down since telling Tanya his story. He knew it seemed insane, and even doubted his own sanity at times. "Tanya," Digby looked up and said, "You may find this hard to believe, but I was thinking of you through all of this. This has all been for you."

"That, I do find hard to believe," she said. "You should stick with the werewolf story."

"I mean it." He stood up and faced her. "You know, I've been a failure in my life. Less than honest most of the time. Permanently banned from re-entering Australia, my own home country for God's sake. But I've wanted to be better. I just didn't know how.

"And you... I couldn't believe I'd landed as crackin' a sheila as you! You get it, the whole fortune hunting thing—even though you care more about actual archaeology than I ever did—but still, you were up for the adventure, and the reward. I thought this was my chance to prove myself to be a great treasure hunter.

"It's all cocked up right now, but we can turn it around. We just gotta play our cards right for just a little while longer and together we can get away from this Skorzeny, and with more gold than either of us could ever spend. So, let's see this through a wee bit longer, we get the gold, and then we can go anywhere, disappear and live a life of luxury together."

Tanya trained her eyes on him, with what he took as perhaps a spark of interest forming. "I also told Skorzeny about your metallurgy skills," he continued, "and you can be of use seeing how we need a new metallurgist for this project. We're a team. You and me. Will you trust me and join me now?"

Digby held up the handcuff key toward her as a sign of good faith. Tanya looked into the big blue eyes of the face she always thought was goofy looking, but somehow irresistible. She didn't answer.

Digby looked back at her and saw the sparkle in her eyes.

He thought it was a clear enough reply.

16: USE OF DEADLY FORCE AUTHORIZED

In what remained of the base at Cimetière du Château in Nice, Val West and Dr. Borge worked on determining the next stop for Otto Skorzeny and Burt Digby, with the captive Tanya Nimble in tow. With the names of two locations in Germany–Waldenburg and Dittersbach– to go on, the five hundred kilometer distance between the two still made it a coin toss as to which location West would find Skorzeny. Choosing the wrong one would waste valuable time. Added to the problem was there still wasn't a match at either location with the points marked on the sketch of the railway tracks.

Borge fidgeted and then jumped up from his chair. "Of course! West, take a look at this." He pointed to a map he was viewing on the monitor, then enlarged it, putting it side-by-side with an aerial satellite view. "We've been looking at the wrong 'Waldenburg' and 'Dittersbach.' Even though there are two unrelated locations with those names in Germany, Skorzeny wasn't referring to Germany. At least not the Germany we know.

"For Otto Skorzeny, in his time of the 1940s, these locations would have been in Germany. Only they aren't there *now*. After World War II, the borders changed and the *other* Waldenburg, Germany of 1945 is now Walbrzych, Poland. What was once called Dittersbach is now known as the Walbrzych Glowny train station, of the Wroclaw-Walbrzych railway line. And yes, it is that Wroclaw—the site of the failed search for the Nazi gold train."

Commander 7 spoke through the speaker. "Good work, Dr. Borge. This has to be what we're looking for."

"Let's follow the railway map," West said. Tracing the railway line from the Walbrzych Glowny train station, he compared it to the sketch with the marks. "Stop there. Zoom in on the location." He looked back and forth between the sketch and the map. "This looks like it fits." The satellite map showed the rail line running into a tunnel under Volovec Mountain, marked *Tunel Pod Malym Wolowcem*.

Borge looked at the sketch and compared it with the satellite image of the railroad. "I concur. This is it. Whatever Skorzeny is up to, it must be somewhere in this area."

"I need travel arrangements to get me there right away." This was the break they needed, and West wasn't about to let it slip away.

"Not yet," Commander 7 responded. "First, you and Dr. Borge are to go back to the Highgate base in London. It's a shorter flight–especially by military plane–to London, than it is to try and get into Poland right now. As soon as you return, we can prepare for the mission and all of the necessary border-crossing credentials will be set."

West bristled. He knew he shouldn't question the Commander, but his emotions began getting the better of him. "What about the girl? What about Cedric?" Cedric's remains were still with them in the underground level of the mausoleum base at the Cimetière du Château.

"Arrangements have been made to transport Cedric back to London. His daughter will be handling the rest. He has 'officially' passed away after a tragic road accident. As for the girl, I do understand that you want to help her, and if there is an opportunity, take it. But otherwise... officially, she is not our concern. You are both to report back to the base at Highgate Cemetery in London as soon as possible."

"Yes, sir," West said, half excited by tracking down Skorzeny's next move, and half disappointed, knowing that every moment was a ticking clock against Tanya's life. She could very well already be dead, but until he knew for certain, he was going to assume she was alive. He got her into this, and it was only right he got her out of it.

***

The journey back to London was solemn and uneventful. West and Borge flew back with the remains of Cedric encased in a casket. They were on a military plane, arranged by Commander 7. No questions were asked, a testament to the level of the Commander's stature.

An hour after departing Nice, the plane touched down at RAF Northolt Air Force station in London. From there, West and Borge were taken by car to Swain's Lane, where they both quietly walked the short distance to Highgate Cemetery in the cold October night.

The mausoleum housing ParaCommand seemed 'lonely as a tomb' without Cedric there. When West and Borge both commented on this to each other, they shared a laugh, knowing Cedric would have appreciated the dark humor. Descending the stone rampway to the subterranean laboratory, they were welcomed by the computer-lined catacombs, the array of blinking lights and chirping machines, all working for Borge even while he was away.

"Commander 7 will be joining us for a briefing," Borge said. "Until then, let's start prepping for what you'll need, now that we know where you'll be going." He looked up at the printed roll of paper spat out by one of his computers. "I see the Commander has booked you a commercial flight to from London to Walbrzych. It should be about a two-hour flight. I'll have to do some additional modifications to your spy suit to get you around the airport x-ray scans. Same for your luggage. Once I have it calibrated properly, a transmitter inside your luggage will send the x-ray machine images of harmless briefcase items and the circulating electronic field inside will hide the metallic properties of your gear and gun. The suit will function in a similar fashion, appearing as your human skin and emitting an inaudible frequency to disguise your NeuraComlink implant."

"Splendid," West said. "But just make sure that the frequency you use is also inaudible to me."

"Roger that," Borge replied, being fully aware of West's heightened sense of hearing. It was also getting close to the next full moon. West's animal senses would grow even more sensitive as the moon grew larger, emitting stronger WLF rays as it waxed toward its peak.

"As you know, we of course always want to keep a low profile," Borge continued. "But if any issues should arise with airport security, hand this card to them. You'll be waved through once they've called the number listed. And for God's sake, don't bring a bottle of shampoo larger than three ounces. We all know that's where the real threats are."

West smiled at this rare show of sarcastic humor from Borge. He also enjoyed the idea of putting one over on the typically rude airport security agents. With his gear ready, West left Highgate Cemetery with his next stop being London Heathrow Airport. Borge's tech tricks worked like a charm and West spent the next two hours in flight relaxing, wondering what awaited him at the target area.

From Copernicus Airport in Wroclaw, West drove his rental car the thirty-five miles to Walbrzych. He had the location figured out but needed to find a way to get close to do some old-fashioned spying. It was a bright and sunny autumn afternoon—perfect for a drive along Poland's southwestern country roads of the Lower Silesian Voivodeship.

He continued driving southeast of Walbrzych, until he could see the large twin hills known as the Wolowiec* and Maly Wolowiec

---

* Pronounced 'Volovec' in English-- *Editor.*

mountains, part of the Black Mountains range. The two mounds rose up, pert and perky, with their mass of evergreen treetops half covered in a sleepy creeping fog. Below the peaks, near the bottom of the northern slope, were the two tunnels of the Walbrzych railway route running underneath.

The two railway tunnels were approximately fifty feet apart and are among the longest man-made tunnels in Europe. Dating back to the late 19th century and early 20th century, during World War II, the twin tunnels served to shelter special trains, and perhaps much more than that.

Parking the car along a dirt side road, West slipped on a dark trench coat over his black spysuit and moved along the thick cluster of trees and brush framing each side of the tracks. Slowing his pace, he went into hunting mode, taking a few steps at a time, and then pausing to listen. The entrance to the tunnel pods was only about a thousand feet ahead. A few feet in front of him a construction barricade was set up with a sign posted (translated from Polish):

WARNING! NO ENTRY!
TRACK IS BEING RENOVATED
THIS IS A CONSTRUCTION SITE- ENTRY FORBIDDEN
RAILWAY PERSONNEL ONLY
USE OF DEADLY FORCE AUTHORIZED

West thought the last part was laying it on a bit thick, but Nazis weren't known for their subtlety, and he was certain this sign wasn't legitimate.

Viewing through binoculars, he could see the tunnels were under guard, and not by typical security guards. These watchmen were armed and looked more like soldiers—most likely Transylvanian

161

troops on loan from General Ferenc, who was entangled somehow with Skorzeny. The Transylvanians had snuck into Poland and were serving as Skorzeny's goon squad. Scanning ahead to the tunnel entrance, there were more workers—without a doubt, more Transylvanian military—doing construction on the tunnel railway line.

Following the wooded area as it continued to the tunnel pods, West crouched low and moved with great care not to step on any branches or any other noises that might get him a bullet to the head. He increased his distance into the sloping woods alongside the tracks, sneaking past the posted sentries. The two tunnel pod entrances were now within view.

West peered through the underbrush down the embankment. The workers appeared to be removing old track from the right-side tunnel and bringing in new, curved rail switching track. The reflection of welding sparks was visible from inside the tunnel, but he could not see beyond. Two armed sentries stood atop the entrance to the tunnel. Another armed guard had come down from the hill and was speaking to one of the sentries stationed above the tunnels. After a few moments, they switched places and the sentry started back up.

There was something going on farther up the mountain and West took the opportunity to follow. The evening mist began drifting down from the Volovec Mountains, bringing a chill with it, along with extra cover. Keeping his distance, he squat-walked in an uncomfortable crouch, following the sentry from the slope to the base of Volovec Mountain and up on to a hiking trail.

A benefit of suffering from lycanthropy was that West could detect the sentry's scent as he followed. Guided by the scent, he tracked his quarry at a distance as the trail wound around the hillside. The sentry left the trail and climbed over a rock bluff topped by a gangly tree.

Keeping low, West scrambled up the bluff, following him to a small swamp filled with ghostly dead trees and jagged rocks jutting

162

out from the marshy ground. Up ahead, another guard stood near a large rock. The man he pursued took position at the rock, relieving the standing guard. Expecting the relieved guard to head back down the trail toward the tunnels, West was surprised by what he saw happen instead.

The two guards grabbed hold of the edges of the automobile-sized rock, lifting it up. Through his binoculars, West could see loose dirt around the rock perimeter and a pair of rusted hinges on the opposite side of where they were lifting. Once the false rock was lifted and open on its hinges, the first guard disappeared beneath it.

Wherever this man had gone, West planned to follow. He sat in silence watching the new guard stand watch over the rock cover, which had slowly descended back to its normal position of looking like an ordinary rock formation. More mist was seeping in, enveloping the swamp, giving West some much needed extra cover. The time was now.

West widened his circle moving around to the back of the rock and slowly moved in closer, behind the guard. In one swift motion he had done countless times, West simultaneously placed his left hand over the guard's mouth, while his right hand plunged a knife blade between the shoulder blades, dropping him in seconds. West picked up the slain sentry and carried him into the thick bushes, depositing the body where it would take some time to be found and covered it with his black trench coat.

He went over to the rock, found the lip and lifted. The rock facade had been here for decades in the middle of this swamp without anyone realizing what it was concealing: a large rust-covered hatch door, ten feet in diameter and opened by a wheel handle. West turned the wheel and with great effort, the hatch creaked open. It opened to a smooth-bored cylindrical shaft, disappearing into the darkness below. He descended the ladder steps down the shaft, with no idea what lay in wait once he reached bottom.

The shaft seemed to keep going forever and at various points on the other side, West saw what looked like entrances to other levels. He kept climbing down until finally, about 200 feet below, the shaft hit ground. His eyes began adjusting to the darkness, revealing a labyrinth of caves, mines and tunnels—a vast network carved deep into Volovec and the surrounding Black Mountains.

At the edge of one side tunnel, a rusted mine car sat on a track, the ground flooded in a pool of slimy brown water. More caverns, some constructed of brickwork and others bored into the bedrock, branched off on each side. The tattered remnants of swastika flags hanging throughout revealed what looked to have been a planned World War II Nazi underground city.

He could faintly detect the scent of the guard he had followed down into this hell, but even without, the tracks of multiple footprints in the thick dust covering the ground led the way. The air was thick and smelled of rot, and despite the enormous size of this installation, there was a choking sense of claustrophobia clinging about it. The trail led to a massive iron door, recently forced open and hanging sideways on its broken hinges.

West flattened himself to the wall and moved through the doorway into a corridor, sparsely lit by torches. Now, he could finally hear echoing sounds off in the distance. The footprints and any scent traces had disappeared in the wet muddy ground ahead, which was under an inch of water from a constant trickle of water coming from a fissure in the wall. Here, the tunnels branched off in three directions. With no lead to follow, West left it up to chance.

He took the tunnel to the left and made note of what he saw to keep some sense of direction to find his way back. He also kept an eye out for still-active World War II-era booby traps. There could be mines ready to explode under his feet or a nerve gas attack among other surprises. If he was going the correct route, Skorzeny and his men would have removed these already. But was he following their route? West passed by some rusted electronic controls installed in the cave wall, next to a slab with hand and leg restraint clamps—an ugly reminder of Nazi experimentations. He could hear the noises again, this time coming from above him.

Ahead was a tunnel entrance about twenty feet up, accessible by a rusted iron staircase. Following the sounds, West climbed up and entered the tunnel. A cold blast of air hit him, along with the sounds of machinery and muffled voices. It was some kind of ventilation shaft, amplifying the sounds. They weren't as close as they sounded, although West hoped this would ultimately lead him to where they were coming from.

The ground shook with his next steps, collapsing beneath him from either a triggered booby trap or natural collapse. Whichever it was, the ground sucked him down, dropping him fifteen feet to land with a crunch, and then he sunk some more. West took a second to catch his breath and try to figure out where he was. He was in a pit, his fall broken by the massive pile of brittle bones surrounding him.

These were likely the skeletal remains of hundreds of victims enslaved by the Nazis to dig these tunnels. Despite the macabre visage of the skulls looking back at him, West saw a human face in all of them, and it strengthened his resolve to take down Skorzeny. He pushed against the bones he was wedged between, but the more he tried to climb out, the more the fragile skeletons broke, the sharp bones jabbing him and sinking him deeper into the pit.

By his estimate, he was seven feet down into the pile of broken bones. A sickening smell rushed through the air, followed by the sound of flowing water. The water rose rapidly and with his arms pinned by the bone pile, he couldn't reach to try and activate

LoneWolf. Still, the water was flowing in from somewhere and West decided that if he couldn't go up, he would try going down.

He kicked downward, the bones crunching with each stomp. As he was slowly moving down, the water level was quickly rising up. The bottom gave out, plunging him into the putrid brown water. Swimming among the grinning skulls and floating bones, West hoped he could find a way out before he ran out of air. He reached the outer wall of the pit and felt along it. It wasn't the source of the water flow, but he had found a sharp ridge. It was a door! Now, to get it open, and fast. There was no handle. West grabbed at the edges and tried to wedge his fingers in. There wasn't enough space to pry it open.

The only hope was that this doorway was fragile enough to force open. He could push the LoneWolf activator, but without knowing the immediate situation, could Borge help? Or would LoneWolf just drown in a sea of bones, far underground where the moonlight would never find him? West fought his body's instinctual urge to retch from the stench of the rotting water. He fought against this as hard as he was fighting against the stuck hatchway. Pulling at the door with all he had, the depleting oxygen made his lungs feel as if they were about to explode. If it wouldn't open to him, he would have to try working it in the other direction. Thrusting both legs into a powerful kick, the door crumpled inward.

The force of the rushing water pushed him through the door and once on the other side, he was finally able to get his head up to breathe in some air. It was reeking, fetid, filthy air, but it was still air and he gulped it in with relief. The water and bones poured in from the chamber, the current carrying West with them.

Fighting against the force of the foul water and skeletal remains, he soon realized he wasn't in another tunnel, but in a metal chute. Ahead, the chute was broken off, leaving an open gap with a drop of unknown distance and he was moving at a rapid pace, unable to stop.

The torrent of corpse water and broken bones pushed him over the edge of the broken chute, and he landed hard on the cave ground below, rolling into a ventilation shaft.

Trying to stop the momentum, he clawed at the ground as he slid in a downward trajectory. He desperately grabbed at the thin metal tubing running along the wall, managing to just barely catch hold of it. The tubing popped its rivets along the way as he continued to bounce down the sloping tunnel shaft.

West held tight to the metal tubing. When he reached the opening at the bottom of the shaft, he swung out on it like a rope. It held and he paused as the swinging came to a stop. He was suspended high in the air, but where exactly was he and how was he going to climb out? The metal piping groaned, and West wondered how long before the remaining rivets holding it also popped, sending him crashing down. He looked down to see he was in a large, cavernous chamber, the size of a warehouse. The smell of soot, grease and oil reached his nostrils. And light—where was it coming from? And also, the sounds—the sound of the noises he was following earlier.

West turned his head to look at the rest of the chamber. Looking up at him from some thirty feet below, was the gaping expression of Burt Digby and the sinister visage of Otto Skorzeny. They were standing near a war train locomotive and cars, all being serviced by Transylvanian workers.

West hung on to the metal piping, dangling helplessly. Within seconds, armed guards gathered under him, rifles pointed.

Skorzeny walked over with the guards. He smiled up at West and gave a wicked wink.

"So nice of you to drop in, mein Freund."

17: NAZI BY NATURE

"Oh, it's our friend from the Canadian Secret Service." Otto Skorzeny grinned at the others, while pointing to the awkwardly dangling Val West. Skorzeny was wearing an all-black uniform in the style of the Nazi SS uniforms, but instead of SS symbols and swastikas, his uniform was emblazoned with the symbol of the Wolfsangel.

After dismissing Digby, who anxiously went aboard the train, Skorzeny walked under West, still dangling from the metal piping twenty feet above. "I didn't even know the Canadians had any secrets worth keeping." He gestured toward two of his workers. "Bring that ladder over and get him down." He looked back up at West. "Do keep your hands where we can see them. I'm sure you know you are completely compromised, and civility is the only option."

"Civility. That's funny, coming from you," West said, the guards training their rifles on him with every step down the ladder. Before he reached the floor, the guards were on him, making sure he stepped away from the ladder without incident, and making sure to remove his handgun. Skorzeny walked over to West. He sniffed, wrinkled his nose, and turned away, repulsed.

Borge's scent solution had worked. The rotting water he had just been in had also helped. The longer Skorzeny thought West was 'just a human,' the better. He was counting on Skorzeny's underestimating him. West looked at the enemy before him, with his wild eyes, the hideous scar running the length of his face, the oddly shaped ears that were wolfish in appearance, and the voice that sounded like a rattle-snake gargling glass. This time, West knew who he was, and also who he was to him: Otto Skorzeny, the infamous Nazi commando and the werewolf who put this curse on him. West wanted to bring him in dead, but as much as it pained him now, he had to bring him back alive—if he wanted a chance at being cured.

West extended his hand. "Val West." Skorzeny snubbed the gesture and West withdrew the token courtesy. "Not with the Canadian Secret Service, sorry to say. I was looking for a different underground Nazi city and seemed to have stumbled through the wrong cave."

"You are quite flippant about the situation you find yourself in, mein Herr," Skorzeny said. "Whichever secret service you are with, it is no matter. Their trail now stops dead with you. Also, you reek. Most likely from your swim with rotting schwein bones.

West decided to push Skorzeny's buttons. "By the way, I didn't catch your name. Is it Otto or Bluto? It's so hard to tell you two apart." Skorzeny's eyes flashed red, and his lips pulled back, baring fangs. West had gotten under his fur. Skorzeny turned away, ignoring the jab, yet incensed that West would even have the knowledge to suggest such a thing.

The two armed guards pointed their rifle barrels into West, prodding him to move. Hearing the commotion, Tanya came down from the locomotive with Digby, pausing on the steps upon seeing West. He glared at her. Here she was, not a prisoner, but walking about freely with the people he was supposed to be saving her from.

"Tanya. So nice to see you. I hope you enjoyed your kidnapping. Seems like you are in good company." She walked up to him and slapped him across the face. "Doesn't anybody here know how to shake hands?" The guards poked him with their rifle barrels and led him away. West turned his attention to Skorzeny while being marched off. "Speaking of hands, it looks like your pet is still missing his."

Skorzeny turned and put his hand up, motioning for the guards to stop marching West forward. Wildebeest the henchwolf was standing obediently alongside Skorzeny. Tiny nubs were forming on the raw stump left by Cedric's silver blade. The werewolf was also wearing a large cone collar around its neck.

"Ja, my poor Húnd could not get his hand back, but a new one will grow in time. Until then, he whines and mewls and insists on licking the raw stump, so he is forced to wear a cone until he can behave himself."

Wildebeest was staring straight ahead with tongue hanging out, panting. Skorzeny turned his eyes to Wildebeest and the beast looked away. "Licking your sore paw… SHAME." Skorzeny raised his hand in a striking motion. Wildebeest cowered, then slinked away and sat down on its haunches in an empty corner, letting out a big yawn, tongue lapping at the sharp canine teeth surrounded by black slimy lips.

"Damn it, Tom," West thought. "I know you're in there. Come on, fight it." He knew it was no use. Thomas Hedison's mind was in the same unknown place West's also went when he was a werewolf. He knew how helpless that also made him, without the control of Borge to override the base animal mind. It was even worse for Tom, with someone like Skorzeny controlling him. Skorzeny nodded to the guards to continue marching West forward. They moved down a corridor and stopped to throw him into a prison cell, shackling his wrists into chains mounted on the wall.

In the dingy cell, West pondered his escape options and how much time he had before Skorzeny enacted his plans. Was he really going to drive this train out of here? It seemed so. West had taken in as much detail as he could before being placed in the cell. The locomotive engine and its seven connected cars were approximately 150 meters long. The engine itself had the armored covering of a war train, with

170

a long artillery railroad gun and battering ram plow mounted on the front. By the smells alone, West could tell the workers had been preparing the train for hours, greasing and lubricating the machinery which had been sitting idle for over seventy-five years.

He saw them adding water from a spigot in the cavern wall, most likely part of the underground water source he had seen leaking through in several places of this old tunnel system. There was no reason to think the train wouldn't operate. It was in immaculate condition and had been covered for decades by the remains of the tattered canvas strewn about. But where would Skorzeny go once he had driven this train out through the tunnel pod?

West's thoughts were interrupted by a guard accompanied by Tanya. She stood outside the cell door glowering at West through the barred window. "Was it the gold that seduced you or just Burt Digby's charm?" West asked. "Or was it Skorzeny? I'm sure you could get a few more flecks of gold added to your purse by performing some 'special services.' I'm sure you're quite well-versed in that."

Tanya swore and told the guard to let her into the cell. The guard was reluctant, but she swore at him as well and he relented. He closed the door with her inside and resumed his post outside the cell.

She stood looking at West and after a moment, flicked open a switchblade knife. West shifted in his shackles as she neared. "Careful," she warned, "I've got a knife." She moved closer grabbing hold of his right arm. She slowly lowered the knife blade toward his wrist. He felt the blade plunge into the cuff and the pressure of its point springing the lock. She leaned down to his ear and whispered, "We need to get the hell out of here. I hope you have a plan because this is all I had." She used the knife to unlock his other hand, standing over him to block any view the guard may have. "Sorry about the slap."

"I've been dealt worse," West said,

"I had to play along. I know this is going to sound crazy, but this scar-face guy Burt's involved with is an actual, for real werewolf... and a Nazi, as in a genuine World War II Nazi."

"You don't say? Well, I admit, it does all sound a bit absurd. Call for the guard to open the door and then fall down as you walk across the cell. I'll take care of him and then we're going to get you out of here. And then I'm coming back to catch a train." Tanya nodded and took a deep breath.

While Skorzeny and his hired men worked on readying the train for departure, Wildebeest sat in the corner, fidgeting to find a way to lick his scabbed paw, the cone collar denying him every time. A noise and the whiff of a scent from down the corridor made his ears perk up and eyes flash with danger. He rose from his haunches and loped off down the cavern's maze of corridors, following his senses.

West had knocked the guard unconscious using Tanya's distraction and the two were fleeing down the corridor. He had figured all of these tunnels were connected somehow and just needed to find a way back to the entrance shaft.

"Any ideas of how to get out of here?" West asked.

"None, except going back where the train is," Tanya replied. "Probably not the best option. This must be an undiscovered hidden base of Project Riese—that's 'giant' in German. The Nazis had miles of tunnels dug out, but they were still unfinished by the end of World War II. The rest of the Project Riese complex is just a few miles away. It's a historical tour site."

"Thanks, but I've had enough of the tour. Hold up... stop for a second."

West saw a narrow tunnel in the wall about five feet up. Wherever it led, it would at least get them farther away before their escape was discovered. He climbed up into it, barely squeezing inside. The tunnel extended beyond his view, and he hoped it would connect with another part of the tunnel system at some point and not come to a dead end.

He reached back and grabbed Tanya's hand to pull her up into the tunnel. She let out a scream. "Something's got my foot!" The jaws of Wildebeest were snapping at her heels. West pulled her as hard as he could, and the momentum sent them tumbling into the tunnel.

They quickly moved up the vertical-slanted tunnel with Wildebeest behind. The snapping, snarling Wildebeest was struggling to enter the tunnel. The cone around his neck was wedged into the small entrance hole and he furiously thrashed his head around, trying to squeeze through. West and Tanya flattened themselves against the tunnel wall and continued moving, while the helpless Wildebeest barked, frothing at the mouth in frustration.

The tunnel widened as they went. Ahead was what appeared to be the dark shape of a connecting tunnel. Tanya asked to stop for a second. West looked ahead and saw the dark shape again, but this time it was rapidly moving toward them. The sound of a thousand flapping wings broke through the air as a mass of bats, their slumber disturbed, filled the tunnel, swarming West and Tanya. He threw his body over hers and felt the stream of bats flow over him with a screeching loudness that drowned out Tanya's muffled screams.

A long minute later, the bats subsided. Tanya was shaking. West could see she was starting to panic and tried his best to console her. They might not get out of here at all, but she didn't need to know that. One thing was certain: if they were to somehow make it, they didn't have time for this. After trembling in his arms for a few moments, she began calming down.

Tanya wiped her eyes. "Val, how are we going to get out of here? There are so many tunnels. We could be lost forever down here."

West considered the situation. Under normal circumstances, she would be right. But nothing was normal about any of these circumstances. "Just stay calm," he said, placing a reassuring hand on her shoulder. "I have a nose for this sort of thing." He hoped it would be true. Once he got nearer to where he had come in, he could follow his own scent trail out. At least he hoped it would work that way.

The tunnel floor levelled out from its ascent at the top of the pathway, and down further was a metal grate in the wall. "Here's our ticket out," he said, and grabbed at the metal, pulling it out of its corroded frame. It was pure darkness inside. He felt around inside the vent shaft, and satisfied the metal bottom was solid, lifted Tanya up, climbing in after her. There was a light at the end of the tunnel, coming through an opening at the end of the shaft, just above eye level.

They both felt a renewed sense of hope and dashed toward the light source. Tanya reached up. "There's something metal and pointy here, like a rod, so be careful. At least's it's something to grab on to." Before she could let go, she was jerked out of the passageway. A blinding light shone on West and Tanya, and they saw it was the barrel of an AK-47 machine gun. It, along with five others, belonged to Transylvanian guards aiming to kill.

With guns trained on them, they both climbed out and were manhandled by the guards forcing their hands up and pushing them into single file line. Standing alongside the soldiers was Wildebeest, growling and salivating. He threw his head back and let out a triumphant howl that echoed throughout the empty caverns.

"Bad dog," West muttered and once again felt the sharp jab of a rifle barrel in his back. He and Tanya were marched back to the train hangar. West thought of how he may have taken a chance but knew they would certainly kill Tanya. In the three seconds it would take to move a free hand to try and activate LoneWolf, they would both be gunned down before he could transform. He didn't like it, but he would have to wait for a better opportunity.

General Ferenc slithered out of his limousine to check on his crew working in the tunnel pod. A curved track was now spliced in off the straight track that went through the tunnel, as instructed by Skorzeny. Pleased with the work, he called over the transmitter.

"Herr Ferenc, report on your progress" Skorzeny said.

"My men have completed the track work to your specifications," he replied as he listened to Skorzeny check over every item. The man's voice alone sent a shudder through Ferenc. "No, they did not breach the second wall behind the bricks. They found the connecting tracks and were able to connect them to the new track switcher rails. Don't worry... yes, all of the route is covered. Payments are in to ensure a smooth and trouble-free flight for us."

Ferenc switched off the transmitter, took a drink from his flask and wiped the cold sweat off his brow. His toupee glue was beginning to run. He had to keep his eye on the prize. A lot of gold would soon be coming to him and then he—and his ulcer—wouldn't have to deal with this Skorzeny anymore.

***

The guards led Val West and Tanya Nimble back to the train hangar, where a dumbfounded Burt Digby stopped what he was doing to see what was going on.

"Tanya," he said. "What the bloody hell do you think you're doing?"

"Back off Digby," West said. "I forced her as a hostage to take me out of here."

"Is this true, Tanya?" Digby asked. He placed his hand on her arm. She recoiled and spat in his face.

175

"No, Burt, it's not. And f---"

"Such language, Fraulein." Skorzeny walked over to her and ran his hand along her face. "Whatever are we to do with you? You need to be tamed, wild minx. Digby—see that she is boarded on the train and does not leave her seat. Verstanden?"

"Yes… yes, sir." Digby narrowed his eyes at Tanya, who met his eyes with a scowl. The guard pushed his rifle barrel into her back, forcing her up the ramp onto the train. Digby reluctantly followed.

Skorzeny barked at one of the guards. "Bind him with chains, schnell!" He turned to West. "You are a wily one, Herr West. However, I do tire of your antics."

"That's a nice train you have there," West said to him. "You know, they do make smaller scales for hobbyists."

"I am no hobbyist, Canadian Arschloch. I once flew a glider into what was called an impenetrable mountain fortress, defeated two hundred guards, and broke Benito Mussolini out of Allied forces imprisonment."

"Not by yourself, you didn't," West replied. "Besides, that's nothing. I once single-handedly stopped a mad professor with a secret formula to freeze the world's oceans."

Skorzeny's glare burned a hole into West. "You would dare measure Schwanzes with me? I am in the history books. You, on the other hand, are about to *be* history."

A guard arrived carrying chain connected wrist shackles. The guard took West's arm to put on the cuffs. With the momentary distraction, he wrested one arm free and sent a blasting punch to Skorzeny's gut. Immediately he felt his hand strike against metal, and it recoiled with vibrating pain. Skorzeny laughed and opened his shirt to show the gleaming gold wolf's head sculpted on the faceplate of his belt. "You have just met Der Wolfsgürtel. Did you like its bite?" The guards locked the shackles on West pushing him away from Skorzeny.

176

"Aren't you going to tell me your plans before you kill me," West asked, hoping to buy some time and also knowing these megalomaniac types loved to gloat about how great they are and how foolproof their plans were.

"Why should I tell you? It will not matter to you. You will be dead." Skorzeny drew his Mauser pistol from its holster. He pointed it at West's face. "However, it does matter to me." He lowered the pistol and shot West in the gut, dropping him onto his knees. "A gut shot for a gut shot. Mine stings more than yours, I should think. That should tame your wild hairs."

West reeled from the pain burning through him. "A shot to the guts like that will take a while to kill you," Skorzeny taunted, "but not before you see firsthand my triumph of piloting this train out."

West writhed on his side, trying to fight the pain. Skorzeny motioned for a worker to bring the hoist placed by the locomotive over to them. The guards wrenched West's arms up and threw the connecting chain over the hoist hook. The hoist lifted him and dropped the chain over the long artillery gun barrel mounted on the front of the train. The gunshot wound drowned out the additional pain of hanging by his wrists, his feet dangling over the track below.

Satisfied, Skorzeny looked up to the pained West and addressed him. "Herr West, this train is loaded with 300 tons of gold. It is a prototype steam train powered by V-2 rocket technology boosters and has magnetic wheels. In addition to the five cars of gold bullion, there is a precious cargo containing the brave soldiers of my elite commando unit and another car with equipment which will win the war. You think the war was won by the 'allies' in 1945? That was Hitler's battle to lose, and he lost it. But it is my war to win, and I've thought and planned how it will be one for all the years I was trapped in a dark hellish nothing, waiting for the day I would be free.

177

"You will not live to see my plans come to fruition, but you will get one last train ride. There are many traps placed throughout this installation. I know. I put many of them there. The curved track Ferenc's men have connected into, are the tracks just behind the outer brick wall of the tunnel. They were not to remove earthen wall behind it. This would automatically trigger the traps. You will get to see this from your front row seat, as the rocket thrusters power this train through the tunnel wall, outrunning all the traps triggered behind it and onto our new tracks... for a split second at least, before you are crushed to death by the impact."

West writhed, the agony of the wound shocking his body. "If I'd known I'd have to listen to all of that, I would have rather you shot me in the head."

Skorzeny smiled up at him. "The next shot wouldn't be to your head, but to your Wienerschnitzel. Luckily for you, I don't want you bleeding out too quickly. I want you to taste your defeat as the last thing that goes through your mind, when your face is obliterated against the tunnel wall as my train breaks free."

Skorzeny let out a laugh that was more of a raspy growl. He went back to his grand plans, leaving West to watch his blood slowly drip down to the tracks below.

18: TRAIN REACTION

West could feel himself fading. Sweat drops stung his eyes as his mind raced, struggling to think of what to do. He had to get free. He wouldn't let himself die at the hands of a maniac like Otto Skorzeny. There was a chance his dead body would be resurrected by the rays of the full moon in a couple of days, but that was no guarantee. He wasn't counting on dying. He was planning on living. The bullet wound was taking its toll and he knew he only had a short window to pull this off.

He had to reach the LoneWolf activator. Damn Borge for putting it in the chest plate. Should he somehow survive this, he would have to remember to talk to him about that. To reach it, he had to get his thumbprint on the activator on his chest plate. His hands were chained above him, and he was losing strength fast.

A blast of steam heralded the locomotive's return to life. A first 'chug,' was soon followed by the rhythmic chugging sound increasing in frequency like a drum beat as the train lurched forward. It was time for West to enact his plan and his plan was simple: He would need to get his legs up and wrap them around the large gun barrel he was hanging from. Then with the slack created in the chain, he could maybe maneuver his hand to activate LoneWolf. Not so simple, even when not bleeding to death.

He strained to swing his legs up, leveraging his chained wrists like gymnast rings. Using all of his upper body strength he pushed through the fiery pain of the bullet in his belly and tried to focus. The train was now picking up speed and the faster it went, the more difficult this would be. West also knew he was running out of time. How many more attempts could he make before his body gave out? He was intending to find out as he pushed himself once again.

He tensed his core once again to raise his legs, the pain shooting through him. That was closer, but not enough. He felt dizziness wash over him. No, no, keep it together, fight off the fading, the increasing darkness overcoming him. The train was now chugging away and approaching full speed. West growled like an animal and let his primal survival instinct take over and with all his remaining strength, he wrenched his lower body up, folding his body in half desperately to reach the chest plate activator... the only chance he had left.

Skorzeny was standing, watching West through the cab windshield. "What is he doing, calisthenics? What a time for gym exercises," he said with a chuckle. "Perhaps I should have shot him again." The train was now moving at full speed, and he turned his attentions to Tanya Nimble, held in her seat at gunpoint by a guard while Burt Digby sat nearby in silence. "Herr Digby says you are trained as a metallurgist. You are good with extracting metals, ja?" She trembled and nodded. Skorzeny grabbed her by her hair and snarled into her ear, "You had better be good, Fraulein. Your life depends on it."

The increasing speed of the train and the vibration of the track made it even more difficult for West. He had to keep going until he got it, but he was running low on time... not just his own, but in minutes, the train would be bursting through the tunnel pod wall, obliterating him in the process. West took a deep breath and gritted his teeth as the excruciating pain of lifting his lower body seared through him one more time...PUSH, goddamn it! His body jerked into the air, the shackles cutting deep into his wrists. A crash had rocked the train, the force of the powerful train moving through the decaying tunnel causing part of the ceiling to collapse. West reeled from the pain and didn't think he had the strength to make another attempt.

A static buzz followed by chirps, pops and a whistling filled his ears.

"West!" It was Borge, communicating through the NeuraComlink. "What's your status?"

"F---ed...," West wheezed. "What took you so long, were you on lunch break?"

"The settings were recalibrated to not auto respond for increased heart rate. However, they still are for low heart rate and what appears to be loss of blood and other issues affecting your vitals..."

"Yeah, a bullet to the gut will do that. And it's about to get lower soon."

"Where are you?"

"Mounted on the front of a speeding Nazi war train and bleeding out. Will you hurry already?"

Borge readied himself at the controls, and called out, "LoneWolf activated."

West slumped his head and in seconds the feeling of primal animal energy took over. He was conscious just long enough to see the transformation begin.

The shackles burst and Borge controlled LoneWolf to grab hold of the gun barrel. LoneWolf was tough, but falling in front of a speeding train and being run over by all of its cars was pushing it. He looked at the surrounding scene through his LoneWolf-eye-view viewfinder. The train was gaining momentum on a downhill trajectory. With a combination of buttons, Borge flipped LoneWolf backwards up onto the locomotive roof. He moved him along the top of the train, planning to get him between the locomotive and cars, where he would then uncouple the cars, causing major problems for Skorzeny, if not stopping him.

Skorzeny looked up to check on West. He watched LoneWolf's leap up to the locomotive's roof. "Impossible!" He turned to Wildebeest, "Húnd! Get up there and stop him." An enraged Skorzeny bit his lip with a fang, blood trickling down his chin, uneasy with what had just occurred. Who was this man? How could he have possibly escaped, while dying from a gunshot wound, no less? Wildebeest would have to stop him. He couldn't afford to have his plans stopped now. Not when he was so close.

Borge moved LoneWolf down between the locomotive and the linked train cars. The train lurched as the tunnel it barreled through was coming undone from the accumulated force and old booby-trap explosives finally detonating. Following behind the train, the tunnel supports were collapsing, a widening crack in the wall now spewing water.

LoneWolf went to work, with Borge guiding him to the coupling. He began disconnecting it, only to be struck by a wild Wildebeest bursting through the rear door of the locomotive. Borge jumped Lone-Wolf up to the top of the train car behind. Wildebeest followed him up and leaped, spearing LoneWolf. The two beasts tumbled along the top, sliding to the edge, their claws sinking in to keep from going over the side. The train and the tunnel were both violently shaking now. The crack in the tunnel wall, now far behind them, had given way, releasing the pressure of the underground river flowing alongside the tunnel. Pieces of the cavern ceiling fell, raining debris down on Lone-Wolf and Wildebeest.

Borge worked the joystick control furiously, trying to control LoneWolf in the middle of the high-speed chaos. The tunnel shuddered and rumbled, knocking LoneWolf off the train car. Beads of sweat formed on Borge's face as he focused intently, moving his controls to keep LoneWolf barely hanging on to the side of the car. Wildebeest had been knocked backwards and was on the third car back.

182

Borge saw and quickly maneuvered LoneWolf back up to the top of the car and prepared to move back to the locomotive and uncouple the cars again. This time, maybe he could do it before Wildebeest could attack again.

"Borge!"

Dr. Borge heard the voice in his earpiece but couldn't believe it. "Borge, did you deactivate LoneWolf?" It was West. How could this be, he thought to himself. He tried to focus his attention back to his top priority—controlling LoneWolf and stopping Skorzeny's plans for this train. But he had to know.

"West? I didn't deactivate. How are you here?"

"I don't know, but I am. I can see through LoneWolf's eyes but can't move or anything."

"However, your consciousness has managed to patch in to this call, we'll sort that out later. For now, I have to concentrate on the mission at hand."

"I can help you."

"You can help by letting me focus." While West and Borge were conversing via the NeuraComlink, Wildebeest charged, leaping at LoneWolf. They fell between the cars and Wildebeest was pushing LoneWolf's head down toward the tracks. Borge smashed the buttons on his controls, sending in turn, a smashing fist into Wildebeest's jaw. Using the distraction to jump onto the side of the train car, LoneWolf stepped on Wildebeest's head, using it as a springboard to propel back to the top of the car.

The tunnel walls quaked with a deafening sound, sounding like an explosion following behind the trembling train. Borge craned Lone-Wolf's neck to get a look down the tracks behind them. Concrete columns and support timbers were collapsing like dominoes, followed by a wall of water surging toward the train like a tidal wave.

"Holy sh…" West exclaimed.

"Indeed," Borge replied. "Skorzeny better hit the gas on this train. Once that wave of water catches up, we'll all be drowned like rats."

"Me, you mean," West said.

"You know what I mean," Borge said with irritation.

Otto Skorzeny must have seen what they saw, and the train responded with the activation of the rocket thrusters. The sudden increase in speed sent both LoneWolf and Wildebeest rolling backwards over the tops of the train cars. The rail line now began a steep descent. The train was now near the bottom slope of Volovec Mountain, which meant it would burst through into the tunnel pod at any moment. The roaring wave of water was crushing everything in its wake and gaining on the train. More of the tunnel shook apart as the train rocketed down the slope like a rollercoaster from hell.

Wildebeest held on with his one paw, the nails dug deep into the roof as he struggled to hang on. The water was now licking the back of the rear train car. Borge fought to stand LoneWolf up only to be caught by a falling timber from the tunnel ceiling. He used Lone-Wolf's claws to dig into the timber, desperately trying to keep him from falling off the train.

The powerful locomotive thrusts sent out another burst. Borge quickly retracted LoneWolf's claws out of the log as it rolled backwards off the end of the train, rolling over Wildebeest in the process. The giant log was swallowed and crushed to splinters by the force of the massive wave barreling down the hill behind them. The wave had almost caught the speeding train.

LoneWolf held tight to the back of the rear train car, the water splashing against him, the pressure crushing him into the car's metal surface. Wildebeest had inched toward the back of the car and swiped at LoneWolf with his one clawed hand. Borge punched at the controls to move LoneWolf away from the strikes and to also get him back up to the top of the car. The train reeled, knocking Wildebeest off his balance. Borge slowly moved LoneWolf up and peered over the top ahead. The locomotive's headlights showed a dead end coming up. The wall the train was to burst through to join the track connectors added to the track in the tunnel pod.

Wildebeest turned and saw it looming as well, let out a yelp and jumped down between the cars to shield himself from the impact. The locomotive's rocket thruster fired once more, and the velocity knocked LoneWolf back. He was hanging by one claw from the back of the careening train, the wave of pulsing water at his back. The train gunned ahead, and Borge and West watched through LoneWolf's eyes as the locomotive charged straight toward the wall.

Outside the tunnel pod, an earthquake-like rumbling heralded the chaos and destruction coming from deep inside the hill. With an explosion of earth and brick, the locomotive burst through the tunnel pod wall. Assisted by its magnetic wheels, it followed the curved track switcher onto the rail line and pushed forward at high speed.

A thunderous bursting wave of water followed behind it, a great geyser exploding through the tunnel opening. On the back of the rear train car, Borge was trying to keep LoneWolf's grip on the edge of the car's roof but was losing it. The torrent of water pushed at him, and he lost grip.

West saw it and knew if LoneWolf died, his conscious would as well. Worse, he could be stuck in this weird state between life and death. "Borge, do something!"

"I'm trying...," Borge said, urgently trying to find some way to get a hold of the edge of the car.

"There!" West exclaimed. "That piece of wood, grab it!" A flat piece of wood was floating by in the onslaught of the wall of water. Borge moved LoneWolf to grab it, and seeing possibility, forced LoneWolf against the crushing pressure of the water to climb on, and stood up to a crouching position on the board.

West watched on in horror, his life completely in Borge's hands. "What are you doing?"

"Surf's up, Big Kahuna!" Borge yelled as West watched half amazed, half mortified.

"I thought you were going to use this as a floatation. I can't surf!"

"I can," Borge replied. "Surfing World Cup, E-Sports Bronze winner, three years in a row."

"Wait… Bronze?!"

"We're going for the Gold today. Hang on!"

Borge surfed LoneWolf onward through the curl as the top of the giant wave loomed overhead, pushing him at a breakneck speed and threatening to crash down at any moment. The rear train car was just ahead, barreling down the tracks staying just slightly ahead of the rapidly flooding tunnel pod.

The speed of the wave pushed LoneWolf closer. Borge leaned him forward to increase velocity. The train was pulling ahead, and the wave's momentum was waning. Borge cut through the surface of the wave and saw his moment. The shaken Wildebeest was just climbing up from between train cars, where he rode out the impact of the train bursting through the hillside.

Borge tilted LoneWolf back and reached forward to grab the front of the board. Using the wave's force, he launched up in the air above the rear car. Wildebeest looked up to see LoneWolf crash-landing the board on top of him. The landing tumbled LoneWolf off the side. Borge scrambled to get him to hold on as the train shot down the tracks.

"Cowabunga!" Borge shouted, pleased he could put his video game surfing skills to practical use.

"Nice work, doctor," West said. "Now, let's get back to what you were doing before… uncoupling the trains cars from the engine. Anything to slow down Skorzeny's plans."

Borge moved LoneWolf up the side of the train car and saw Wildebeest standing on the opposite side, staring with a rabid glare. LoneWolf leapt to the top of the car. Wildebeest charged at him, jumping in the air with both feet aimed at LoneWolf. The impact caught LoneWolf straight in the chest, flipping him backwards. He landed with a crushing thud on the ground beside the tracks. Borge and West watched the train speed away, Wildebeest standing atop, howling in triumph.

The great wave of water had now calmed to that of a bubbling brook. LoneWolf lay on his back, water pooling around him.

"Borge, get me moving. We can still catch up with the train."

"Not at the rate of speed it's moving. LoneWolf can run fast, but not that fast."

"It doesn't matter. Skorzeny's got to stop the train somewhere for a rendezvous point."

Borge raised LoneWolf to his feet and sent him sprinting down the tracks in pursuit.

"How far ahead is the next border crossing?" West asked.

Borge looked at the rail map on his side monitor. "It's about 12 miles by rail to the border crossing at Czechia. Do you think he'll stop? He is kind of crazy."

"He is all kinds of crazy, but he may also have a deal in place with the Czechs. Either way, the train is carrying five cars filled with gold, along with two other cars filled with equipment, including dead Nazi werewolf soldiers."

"Whaaaat?"

"Yes, his plans keep going from bad to worse. He's going to need to unload the cars for transport at some point. There are Transylvanian soldiers working with him, so whatever arrangements he's made, he's getting help from General Ferenc."

Borge pushed LoneWolf to run as fast as he could. There was nothing but countryside surrounding the tracks with no sight of the train. Borge decided to find out more about West's curious situation. "I don't know how your consciousness is aware and connected right now. It's truly baffling. All I can think is that because you were losing consciousness at the time of activation, somehow your mind separated from your werewolf form at transformation. We will have to do some tests to see if this will happen again. The NeuraComlink is connected to your brainwaves, so it must be accessing your mental self while your physical self is being controlled by my digital interface."

"Whatever you say, doctor. All I know is right now we're linked, and we need to make the best of it."

"Up ahead," Borge said with excitement. "That looks like the train."

"Strange place to stop," West said. "There's no roads, just wild marsh country."

"It's about to get wilder," Borge replied. "I'm moving LoneWolf off the tracks, and we'll come in from along the side. There's a bridge over a deep ravine coming up. That's where they're stopping."

Borge slowed LoneWolf down and crept him along the underbrush, stopping him at the edge of the bridge. The gorge was perhaps 300 feet to the bottom, with the tops of tall evergreen trees looking like tiny shrubs sticking up from the ground below. Using LoneWolf's telescopic eyepiece, Borge estimated the railway bridge stretched some 600 feet to the other side of the mountainous terrain. The old bridge was a viaduct in the stone arch style, with six large arches supporting it. Skorzeny had his train stopped dead in the middle of the span.

"Do you think he's having engine trouble?" Borge asked.

West surveyed the scene through the eyes of LoneWolf. "No, the engine is still running. Listen... you can hear the air pressure brakes. He's stopped on purpose."

"What for? The middle of a bridge over a deep canyon is about the last place I'd want to stop."

In answer, the chopping sound of whirring helicopter blades filled the air. West and Borge looked around and were surprised to realize the sounds were coming from below. Seven large black helicopters rose from the bottom of the gorge up to the bridge, surrounding the train.

Though they were painted completely in black with no identification markings, West had seen this type of helicopter before. These were Mil Mi-26 Soviet Russian heavy transport military helicopters. The helicopters swirled around the top of the train. Otto Skorzeny stepped down from the train and waved to the pilots.

The helicopters lowered to the level of the bridge. The Transylvanians who had accompanied Skorzeny on his train ride climbed down and into the hovering helicopters. Skorzeny pointed at Wildebeest, barking out orders to get to work uncoupling the train cars. Burt Digby led Tanya down the side of the locomotive, followed by the Transylvanian guards pushing them into one of the waiting Mi-26's. The helicopters lifted and hovered over the train cars, deploying cable slings attached by the Transylvanian troops.

"Ok, Borge," West said. "Get me closer. I want to get in on this helicopter ride."

"With the steep drop off, it's going to be hard to get close without going straight down the bridge."

"Then damn it, let's do it while they're occupied."

Borge ran LoneWolf down the tracks at top speed, hoping to get as close as he could before being noticed. By the time LoneWolf reached the train cars, the Mi-26's were already climbing and the boxcars were rising off the tracks into the air. LoneWolf grabbed the back end of the rear car and held on as the powerful helicopter lifted it up. The car was rising higher with LoneWolf clinging to its side. Digging his claws

189

into the metal roof, he moved toward the cable sling supports. A zinging sound zipped past LoneWolf, pricking his ears up. "What the hell was that?" Borge yelled.

"Damn," West replied. "Looks like they made sure to bring an escort service." From the bottom of the gorge three Havoc attack helicopters, also all in black, flew up to accompany the Mi-26s, ensuring safe delivery of their cargo. LoneWolf dangled from the cable, bullets zipping past him. The next one hit, striking his hand. Falling from the cable, he bounced off the roof of the boxcar. The helicopters picked up speed and flew off. He kept falling down into the gorge.

Borge could only watch LoneWolf freefall into the depths of the mountain gorge and hoped his next move would work. The treetops were coming up fast. Borge deftly moved LoneWolf to grab the top of a tall evergreen tree, swirling around the trunk until stopping by crashing into the larger branches below.

Above the bridge, the attack helicopters stayed back, circling locomotive engine left behind. The three copters each blasted it with rocket launchers. From LoneWolf's treetop position, West and Borge watched the Nazi war train explode into a fiery ball of flaming hell, sending burning shrapnel crashing down to the bottom of the gorge. Off in the distance, the flight of helicopters disappeared into the burnt orange evening sky.

"Well, Borge," West said with a sigh.

"Looks like we're up a tree again."

19: THE BEAST COMES

General George Ferenc was a nervous passenger. He dotted the sweat off his brow with a handkerchief stained by the running hair dye and hairpiece glue. Looking down at the view from the Mi-26 military transport helicopter, he was relieved they were now over the Transylvanian border. His nerves had been frayed since that fateful day when Otto Skorzeny walked into his office waving a gold bar.

It all seemed too easy, and while it started relatively easily, his hope was that it would also end that way. He had used his Transylvanian Military power to secure the equipment, manpower and transport. He had been forced to work with the Corsicans, whom he despised, but the hard work and his dealings with them were now over. Soon, he would reach beyond anything he could have imagined, more than his military salary and all of the bribes and shady deals he ever pulled combined. Not bad for someone who had always been described as "failing upward."

As the head of the State Security Committee in the Transylvanian National Alliance, General Ferenc had always had a not-so-secret reputation as someone who could always be bought for a price. This doughy, mustachioed toad of a man wore the Transylvanian flag and coat of arms on his uniform, but he was truly always working (when he actually did work) for his benefit alone. Now, he was to be 100 million dollars richer, and the thought aroused him, more than any beautiful woman ever could. These were the dreams he tried to focus on. Not the nightmare he tried to ignore, haunted by Otto Skorzeny.

The helicopter swooped down over the Cozia Mountains, part of the Southern Carpathians range also known as the Transylvanian Alps. It lowered near the base of the mountain known locally as *Muntele Lupului*, which translates as *Wolf Mountain* in English. A large drawbridge stuck out of the gaping mouth carved into the side of Wolf Mountain, bridging over the deep drop to the jagged cliffs below. The spotlights illuminating the work area bounced off the thick fog moving in. As the helicopter lowered the cargo of a gold bullion-filled boxcar to the ground, workers—Ferenc's own troops being employed under the guise of this being a national military installation—waited with cranes and motorized carts. They hurriedly unloaded the car, transporting the stacks of gold bars through the large cargo doors into the mountain base.

Wolf Mountain had its own secrets, unrevealed until Otto Skorzeny and Burt Digby led Ferenc on an expedition to show him what had been undiscovered for decades. Clearing away a pile of rubble, the men climbed into the cave and into an unfinished Nazi war base. The Wolf's Lair… that's what Skorzeny had called it. He told of how Adolph Hitler had been working on his own war Command Center that he called the Wolf's Lair, but this was to be Skorzeny's.

He had sniffed dismissively when he spoke of Hitler calling himself a wolf, and how he wasn't worthy of such a title. With the promise of a huge personal payday, Ferenc readily agreed to go to work for Skorzeny. He was not concerned with who Skorzeny was, or at least claimed to be, as long as the check cleared. This was to be the culmination of their joint efforts: Skorzeny's own Wolf's Lair in Wolf Mountain, finally completed by Ferenc and his men, and the protection of being in Transylvanian territory.

The wicked wind of a chilly late October night howled through the tombstones and mausoleums in London's Highgate Cemetery. Beneath the mausoleum housing the secret base of ParaCommand, a different kind of chill filled the air. Val West paced back and forth, filled with an anxious energy. He had to get back to Transylvania. Tanya Nimble was in even more danger now after the unsuccessful escape attempt in Poland. She had once successfully convinced Otto Skorzeny and Burt Digby she was on their side, but likely wouldn't be able to pull that trick again. Even if she was still alive, she wouldn't be as soon as Skorzeny had no further use for her.

He had, whether it was professionally right or wrong, decided her safety was an important part of this mission and waiting around in London wasn't going to get her out of danger. He and Dr. Borge had argued the entire flight back about his consciousness now being aware while transformed into LoneWolf. Borge didn't want him to get involved. West argued that it was his body, even though wasn't controlling it and that he would have say in what Borge did with the controls.

Commander 7 was in a foul mood and curtly broadcast via the speaker box that he had to call in an extra special favor to the Royal Air Force to get them out of there and back without the Polish government finding out, and he never wanted to have to put the RAF in that position. West wanted to get to Transylvania, immediately. Commander 7 ordered him to wait. He was expecting an intelligence report from Double Agent Gypsy, and they would plan accordingly based on her briefing.

Borge walked into the room and poured himself a glass of beet juice. Neither man spoke to each other. West continued to pace anxiously, when finally, he decided to break the ice with Borge. "Listen, I didn't mean to bark at you on the plane ride back. It's just... well, this isn't how I'm used to doing things and when we're in the field, my experience is more important than being good at video games."

West's explanation only inflamed Borge. "You like to downplay my e-sports accomplishments, but they seemed quite useful to you 'in the field.' Don't forget, you did finally catch that bullet, and if not for me, you'd be lying dead in a flooded train tunnel, a place that probably doesn't catch much moonlight, if there was even enough left of you to be revived."

"That's easy for you to say when you're safe in the lab, hunched over your joystick and I'm the one whose neck is on the line."

"Is that supposed to be referring to my hunchback?" Borge yelled back. "You know, if you wouldn't keep getting captured, I wouldn't have to work so hard to get you out of these situations!"

The speaker box with the waveform monitor placed in the center of the command console crackled and the audio wave form started jumping. "That will be enough from both of you gentlemen." Commander 7 had joined the conversation. "This is new to all of us. We can't expect everything to go perfectly, but what is expected is professionalism on both your parts.

"Before the next phase of this mission begins, I want the two of you to work with the simulator to figure out how to make the fact that Mr. West is mentally communicating through the NeuraComlink an advantage. I want you to spend the next two hours working on how to maximize this new development. By then, I should have Gypsy's report and we will plan from there."

Both West and Borge answered with a 'Yes, sir," and like two boys being scolded by their father, went into the simulator to do as ordered.

***

Tanya Nimble looked over the equipment in front of her and felt a sense of hopelessness. She had been provided with an array of metallurgical equipment but wasn't sure how to go about the task before her, which, if successful, was supposed to guarantee her life would be spared. In the past she had successfully extracted silver, and also gold, but that was from ore deposits. The metallurgical operation before her was something else entirely.

She looked at the large, rusted metal container placed near the equipment, retrieved from one of the train's boxcars. Inside the container was a large solid chunk of silver, and somewhere inside the silver were the bodies of seven Nazi werewolf commandos. These were Skorzeny's boys, and the utmost care was to be taken to remove the silver they were encased in, as well as in their bodies, so they could be restored to life. It was their lives for hers. Even though the idea of resurrecting these monsters went against all she believed in, Tanya knew she had to do it, and do it successfully. Now she was truly scared.

Burt Digby arrived and walked over to Tanya. "Cheer up, girl. After what you pulled, you should be grateful I put in a word for you. If you didn't have a metallurgy degree, you'd be treats for Skorzeny's Húnd right now. That's what happened to the metallurgist who had first been hired and then tried to play games."

She turned away from him and said nothing. "Tanya, you had your chance, and you blew it! I was going to get us out of this and with a shit ton of money to boot. But you just had to run off with your new spy boyfriend, and guess what? He's dead now, too. He couldn't have survived getting blasted off the side of that gorge. No way, no how."

He turned to her and put his hand on her shoulder. She recoiled. "I'll tell you what though. You still got me. Even after all that. You do this for Skorzeny, and we still got a shot at this. At us." Tanya looked down at the floor and Digby waited for a response that didn't come.

He muttered under his breath and walked off, slamming the door with a thud behind him.

***

For the first time since being awakened to this strange new time, Otto Skorzeny felt at ease. Technology and many other societal trappings had changed drastically since 1945. One thing that had not changed was basic human nature and using the sin of greed he had been able to bring his vision to fruition. He had thought of these plans while trapped in the limbo between life and death for decade after decade. The only thing that kept him going was the hope he would be set free and the plans he had, for everyone. He would get revenge for the betrayals of Heinrich Himmler, Josef Mengele and his bastard cousin Bluto Skorzeny. They were long dead now, but he would still have his revenge, only now all the world would pay.

Satisfaction filled Otto Skorzeny as he beamed with pride over his now operational *Wolfsschanze*, his Wolf's Lair. He remembered back to when Adolph Hitler and the Nazis abandoned its construction in 1944. How, when confronted by a Transylvanian Count, Hitler had shown fear in a way he had never seen him show fear before. The entrance was immediately dynamited, followed by a hasty retreat back to Germany, with plans for any further incursions into Transylvania abruptly cancelled.

Der Führer. Skorzeny laughed a snarling laugh at the thought of Hitler's weak leadership. If he and his SS Werwolf Commandos, his Wolf Pack, had not been trapped and taken out of action, Hitler and his inner circle would have become a feast for the hounds. The war would have taken a much different turn once the surprised Allied Forces realized what they were up against. Now, without the weakness of inferior men like Hitler and his cronies, Skorzeny's destiny was to be fulfilled.

***

The high-speed clatter of the teletype machine urgently spit out an encrypted message. Dr. Borge pulled off the perforated paper and re-layed its contents to West and Commander 7. In the time leading up to receiving the teletype, West and Borge had been working in the simulator. As in the previous transformation into LoneWolf, West's consciousness was again aware and able to communicate with Borge via the NeuraComlink. Arguing wasn't going to get them anywhere, but that didn't stop them.

By the time they had finished in the simulator, they had begrudg-ingly accepted their new working arrangement and had devised a new working method that both men accepted. While in LoneWolf form, Borge was in control and West would only observe until needed. He would then tell Borge when to transform him either to or back from LoneWolf and Borge would cede control. Over the course of the sim-ulator's practice drills, they found a rhythm and felt hopeful about the mission ahead. And Borge had a new surprise: a 'turbo' button con-nected to the spysuit which would give LoneWolf an extra blast of WLF light particles for an extra burst of power when needed.

"Gentlemen," Commander 7's electronic voice said over the speaker box, the waveforms on the monitor above it dancing to his words. "You both heard what Double Agent Gypsy's teletype message relayed. What do you think?"

Gypsy's message stated that new activity had resumed in the area where Val West and Thomas Hedison were attacked in Transylvania. Since that night, it had been seemingly dormant from what she had been able to tell. This had led Commander 7 to believe this was another gold cache site and had been abandoned once the gold had been recovered.

Gypsy's latest information showed this wasn't so. She included details from a file she had obtained from Ferenc's office safe. The file, labeled *Operation: Wolf's Lair*, showed the use of Transylvanian military construction for gold payoff in the Cozia Mountains, just beyond the construction site West and Wildebeest had been investigating. The construction was at Muntele Lupului—Wolf Mountain.

Just yesterday, black helicopters had been spotted by villagers. Her report concluded with the disappearance of International Command agent Luther—most likely West's replacement in IC—who had sent her a message he was on his way to investigate Wolf Mountain. West knew Luther. He didn't like him, but the poor bastard didn't deserve the grisly fate he most likely found at Skorzeny's Wolf's Lair.

"Sir," West said to Commander 7, "we know the location is Wolf Mountain. That's confirmed and is the easy part. The hard part is getting past the Transylvania border and into this section of the Carpathian Mountains. With General Ferenc's involvement, it's going to be the equivalent of breaking into a military base."

"Indeed, it is," replied Commander 7. "And it comes with the same international incident implications. We are alone in this, so no matter where the other intelligence organizations are in their own investigations, there will be no backup from them. It's too risky, especially considering the high level of concern regarding their trustworthiness. I would normally not send one man in on a mission like this. But you're more than just a man now, LoneWolf, and I have no doubt you—with Dr. Borge's assistance—will successfully dismantle this operation before Skorzeny can proceed with whatever he has planned next."

***

Tanya found it difficult to work with a machine gun pointed at her but tried to ignore the ever-present threat of the posted guard and focus on the task at hand. Skorzeny had brought in all the materials for several different metallurgical extraction methods. Before her stood the large block of silver. It had been placed in a tub with drainage pipes to pump the extracted silver into an industrial melting vat located out in the main floor area of the base.

The work was coming along, but the process was hot and stifling. She had to slowly heat up the silver from the outermost layer, melt it inward, and wait for the melted silver to drain out of the containment unit. After long hours of slowly removing the silver, she could see another structure inside the block.

While the silver was still malleable, she worked to clear it away and discovered a lead container was underneath the silver. She instructed the Transylvanian soldiers assigned to work with her to quickly cool the heated lead to protect the contents inside. Despite the fact the contents contained the remains of seven Nazi werewolf commandos, she still found herself feeling the excitement she had felt on archaeological digs and, when treasure hunting with Burt in better times. The lead had cooled to room temperature and the front of the lead container was pried off. Skorzeny came in to watch the work.

Tanya shined a light into the lead container unit and inside were seven glass cylindrical tanks. Each one contained the shadowy image of a human body, submerged in a type of thick, briny liquid. She was sickened knowing there was already the risk of safely getting through the silver and lead layers and now she faced the potential biohazard from these monsters soaking in a mysterious liquid for over seventy-five years.

"Fraulein!" Skorzeny said with genuine delight. "You have done well with a difficult task. Now, let's open these capsules and free these soldiers."

Tanya examined the horrifying display in front of her and decided that a sample of the liquid was needed. A tiny hole was drilled, very delicately, into the glass and she capped off a test tube filled with the fluid.

Skorzeny impatiently urged her to get on with it, and walked off, leaving her to test the liquid to determine its composition. It was Formalin, a ten percent solution of formaldehyde mixed in water, standard for preservation of specimens. The Formalin had been mixed with a silver solution which had also saturated the bodies, still clad in their SS Werwolf Commando uniforms. The silver would need to be extracted.

Skorzeny began shouting at Tanya to get the silver out of them. He wanted it done before nightfall, which was still a few hours away, but she needed time to rig up a system to filter out and extract the silver embedded into the flesh of the corpses. Skorzeny didn't want to hear any excuses or explanations and stormed out of the chamber.

What now? Tanya frantically wracked her brain for a solution. She looked over the available equipment and at the clock to find a way to accomplish this task and maybe, just maybe, save her own skin. She thought about her lab experience in college. She remembered back to experiments with the electroextraction process known as Electrowinning, and quickly began setting up the electrical equipment and hoped she had paid enough attention in her college classes to make it work.

***

"West," Dr. Borge called out. "Come over here. I have something I've been working on that may be of interest to you." Val West followed Borge down a twisting catacomb tunnel. They stopped at an earthen wall with a partial skeleton embedded into it. Borge reached to the grinning skull and flipped open the top, revealing a keypad. He entered in a code and the earthen wall slid aside. They walked into darkness, their footsteps echoing off the cavernous walls. Borge flipped a switch and with a loud hum, the lights powered up. In the center, placed upon a platform, was a jet no larger than a small sports car.

"It's hypersonic," Borge explained. "Undetectable to all currently known radar systems and can exceed the speed of sound, reaching a top speed of 350 miles per hour… at least that's the theory. It hasn't been tested yet."

"Seems like a good time for a trial run," West replied, looking at the all-black coloring of the strange, avian looking design with its beak-like nose cone and talon-esque landing gear covers.

"I call it the ThunderBird. Not like the car, of course, but like the large Thunderbird of American Indian legend. The bird-like aspects of the design are intentional. The idea is, if spotted from the ground that there is a small chance it could be taken for a Thunderbird or any of its cryptozoological counterparts. Any reports would be, per usual, laughed off by the authorities and media, thus keeping the vehicle's cover."

Borge walked around the craft and pointed to its underside. "If you look here, you can see the drone—the one I used to recover you in Transylvania—is affixed for transport. I've also modified the drone to function as what I call a "dronepack." Being that it has enough load capacity to carry you, it can now be strapped to your back."

West eyed the upgraded drone with some skepticism. "You're certain about this?"

"Reasonably certain." West had been served well by Para-Command equipment so far and would just have to put his trust in Borge with this as well.

Borge continued. "From what we can tell there's some sort of Doppler pulse radar system, and most likely positioned surface-to-air missiles, meaning you're going to have to trek in on foot from quite a distance. Getting past all of the security is going to be hairy."

"Good thing I have that part covered."

"Precisely. I can also control the drone remotely, so when you are in LoneWolf form, it can still be piloted. Any questions?"

"Only one," West replied. "What time is our flight?"

***

The bloated, discolored visages of seven long-dead Nazi soldiers stared back at Tanya as they floated in the glass cylinders. She avoided looking at them during the electrolysis process, the silver saturating slowly being filtered out. The applied electricity attracted the silver and pulled it from the waterlogged tissue, mottling the flesh with small holes. The electrical current made the corpses seem to dance animatedly, sending a shudder through Tanya.

She had remembered the process correctly and now heaved a sigh of relief while watching the silver drain away. The only thing she could do was focus on the work. These things would conceivably be revived soon, and the thought was terrifying. She looked down at the silver being pumped out into a large open tank outside of the small laboratory area she was locked in. The voltage meter showed no more silver was being attracted and she shut the generator down. The corpses swirled around in the preservative, the sight causing her hands to shake uncontrollably when connecting the hose pump to drain out the Formalin solution.

The last of the liquid was dripping out of the cylinders when Otto Skorzeny came in again to check on her progress. He flashed a grin

seeing the corpses of his team being freed from their long entomb-
ment. He turned to Tanya and praised her skill and efforts.

"How can I be sure after all this you won't just kill me anyway?
Tanya asked.

Skorzeny paused, irritated by the question. "You don't. I said if
you did this, I would set you free, and I am an honorable man."

Tanya was feeling brave. "You're a Nazi."

Skorzeny glared at her. "I am more than that. And I am also more
than a man." He turned to two of the soldiers and instructed them to
bring the corpses, and Tanya, to a long narrow cavern room. A large
round hole had been carved into the cave ceiling and was framed with
steel bars.

"Please keep an eye on der Fraulein for now," Skorzeny said to the
guards. "Soon, the moon will be up. I want her to see the fruit of her
labors as the moon shines down, bringing life once again to my seven
soldiers of death, my Wolf Pack."

Otto Skorzeny walked up the metal scaffolding to his Command
Center and stood looking at the view from the great window he had
specially carved out of the side of Wolf Mountain. The orange embers
of the sinking sun painted the view of the crisp October evening. He
breathed in the smell of the cascading leaves and looked down over
the Transylvanian wilderness and saw beyond it.

Far beyond.

The world was his for the taking.

Tanya backed away into a corner, feeling both helpless and hope-
less. The moon was just rising in the fading evening sky, its amber
beams shining dimly through the open ceiling. The seven corpses were
all laid out on concrete slabs directly under the window. One of the
guards came over to her and prodded her toward the slabs, per

Skorzeny's instructions. She shivered, keeping her eyes turned away from the grotesque display.

The room was quiet aside from an increasing wet, slithering sound, followed by dripping. A skeletal hand barely covered by its water-logged, blotched gray flesh reached toward her.

They were hungry.

20: WHERE WOLVES DARE

October 31st. Halloween. The night where the veil between the worlds of the natural and the supernatural is at its thinnest.

On this night, the moon would be full. Being the second full moon of the month, it would also be a blue moon. Otto Skorzeny could not think of a better time to claim his power and set his plans into motion come nightfall.

He left the large war room he used as his Command Center and walked down the steps of the steel walkway to the lower level. Ahead, carved out of the mountain rock interior, was a prison cell. He paused to look in the barred window of the door. Inside the cell, chained to the wall, was his pet Húnd, his Wildebeest. Thomas Hedison, the man cursed with this existence, looked up toward the door once he sensed Skorzeny staring at him.

"Happy Halloween, Mr. Hedison," Skorzeny said with a raspy chortle and walked on. Hedison looked through the barred window at the twilight sky. Skorzeny's taunting comment was the first reference to a date he had known in a while. Everything was so hard to remember, and time didn't seem to exist for him. He struggled to remember what he could, but it always came in flashes, just bits and pieces. The weird hallucinations and constant blackouts. All he could figure was he had been drugged the whole time, as part of interrogation and... torture. He looked at his hand—the bastards had cut it off! Still, there were strange little finger nubs sticking out and he had no idea what was real anymore.

He did remember his recent escape attempt. One of the clasps of his shackles came loose and with great pain, he was able to slide the nub out of the other shackle. The cell door was unlocked, and he fled outside, making his way across the bridge. Hiding near the cable car station, he found a familiar face.

It was Agent Luther of International Command, hiding in the tree cover doing reconnaissance, under the cover of a "lost" climber. Hedison thought about how he didn't actually see him. It felt like he sensed or even smelled Luther's scent first. On recognizing him, Luther came out of the brush to assist. He then remembered the feeling of dread creeping over him. The overpowering force making him stop in his tracks. The low, rumbling growl he heard while turning around to see Skorzeny standing in the shadows.

The wild eyes burned a feeling of absolute terror into him. He turned to run toward Luther, and felt the delirium once again coming over him, the hallucinatory feeling of his body changing along with the crazed uncontrollable drive. He knew he was somehow under the command of Skorzeny. He remembered lunging at Luther, towards his throat, and then crimson filled his vision and he could recall no more. Was it real? Was any of it real?

It would seem all-too-real when Hedison later looked across the cell and saw the gnawed remains of a severed arm lying in a pool of dried blood. The skin was a dark brown and he could only think of how it looked like it belonged to Luther. His thoughts connected with a memory of Skorzeny coming by at another point and asking him if he enjoyed his 'dark meat,' amused with himself as he strolled away.

He had escaped once and would try again. He had to keep trying, even if he died in the process. Death would be preferable to the horror he had been living since the night he had come to Transylvania. Poor

Val. He must have been killed by the same beast that had mauled him, leaving him wounded and easily captured by Skorzeny and his men. Once he found a way to free himself, he would get revenge for his friend Val West as well. There was a wonderful woman waiting for him back home and he was determined to get back to her. He chafed in his restraints, desperate for any opportunity to break the shackles again and make a run for it. *Give me liberty or give me death.* That's what Patrick Henry had famously once said. Thomas Hedison was planning for either option.

***

Val West went over final preparations with Dr. Borge as he strapped himself into the sleek ThunderBird microjet. After he gave Borge a thumbs up, the jet blasted down the long tunnel underneath Highgate Cemetery, the guidance system piloting the small aircraft through the winding catacombs. The tunnel angled upward, leading to a seemingly crumbling chapel. Using a hydraulic system, the stone structure rose up and tilted backwards, opening the passageway for the ThunderBird to blast out and up into the dark clouds over London.

At its top-flight speed, the ThunderBird could reach Mach 1—over 770 miles per hour—and was engineered with stealth technology to prevent a sonic boom from being detected. West would be arriving at the Transylvanian Alps in about ninety minutes. The plan was clear as mud. There were no recent satellite images available for the Wolf Mountain region. All images were blocked with a satellite jamming frequency, the type typically used by top-secret military installations. West had spent the time in the air studying the maps of the mountainous terrain surrounding Skorzeny's Wolf's Lair. Maps, as he knew, would not prepare him for the other dangers lying ahead. Now, as the

ThunderBird rocketed towards its destination, West eased up on the controls and connected with Borge over the secured channel.

"Okay, Doctor, we're coming into target range, ETA ten minutes."

"Very good, Mr. West," Borge replied. I'm taking control of the ThunderBird. Is the dronepack ready? West shifted in the cockpit, assembling the attachments of the drone to the framework strapped to his back.

"Affirmative. Ready for deployment."

Borge checked over his control panel. All systems were operational—time for action. "Standby for LoneWolf activation," he said, feeling the anticipation of the coming battle rolling in his stomach with a nervous energy.

The ThunderBird swooped downward into the dusk, leveling out over the twilight-highlighted mountaintops. West waited for the bombardment of WLF rays that would start the transformation process. The full moon was also on the rise. How would the wild power of the full lunar rays affect him? Would Borge be able to maintain control over LoneWolf? West involuntarily closed his eyes tightly as the first pangs of the transformation began. He once again felt the wild fever coursing through his veins, the primordial beast within growing and taking over his very sense of self. His mind reeled in the feeling of rushing forward in slow motion, as his consciousness fled to the back of his brain, and the LoneWolf howled to life.

Borge entered in the coordinates into the navigational computer for these crucial next steps. LoneWolf was strapped to the dronepack and placed into position. The seats shifted back, moving him down to the floor into a commando crawl position. With a deep breath, Borge opened the sliding panel and LoneWolf dropped out from under the ThunderBird. The drone pack activated, its autoburst thruster shooting LoneWolf like a missile out from the retreating ThunderBird. Borge pulled back on the thruster to conserve power. Under his control, he glided LoneWolf over the foothills up toward the towering peaks casting sinister shadows below. The target: Wolf Mountain.

The sky blazed an ominous red over a horizon line blanketed by a creeping fog. West was again consciously able to observe and communicate with Borge through the NeuraComlink. Together, as Lone-Wolf soared over the jagged spires of the Carpathians, they looked through his view, looking for the first outer perimeter guards.

The dronepack flew over the river below the cliff West had fallen into, where this same drone had found him and brought him to Dr. Borge and ParaCommand. Flying upward over the cliff's edge, they spotted a perimeter guard patrolling the rock-strewn plateau of an overhanging crag. This would be LoneWolf's landing and starting point.

Borge banked the controller left, swooping LoneWolf around, ready to come in fast for attack. With the rising moon behind him, LoneWolf flew in with the drone pack. A shadow crossed the guard's face and he turned to see a giant black winged monster coming at him. Before he could aim his rifle, the dronepack released LoneWolf, who came hurtling at the guard headfirst, his fangs tearing out the guard's throat before he could realize he was dead.

Borge stopped LoneWolf and piloted the drone to land nearby on the plateau. The ThunderBird was sent on autopilot to be landed miles away. From here on in, it would be on foot, and Borge let LoneWolf get the scent of the trail the guard took to get here. Once his screen readout indicated LoneWolf had made an olfactory scent match, he moved him along the trail to Skorzeny's mountain fortress, Der Wolfsschanze... the Wolf's Lair.

***

Tanya's scream was enough to unnerve Burt Digby to the point where he had to intervene. Whatever Skorzeny was doing, he was going too far. They had a deal, and part of that deal was the girl wasn't to be harmed. In fact, Skorzeny had specifically said she would be set free once the silver was successfully extracted from his Wolf Pack. She had done it, and as far as Digby was concerned, she had fulfilled her part of the bargain, no matter how reluctant she was to do it. He found a guard and ordered him to let him into the chamber. Inside Tanya was under watch by two guards and a room full of long dead Nazis about to wake up.

"Tanya!" Burt ran through the door to her. He looked on in horror when he saw the shadowed figures on the platforms writhing in the moonlight. There was a guard at each end of the chamber, each sweating, unsure what to do with the increasingly animated corpses. Digby's arrival stirred them even more and the one nearest him sat straight up. The decaying flesh over the skeletal face was slowly growing bits of fur, the rotting teeth slowly pushing canines out through the blackened gums. They were stuck in a state between reanimated corpse and werewolf. They needed to feast to fully regenerate and the smell of fresh meat filled their rotting nostrils.

On the other side of the chamber, two of the corpses rose, shambling towards the guard near the far wall. They came closer than he would have liked, and, in a panic, he began firing his rifle at them. Bits of yellowed flesh and darkened blood splattered into the air with each bullet strike. The unfazed creatures continued to advance, clawing at the guard. He tried to use the butt of his rifle as a weapon, also to no effect.

Tanya instinctively latched on to Burt as the first pained shrieks from the guard echoed across the chamber, chunks of flesh being torn off by the ravenous zombified werewolves. More of them shuffled off the platforms, shambling toward Tanya, Digby and the door guard, others moving toward the blood feast happening on the other side.

Digby grabbed the door guard by the arm. "You just gonna stand there, mate? Let's get the fooking hell outta here!" The guard looked again at the situation and agreed and the three of them ran for the door. Before the door had closed behind them, a shriveled, hairy hand reached its claws through. The talon-like claws tore into the guard's arm, pulling him through the narrow door opening. Digby ran and kicked at the door, pushing the rest of the screaming guard's body back through the door until it latched. Taking Tanya's hand, they ran off down the winding cave corridors, the sounds of shrieking terror and ripping flesh echoing behind them.

***

LoneWolf ran along the trail, ascending deeper into the wilds of the mountains. Following the scent of the guard's footfalls, he continued along until Borge stopped him when he came to a corner. Around that corner was the lower tramway station for an aerial cable car, along with a posted guard.

"Well," Borge said to the consciousness of Val West. "What do you think?"

"You mean, what would I do, now that we're in this particular situation?" West answered through the NeuraComlink. "Now, that's a nice change of pace, and I feel honored to be consulted. Let's see if we can get a look up past this cable car."

Borge turned LoneWolf's head and activated the telescopic lens, the lens springing open from the headpiece and locking into position over LoneWolf's right eye.

West studied the view of the mountainous terrain before them. "Look over to the left. Now, up. Zoom in there." The viewfinder showed the cable car's route leading up to a wide, flat ledge housing the upper cableway station. The retractable thrust bridge leading to the main entrance of the Wolf's Lair was still in place and connected to the ledge. On the other side of the bridge, the main face of Wolf Mountain rose up beyond the large bay doors of the base, with smaller crests and peaks jutting up to the summit. Off to the right and above the doors, a row of smaller openings in the steep rock face looked like they could be windows.

"Before we go anywhere," West said. "We'll have to do something about this guard. Quietly. There's bound to be another guard, probably more, at the upper station. They're going to want to know why the tram is coming up without word from the guard at the lower station."

"I concur," Borge replied, while working out some calculations. "I think climbing the tramway cable is too risky with this trajectory. LoneWolf can make it, and an accidental fall may not necessarily be fatal, but by the time it would take to get back to this spot Skorzeny would be on full alert."

"One guard is down, and we have another about to go down just a few yards away. It's only a matter of time before the rest realize the guards aren't responding. Then it's high alert. That's bound to happen, but the closer we can get before that happens, the better."

"West," Borge said with hesitation. "Listen, I know in the field these things must be done, but do we have to kill this guard?"

"Getting to you, is it?" West replied. "I'm glad to see you're realizing this isn't just some video game, but I'm not going to razz you about it. What you're feeling is serious, and sometimes I wish that basic compassion hadn't been driven out of me years ago. But, for what it's worth I do understand. So, let's plan to just knock this guard unconscious."

"Thank you," Borge said with a sense of relief. "Now, how do we go about doing that?"

"Ok. I'm going to need you to work LoneWolf's right hand into an open palm strike formation. Then tighten the fingers for a judo chop." Borge practiced with the controller and soon had LoneWolf doing a swift chopping motion. "Got it?' West asked. Borge answered that he did. The guard was standing outside the parked cable car and Borge crept LoneWolf closer. "Now, quickly move up to him and before he turns around, strike him hard on the back of the neck with that judo chop."

Borge moved LoneWolf silently to the standing guard. The guard sensed something moving toward him. Before he could turn, Borge hit the button controls furiously, using all of LoneWolf's strength. The chop struck the guard across the back of the neck; however, the force of the strike took the guard's head clean off his shoulders. The decapitated head dropped to the ground and tumbled over, stopping with its empty eyes staring up at LoneWolf.

"We'll need to work on that," West said. As a matter of habit, he was about to follow up with a pun about losing one's head, but then remembered the very real effect this was having on Borge, who likely had never killed before tonight. Even though it was indirectly through LoneWolf, the death was very real. "Don't take it personal, Hector. Let's just move on."

LoneWolf entered the lift station and started the engine. The guards at the upper station looked down at the slowly rising car. There had been no signal from the guard at the lower station. They tried to reach the perimeter guard on the two-way radio. No answer there either.

Deciding trouble was afoot, three of the four guards climbed into the car docked at the upper station, released the grip, and began descending on the parallel cable towards the lower car. The remaining guard stayed at the upper station as gripman, waiting by the huge levers for the signal to apply the grip brakes to both cars. The cars met halfway, and the gripman pulled the lever back, stopping the cars as they hung over the vast gaping chasm below. The guards cautiously looked at the car stopped opposite them, about twenty feet away. From their vantage point, it appeared no one was inside.

The guards opened the windows and trained their automatic rifles, watching the tramcar gently sway in the cool mountain breeze. The lead guard picked up his two-way radio and was about to inform the guard at the upper station that the other car was empty, when all three guards whipped their heads around at something coming at them fast.

"Borge, what are you doing?"

"Don't worry, I got this," Borge replied as LoneWolf leaped from the roof toward guard's car.

"Aww, hell!" West exclaimed as a volley of gunfire sprayed at the leaping LoneWolf. He landed on the roof with a thud that shook the car. The soldiers leaned out the windows, shooting wildly up at the rooftop. Borge smashed at the controller buttons, jumping LoneWolf into the air to dodge the fire. A barrage of bullets sliced through the wire of the lower track cable, fraying the braids. The damaged cable sent shockwaves up the line, rocking the car as the remaining wire unraveled.

With a crack, the last of the wire braids snapped. The car swung like a pendulum, smashing into the side of the mountain. The death screams of the falling guards echoed from the misty depths like a morbid yodel. The car was still swaying from the momentum, but the rooftop grip brakes held on, biting into the cable as the upended car dangled over the abyss. LoneWolf's grip had also held. Borge moved him to grab the cable, rapidly moving him up the line.

The guard at the upper station had watched all of this unfold from the station building and saw LoneWolf speeding upward along the dangling cable. The guard ran out and began firing. He stopped, distracted by the sound of the large steel bull wheel inside the station groaning at the strain of the suspended cable car hanging over the steep precipice. The groan turned into a loud screeching shriek as the stressed supports bent and popped, pulling the station building toward the edge of the cliff drop.

LoneWolf used the few seconds afforded by the distraction to get near the top, while trying to keep a grip on the shaking cable. The overstressed wheel finally gave way, snapping off the frame and rolling through the building wall with massive force, crushing the stunned guard as it bowled over the cliff side. LoneWolf made a powerful jump, holding tight to the cliff wall. Just above him, the rest of the entangled cable pulled what was left of the building over the side with it, crashing down into the chasm behind the cable car.

"That was a fine mess," West said, disapproving of Borge's reckless actions.

Borge took a deep breath and wiped the sweat off his brow. "Did you have a better plan?"

"I was thinking of a leisurely ride up to the top, but now that we're here, let's get across that bridge. Looks like we're coming in right through the front door without knocking."

"No time for manners," Borge said and readied his controls for the next level.

West looked across the great gaping chasm to the large—and still open—bay doors. "And that retractable bridge is retracting, so let's invite ourselves in already."

LoneWolf raced to stay one step ahead of the bridge as it retracted under him. The guards at the bay doors saw him charging across and began firing. Borge pushed LoneWolf hard, straining to keep him moving faster than the disappearing bridge beneath his feet, all while trying to dodge gunfire along the way. The guards retreated and quickly went into lockdown, the heavy bay doors dropping down with a thud in front of LoneWolf. With the guards now behind the closed doors, Borge pushed LoneWolf as fast as he could go, grabbing hold of the outer framing just as the bridge fully retracted inside and vanished under him.

"Well, that was fun," West said. Borge lifted LoneWolf's neck upward and he and West looked at the jagged crest of the ridge at least 100 feet above. "Borge, switch me back into my body. This will need to be free climbed, and I don't think 'ol LoneWolf will have the manual dexterity for it."

"But…"

"Just do it. I can handle this. You act like I've never been on a mission of this nature before."

"Of *this* nature?"

West sighed with irritation. "You act like I've never been on a mission before."

"Correction noted. Standby for LoneWolf deactivation."

West mentally prepared and braced himself for the sudden shift. As soon as he could feel bodily sensation, he tightly grabbed the bay door framing to keep from falling and winced as the bitter wind whipped against his face. He removed his gloves, clipped them to his belt, and took a deep breath to calm himself. Moving cautiously, he found a foothold in the textured rock face. Groping the cold, rough rock, he found a suitable crack line and began the arduous process of moving upward, hand over hand. Even though the true depth of the deadly drop was obscured by fog, he dared not look down and kept all his focus on the climb. He was now over the top of the cargo bay door and was painfully digging his fingers into a pocket in the rock when the NeuraComlink buzzed in his ear.

"You know," Borge said, "this is very risky."

West fumbled slightly trying to find a foothold. "What would give you that idea?"

"Yes… well, I'm not sure that even if you managed to activate LoneWolf, you could survive this fall. It's far beyond what we tested.

Have you looked down to see the distance involved? You're a thousand feet above the ground."

"Borge! Could you maybe please stop talking? I'm trying to concentrate."

"Hmmph. Now you know how I feel. Let me know when you're at the top, or just holler on your way to the bottom."

West heard the static sound in his ear of Borge signing off the NeuraComlink. He once again put all of his attention to the climb. After struggling the next few lifts, he was relieved to see the ridge leveling off up another twenty feet or so. The wind whipped icy daggers at him, and more than once it pulled him from the surface of the mountain, making him dig his fingers in with all his strength just to hang on. Finally reaching the ledge, he dragged himself over and rolled onto his back to shake the tension off.

After a moment, he got up and looked over his surroundings. The ledge was near the peak of Wolf Mountain, and widened as it ran along the ridge. Down along the side, he spotted the window-like holes he had seen through the viewfinder. With the steep sheer rock face, they were inaccessible to him from this position. Knowing the installation would need some openings for ventilation and exhaust ports, West scrambled over the rough, rocky terrain in search of one.

The full moon was faintly peeking through dark clouds moving over the horizon. He could feel its energy calling to him. Soon it would move around the front of Wolf Mountain and its light—and its power—would be inescapable.

***

Tanya and Burt stopped running for a moment to catch their breath. After a few seconds, she moved to run on, but Digby stopped her by grabbing ahold of her arm.

217

"Burt, what are you doing? Let's move!"

Digby gulped air. "Hold your shirt on a bit now, we need a plan."

Tanya pushed his hand off her arm. "We have a plan. It's called 'let's get the f--- out of here!"

"I mean for the gold. We ain't leaving here empty-handed. Skorzeny owes me."

"And how do you propose to carry it? It's not exactly light."

Digby paused. She brought up a good point. There had to be a way to get out as quickly as possible and still take gold with them. Perhaps General Ferenc could get them out? "Hold on, I'm thinking," he said to the impatient Tanya.

"Time's up," Tanya said. "I'm leaving now, and Skorzeny can keep the gold."

"Wha-what?" Digby couldn't believe what he was hearing. No way was he leaving empty-handed after all of this.

"You heard me." She bristled to move, and Digby tightened his grip. "Let me go, right now!" Burt held on and in response, she swiftly kicked him in the groin, which loosened his grip considerably. She ran off, leaving Digby squirming on the ground.

The tunnel she was running through connected to the main floor. She would find a guard, get him to open the bay doors and then she'd take the cable car back down. She wasn't sure how she would convince the guards, but clearly things were going in a strange direction, and she hoped that would be enough to afford an escape. Turning the corner, she ran straight into a dark shadow. She looked up to see the shadow belonged to Otto Skorzeny.

"Going somewhere, Fraulein? You know, your feminine scent is quite delicious. It follows you wherever you go. And so it goes that I can as well. You aren't going anywhere, dear liebchen." He reached down and grabbed her by the back of her neck, his steel-grip fingering it like a scruff. "You are coming with me. The night is still young, and we have so much to do."

***

West waited on calling Borge over NeuraComlink. He was used to working alone and even though they had found a method for working together, he took this time to use his experience to plan his next steps. He also thought about what he would do when he next crossed paths with Skorzeny. If he wanted to be cured of lycanthropy and be a full man—not a monster, he would have to find a way to bring him back alive, while stopping whatever plans he may have. It was a tall order. He knew if he was able to get inside without being seen, a kill shot opportunity would most likely present itself. He knew it ultimately was what was best for the mission. It always was, no matter the scenario. However, he convinced himself this was different, with very extenuating circumstances, and he had to find a way to capture Skorzeny and still successfully complete the mission.

Ahead, he saw what looked to be a promising opportunity. Cut into the rocky ground was a large oval opening. It was open-air but covered with a steel grating. The bars of the grating looked large enough to climb through. West cautiously moved closer and looked down. The moon provided enough light to see a large room but was still dark enough he could not see any details. It had a terrible scent but seemed empty. It would have to do.

He took a spooling of high tensile string from his belt-pack, connected it to the bars and lowered himself down. As his eyes adjusted, he could see a flat concrete platform below him, and swung over it. He dropped onto the platform and looked around. His night vision was very good, but he still took the small penlight from his belt and shined it around the room.

It was a large chamber, and alongside him were other platforms. Blood spattered the walls, various unidentifiable body parts strewn about. He sniffed and could tell it was human scent. West reeled around, his ears pricking up at the sounds of shuffling movement. The rock walls began echoing whispery, rumbling growls. His moved his light and saw seven very ravenous Nazi werewolf ghouls surrounding him, rancid saliva dripping from their clacking decayed canine teeth.

"Borge," West said into the NeuraComlink. "I'm going to need a bit of assistance."

21: SHOWDOWN AT WOLF MOUNTAIN

The dark clouds broke, and pale moonlight streamed into the dark chamber, spotlighting Val West as he stood atop the concrete platform. Encircling him was a pack of seven very hungry reanimated Nazi werewolves. The remains of two Transylvanian soldiers were strewn about the floor and walls, bloodied chunks of the devoured men hanging from the creatures' dripping mouths. They sniffed, growled, and licked their rotten chops in anticipation of more food to regenerate their part-werewolf, part-corpse bodies.

Snapping their jaws, the Wolf Pack closed in around West. Finally, he heard a crackling in his ear. "Borge! What, were you taking a nap?"

"I had to use the restroom. It happens you know, especially after eating tacos. You know how they…"

"Okay, okay. I have company… a whole pack, in fact, and I need you to activate LoneWolf right now."

"Standby. Here we go in three… two… one."

The rush of adrenaline and animal vitality burst through West as the shapeshifting took place. With the transformation complete, Lone-Wolf lowered his head and glared into the red eyes of the surrounding pack. The closest creature leaned back on its haunches, and then sprang at LoneWolf. With lightning speed, he clamped his sharp, gleaming fangs on its throat and tore it open with ferocious force. The limp body dropped to the ground, dark rancid blood fountaining from it as it slowly turned back into the shriveled corpse of a long dead Nazi soldier, now truly dead.

LoneWolf stood, ready for attack. Another came at him, teeth bared, claws out. It jumped onto LoneWolf, and he wrestled to stay on his feet. The beast snapped and spewed its vile saliva, the fangs moving toward LoneWolf's throat. Borge worked the controller as fast as he could. He gained a grip on the opposing werewolf's head, prying it back away from him. Pushing LoneWolf's forearm into the creature's neck, he used the other hand to push its head backwards. Next came the sickening snapping of bone and tendons. With the neck weakened, LoneWolf tore into it, the ruptured jugular jetting gore into the air. The limp body dropped to the ground and as had the other, turned back into the waxy corpse of a dead commando.

The remaining five moved in a circle, each ready to make an attempt. LoneWolf barked and lashed out at each of them. He jumped down from the pedestal and attacked the closest one, grabbing it by the head and smashing its nose first on the ground. LoneWolf's foot was on the werewolf's head, pressing its face into the gravel. The circling of the others slowed, and then came to a stop.

LoneWolf leapt back up on the platform and looked over the remaining pack. The werewolves lowered down onto their haunches before him. One by one, they turned their heads to the full moon shining down from above, and let out a long, slow howl. The howling turned into a chorus as each of them came to heel and bowed to the dominant alpha. Borge eased off the controls and let nature take over. He and West observed the scene in silence, as LoneWolf stood tall as master and howled, his savage battle cry echoing throughout Wolf Mountain.

***

Thomas Hedison began sweating profusely when he saw the glow of moonlight creeping into the edges of the view from his cell window. Whatever this scar-faced man, this Otto Skorzeny, had been doing to him was happening again. The sweating, the trembling, the feeling of losing all sense of self and control. Was it a drug? Hypnosis? He still did not know. He chafed against the chains, knowing he couldn't break them, but was unable to stop himself. His ears pricked up and he could hear the strange echoes, the echoes of howling somewhere in the distance. This howling was different. This howling did not come from outside his window. This howling was coming from somewhere inside.

***

LoneWolf had reigned dominance over Skorzeny's Wolf Pack. Now, it was time to move. Tilting LoneWolf's head toward the chamber exit, Borge next pushed the turbo button to full power. LoneWolf jumped off the platform, ran at the metal door, and smashed through it, along with part of the wall. He bounded out through the rubble, the others following behind. Sending the Wolf Pack in other directions, LoneWolf ran off down a dark tunnel. Once out of sight, Borge deactivated him. West shook off the strange feeling of reawakening in his own body and took a moment to adjust.

"All right, Borge. I'm going to do a little scouting and see what we're looking at here. I'm deploying the LoneWolf eyepiece viewer so you can follow along visually." The eyepiece control unfolded from behind his collar and automatically moved into place, attaching over his left eye. Once the autofocus locked in, West kept to the shadows and crept along the tunnel until reaching the exit. The tunnel came out near the cave ceiling and from there he could view the entire installation. The interior of Wolf's Lair was a vast cavern with a large, immaculately polished floor surface housing various equipment, including landing pads for the squadron of helicopters.

Scanning the area below, he saw a giant vat filled with molten gold. Standing next to it were tall racks filled with freshly cast gold bars. Hanging from the interior steel framework were a number of giant Wolfsangel symbol flags, the symbol now adopted by Skorzeny. Several Transylvanian guard soldiers patrolled the main floor. Across the expanse, a wide windowed wall loomed over the main floor, a steel walkway running the length of it. Below it, along the wall, was another large vat, bubbling vapor rising from within—the silver extracted by Tanya. All along the perimeter of the interior were a series of tunnel corridors. He turned and walked back through the tunnel he was in and found a connecting tunnel.

"Borge. You there?"

"I've been waiting with bated breath for your call. I saw the visual of the base. Quite impressive."

"Skorzeny's been on a spending spree with his interior decorator, namely the Transylvanian military. But as you can see, he still has plenty of gold left for whatever his next move is. I'm moving down a side tunnel now, hoping to get over to the other side without alerting the guards on the main floor."

West slowed down his pace. Up ahead, along the torch-lit walls of the corridor, he saw a row of medieval-styled dungeon cells carved out of the rock interior, each with thick iron doors and a single barred window. "Borge, by the distance I've gone, I'd say I'm nearly across to the other side, but before I go any further there's some doors up ahead I want to check out."

West slowly walked up to the first door, looking in through the barred window. Empty. So was the next one. But not the third. The filthy cell had a tiny hole of a window providing light from the moonlit mountaintops, and this light was shining on a trembling prisoner chained to the wall—Thomas Hedison. West walked up to the door and peered through the bars on the door.

"Tom," West whispered. "Tom, it's me, Val. Val West."

Hedison looked around, seeming confused. "Val? My God, please don't be a delusion."

"Quite the real thing, I assure you. I'm going to get this door open, hang on." West took out his standard-issue master lock pick and went to work. The lock sprang open, and the first thing West noticed was the sickening smell of rotting flesh coming from the other side of the darkened cell.

Hedison trembled as he spoke. "I... I think that might be the remains of Luther. You know, Luther? Agent Luther, from X-Division? I think I, uh, I think I maybe killed him. I don't know, Val, I've been drugged or something. I can't tell what's what and I think I've lost it."

"I'm afraid it's worse than that, Tom. We will have to deal with that later. First, let's get you out of here. Do you have enough strength to walk?"

"I think so. But I'm feeling weird again. Whatever they've done to me seems to be kicking in again. I can feel it... crawling through my body. It's like a 'wild' feeling. I don't know how to describe it."

"I think I know what you mean," West said. "Hold on. I'm going to break these chains off the wall."

A dark shadow fell over the cell. A voice spoke, one that sent Thomas Hedison into convulsions of fear... the raspy, steely hiss of Otto Skorzeny. "I'll decide when Herr Hedison leaves. And I say he shouldn't go out with an empty stomach." The door slammed with the clicking of the lock turning from the outside.

Through the bars, West could see Skorzeny gripping Tanya with one arm. Burt Digby walked up and looked in on the happenings inside the cell. Skorzeny snarled and released his hold, throwing her at Burt. "Herr Digby. Keep her on a leash." He then grabbed her by the head, pushing her face into the window bars. "But first, a closer look, Fraulein. Look at your Canadian hero about to become supper for the Húnd." Skorzeny gave West a mocking look. "I hope you have finished your conversation. You'll find the Húnd to be less of a conversationalist than Herr Hedison."

Skorzeny raised his hand with his long fingers outstretched and gave a mental command. Hedison gave an involuntary growl and began to writhe. Tanya watched Hedison's face twist into the beastly features of the henchwolf, Skorzeny's Húnd. He reached his hand out and it rapidly extended into long-nailed, fur-covered claws. The other hand twitched with its little nub, its claws still re-growing.

West readied himself for the coming attack. Hedison was now once again the Húnd, the former Agent Wildebeest, now just a wild beast. He snapped at West, his arms still pinned back to the wall in their restraints. Skorzeny turned to Tanya. "Now, Fraulein, you will see the superior race of der Werwolf defeat the inferior human race. With great ease, and for your enjoyment."

Tanya watched on through the bars of the window. She tried to keep herself together, but right now, the one man she was hoping was alive and coming for her, was alive... but for how long? A tear of frightened resignation fell from her eye as she was forced to watch her one hope be devoured by this horrifying beast. She saw West take up a fighting stance. Skorzeny gave the command to Wildebeest to break his shackles. She then felt Skorzeny's grip leave her head as he uttered in surprise, "Was ist das?"

Skorzeny had a puzzled look on his face as he, along with Tanya and Digby, all in disbelief, watched West transform into LoneWolf. With the transformation complete, he growled through bared fangs as a challenge to Wildebeest. The enraged Húnd ripped the chains out the rock wall and charged at him.

Tanya could not believe what she was seeing, despite all she had recently seen. She didn't want this to be true, that West was just another monster like these others. At the same time, she could see he was somehow different, as he fought against the Skorzeny's Húnd. She felt a glimmer of hope returning. Skorzeny pulled her from the window and barked at Digby to take her away. Struggling against Digby, Tanya pushed off him to get another look through the window as LoneWolf and Wildebeest threw each other around the cell. Digby grabbed her tightly, Tanya kicking and attempting to break free as he dragged her away.

"It's you or him," Borge yelled to West as the fight raged on. "He's not in any capacity to be taken alive."

"Goddamn it, I know that," West replied watching while trapped in his own mind. "But I had to try." He paused, knowing what had to be done. "Tom was a good man. He didn't do this. He didn't kill Cedric... this monster did."

"I'm sorry, West."

"I'm sorry, too. Now do it."

Borge maneuvered LoneWolf's controls to pick up Wildebeest and slam him against the wall. The dazed Wildebeest reeled as Borge pushed the turbo button on his controller and barreled LoneWolf straight into the monster. Wildebeest tried to shake off the damage, but it was too late. LoneWolf bared his fangs, his eyes flashing a glowing red. He tore straight into Wildebeest's neck, tearing out the jugular vein, gore spraying out of the shredded throat.

As the mortally wounded Wildebeest completed his final metamorphosis back to the dying form of Thomas Hedison, Borge deactivated LoneWolf so the two friends could have a last moment. West knelt down alongside Tom and put his hand on his chest. The blood loss was too great and Hedison could not speak. He looked up at West and without saying anything, seemed to know what had happened, giving a feeble nod as he faded into the darkness.

West turned and looked through the barred window of the door at Skorzeny with rage in his eyes. The door creaked open and Skorzeny walked in, sniffing the air. "Whatever you're wearing has been convincing enough to conceal your scent from me. I should have known when I saw the white streak in your hair that you were one of mine. I thought you had fallen to your death that night in Transylvania.

"If it makes you feel better, I never could get any useful information out of Hedison. His will in human form was too strong to even tell us who you were. 'Good boy,' I suppose," he said with a sinister chortle. "But now that mein Húnd is dead, you shall take his place."

West stared him down. "He was not a Húnd, not a dog, not even a wolf. He was a man, which is more than I can say for you."

"Indeed. We are not men. Are we not wolves? Nein. We are der werwolfen. The true master race." He raised his arm and pointed a finger at West. "Now, you be a 'good boy' and come here."

Borge was listening in through the NeuraComlink and sensed trouble coming. He activated LoneWolf without alerting West and watched through the viewfinder to see Skorzeny pulling LoneWolf toward him with his primal psychic command. Borge gripped the controller joystick and pulled back on it, noticing how hard it was to stop LoneWolf's movements.

"I SAID COME," Skorzeny commanded with an inhuman voice that echoed off the cavernous walls. LoneWolf started moving toward him but was stopped again by Borge fighting back with his controls.

West watched helplessly. "Stop him, Borge."

"I'm fighting with all I got. His powers of command are stronger than you can imagine."

"I don't need to imagine it. I can see it with a wolf's eye view. If he gets LoneWolf under his control, it's game over."

Borge fought with all he had without breaking the controller. He watched as Skorzeny put his hand down and looked curiously at Lone-Wolf.

"I see you have someone pulling your strings somehow. You need to come to heel to your true master. You are one of the Pack, and you do not turn your back on the Wolf Pack." Skorzeny's face morphed into that of a huge gray wolf, with glowing red eyes and a large set of fangs, the lips pulled back in a sinister grin. In a deep, guttural, demonic voice that pierced LoneWolf's ears and forced him to his knees, Skorzeny roared, "You will kneel before me, Húnd!"

Sweat rolled down Borge's forehead onto his glasses as he fought for control of LoneWolf against Skorzeny. He thought about his options. He had one ace up his sleeve and at this crucial point felt he had no choice but to use it. "Dammit," he said to West. "I was hoping to save this."

Before West could ask what it was, Borge activated a control to open the top of LoneWolf's right hand gauntlet. He held the button down and a fireball screamed out. The bursting flame singed the wolf hair of Skorzeny, causing him to yelp and retreat backwards. With the control broken, Borge ran LoneWolf out through the cell and down the long corridor. He ducked into a short side tunnel to regroup.

"What the hell was that?" West demanded. "You didn't tell me we had a flamethrower."

"It was a lighter, but I put extra pressure on it and used all the fuel for one fireball burst. Hopefully, we won't need to start any fires later."

"We'll just have to improvise in that case, but don't worry. One way or the other we're burning this place down. Let's get me back into my body and get Tanya and Digby out of here. Once they're safe, I'll work on Skorzeny. And I'm still taking him, alive."

Borge grimaced at the thought. He knew how much it meant to West to be cured, but he just wanted him to kill Skorzeny and end this whole affair. "I don't know which is going to be tougher… killing him or bringing him back alive. Or even just bringing you back alive."

He deactivated LoneWolf and West crept out back into the corridor. Seeing it was clear, he ran off in the direction that would bring him out near the walkway leading to the upper level with the large wall of windows—Skorzeny's command center. With the tunnel exit looming ahead, West slowed down and looked as far down it as he could see. The passage would bring him to the walkway, but he would have to go past the large vat of molten silver bubbling away below it. The fumes wafted up toward him and he felt a slight dizziness from the vapors alone. He snuck up the steps to the upper level and was surprised to see Burt Digby standing in the shadows along the side wall. West whispered to him, and the jittery Digby made his way closer.

"Digby, what's going on?"

"Mate, am I glad to see you," Digby said with desperation. "Can you get us out of here?"

"Yes, I think so. Where's Tanya?"

Digby paused for a moment. "I had her wait in a side room over there."

West looked in the direction Digby pointed and saw her hiding place. Off the side of the walkway, a thick tarpaulin concealed the room entrance. "Let's get her and then I'll get the both of you out of here. Once the two of you are safe, I'll come back in for Skorzeny."

Digby looked around, then motioned for West to follow him along the walkway to the room. West went in first, pulling the tarpaulin aside. No Tanya. The tarpaulin fell away and the sound of a metal door slamming down reverberated off the steel walkway. There was no room, just a cage, and now West was locked inside it. The cage was suspended from the girders above it by a chain on a hoist. Digby worked the hoist's control unit, moving the cage out and away from the railing edge.

"Digby, what the hell are you doing?"

"Sorry, dog. You're not the man, mate." Digby moved the cage until it was positioned directly over the silver pit and lowered it until it was suspended just a few feet above the bubbling surface. "As they say, gold talks and bull dust walks. You think I'm leaving here without payment? You've gone barmier than Skorzeny then. And at least he didn't try to steal my girlfriend."

The silver vapors wafted up into the cage and West could feel his strength draining. "You really think you can trust him, Digby? And what makes you think I was trying to steal Tanya away from you?"

"It's quite obvious she fancies you, you bloody fleabag. And no, I don't trust Skorzeny, but I'm taking the gold—and the girl—and we're leaving you lot to faff around. I've had enough bloomin' werewolves. Now you just hang tight right there, mate, and now that I've done my part, I think it's about time for me and Tanya to get paid and say our bye-byes."

Unable to stay on his feet, West staggered down to his knees. He wearily looked up through the cage bars. A dark silhouette watching from the large windows directly above the walkway came into view. Otto Skorzeny peered out and told Burt Digby he had done well.

The voice sounded far away, and everything went black as West dropped to the floor of the cage.

22: IN HIS OWN REICH

"My good General Ferenc," Otto Skorzeny leaned back in his chair
and took a sip of his Cognac. "Why such a hurry to leave? It is All
Hallows Eve and what better way to spend a holiday than in the company of good friends?"

General Ferenc looked around Skorzeny's Command Center and
tried not to appear nervous. He stared at the wall filled with control
banks, all with lights blinking and gauges reading levels, performing
all the functions needed to operate the base and its power sources. All
of it built by his men of the Transylvanian National Army. Under his
command, they had also refurbished the long-abandoned remains of
this hidden and unfinished World War II Nazi base—Hitler's pro-
posed "Wolf's Lair."

Looks could not deceive, however, and Skorzeny also had the stra-
tegic advantage of being able to smell the fear creeping through Ferenc
and he reveled in the sensation. Ferenc shifted in his seat, then stood
up and walked over to the large wall of windows overlooking the main
floor of the base below. He focused his gaze on the large stacks of gold
bars on the far side. "Mr. Skorzeny," Ferenc began, trying to project
some measure of authority, if not intimidation. "My men are being
eaten by those... *things* running loose down there. We have a deal,
and I am intending to collect the gold owed to me, and then I, and
whatever is left of my men are leaving."

"Tsk, tsk, mein Freund. You know tonight is a night of the supernatural. Why, as a Transylvanian, you should also know travel is not advised. Besides, the cable car is… out of service… and it would be best if you and your men waited until morning, when it will be much safer for all of you."

"I know all about the cable car. Something attacked those men—my men, and on loan to you, I might remind you."

"And you will be fully compensated for the loss, I assure you."

"Very well. We are still leaving now. My remaining men will load the gold onto the helicopters, and we will be flying out of here."

Skorzeny looked Ferenc dead in the eyes. "If you insist. I, of course, want to be a good neighbor and we will be doing much more business to come, I'm sure. As for now… let us say an extra 100 million dollars in gold should alleviate some of your discomfort, no?"

The thought of doubling the initial agreement made Ferenc smile involuntarily. Maybe Skorzeny wasn't so bad after all, he thought. So, it cost him a few soldiers. They knew the risks of being in the service. 200 million would be far more than enough to flee Transylvania if this all fell apart and live in comfort somewhere far away, and stay paid up with the right people.

"You do understand it will take some time to get the helicopters ready and to load the gold bullion," Skorzeny said as Ferenc nodded in agreement. "If you will please go down and instruct your men on the plan, I will join you once I have concluded some important business I must attend to."

"Yes, of course. Thank you for your understanding, Mr. Skorzeny."

"Please," Skorzeny replied with a smile, "Otto."

"Otto, yes, yes. I will get started at once." Ferenc nearly tripped over himself in excitement on his way out. Skorzeny glowered at him and ran his tongue across his fangs. He walked out of the Command

233

Center and on to the walkway, eyeing up his captured quarry. Val West was still lying unconscious in the cage above the bubbling silver vat, the dangerous silver vapors wafting up through the cage bottom.

"Herr Digby, please bring in the cage so our guest may join us. I think being suspended over the silver has tamed his wild hairs a bit." Digby used the controller to pull the hoist's chain in and lowered it onto the walkway. He disconnected the chain, sending it swinging back over the vat of molten silver and dragged out the prone West. Skorzeny stayed back, not wanting to get any closer to the power-draining silver fumes. "Bring Herr West into the Command Center." He looked down at West and smiled. "It's Halloween and I have a special horror planned, just for him."

The unconscious West was bound to an operating table, courtesy of Burt Digby. Across the room was Tanya, tied to a chair near the wall opposite the control banks. She looked at Digby with narrowed eyes. He turned away from her glare and looked down. Of course, she was beyond upset with him, but he felt he had kept his part of the bargain, even if it was a deal with the devil. Once they were on their way out in a helicopter filled with gold, she would see he had done the right thing. Now away from the deadly silver, a groggy West tried to focus on where he was. Still too weak to move his limbs, he looked around to assess the situation and did not like the look of it.

Digby pulled the leather belt restraints to ensure they were tight enough and walked over to where Skorzeny was standing. "Well, that looks to be about it. If we could get the gold loaded up on the chopper and get going, that would fan-bloody-tastic."

"Perhaps it would be better to wait until morning."

Digby needed to keep his nerve, but still found himself looking down at the floor as he spoke. "Listen now, I appreciate everything, but I think with all that's gone on, I would like to stick to our arrangement and leave with Tanya. We've already talked to Ferenc and we're leaving with him and his men."

Skorzeny frowned. "I'm not sure that's a wise choice, Herr Digby. And what makes you think Ferenc is leaving?"

The confidence Digby had found to face Skorzeny visibly drained from his face. "I... I did everything you asked. You promised me you would let us go, and with our gold, if I could get you the Canadian. I kept my end of it. Now... we have a deal, mate!"

Skorzeny's eyes flared with fire, fury dripping from his teeth. "I told you never to call me 'mate.'" Digby began shaking and slowly backed away.

"Herr Digby. Your services are no longer required." Skorzeny suddenly leaped up into the air and came down as a vicious beast. Shredded pieces of Digby dropped to the ground in a bloody splatter. Tanya screamed at the sight of the gory jigsaw puzzle that just a moment earlier was Burt Digby. Skorzeny sniffed the air with his snout, enjoying the deliciousness of the fear in her scent and howled along with her screams.

When Val West finally regained full consciousness, he was bound across the arms and legs, with no way to reach the LoneWolf activator. Perhaps he could reach Borge through the NeuraComlink. It had been some time since their last communication. Even though he told Borge he would contact him when he was to activate LoneWolf, he hoped Borge would become concerned and disobey him. When he heard the static crackle in his ear, he was glad they were on the same wavelength this time.

"West," Borge shouted over the communicator. "What's going on? I'm opening up the speaker in case you can't push the microphone button."

West wriggled his head and tried to speak softly. "I'm a bit tied up, if you know what I mean. I need you to— "

"What's this?" Skorzeny turned his attention from the control panel wall to West and walked over to him. "Talking to yourself? More like someone else, ja?" He wrenched up West's head. Running his long fingers along the back of West's head, he felt the implanted jack with the thin wire leading down the back of the neck to the NeuraComlink microphone. Skorzeny dug his sharp fingernails into the flesh surrounding the implant and grabbed hold of the jack, yanking it out with one swift, painful motion. Skorzeny held up the blood-covered implant to examine it. "What a fascinating device." He closed his fingers around it, crushing it to dust. "I would, however, like your undivided attention."

West felt woozy from the blood pouring out of the back of his head. Skorzeny focused on preparing a mechanical contraption, while Tanya appeared to be working on loosening her bonds while Skorzeny was occupied. He stopped and walked over to her.

"Are you trying to free yourself Fraulein? You must understand my sense of hearing is quite keen and I can hear your attempts quite clearly. You can try if you like, but you will not be able to undo those knots."

West turned his head toward them. "You know, I can think of better things to do with her than kill her. Of course, it is quite obvious you are of a different persuasion and not interested in women."

"As it happens, Herr West," Skorzeny sneered, "I am quite attracted to females... and female wolves, in particular. As an alpha wolf, I love nothing more than the wild feeling of roaming the forest and taking the bitch-wolves I find. Animal sex in its purest form, the way nature intended."

Tanya was beginning to mentally question all that had been unfolding before her. "Wait, wait. I want a werewolf break." She pointed at West, then at Skorzeny. "You're a werewolf, you're a werewolf, and there's all those other dead, now not-dead werewolf... things. Is anybody around here *not* a werewolf?"

Skorzeny looked at her with a bemused reaction. "You. And you could just end up a morsel to be wolfed down."

"But you said if I was able to free your Nazi werewolf army buddies, you'd let me go."

"I never said I would let you go," Skorzeny replied with a twinkle in his red eye. "I said I would set you free. I may make you my bitch-wolf. Then you will know freedom as a member of the super-species, under my command until I tire of you and after you've sired enough litters of my seed."

Tanya recoiled in horror at the thought. From across the Command Center, West shouted to Skorzeny. "You really know how to talk to the ladies. Quite the Romeo, I must say. Did you used to chat up Adolph like that?"

Skorzeny curled his lip into a snarl. "The difference between you and I, is I am a werewolf who can turn into a man, and you are just a man who can turn into a werewolf, and badly. You are a mindless beast. With der Wolfsgürtel, my wolfskin belt, I have both the power of my mind and the power of the werewolf. Soon, I will be taking your werewolf powers and leaving you as nothing, which is a fitting end for you."

Skorzeny used his long thumbnail to open his shirt. He pointed to a large scar on his chest. "Once you're gone, I will always have this to remember you by: the scar left by your silver dagger, the first time we met. Your parting gift as you fell off the cliff and unfortunately survived due to luck." He then ran his fingers along the deep scar that marked the length of the left side of his face. "Another souvenir, left long ago. My enemy only got lucky once, and then met his doom. The same fate will now happen to you, as your luck has finally run out."

A drumbeat of machine gun fire echoed from the main floor below. Skorzeny's ears pricked up and he left the Command Center to check out the commotion.

"You know," Tanya said while working to loosen her bonds. "I thought all of this was too much. Then, I find out on top of it, you're a werewolf, too. How long have you been one of them?"

"I'm not one of *them,* exactly," West said as he shifted back and forth, trying to create some movement in his restraints. "I'm trying to bring Skorzeny in alive, so I can be cured. And I've been on his trail since before I met you. I work for a secret organization called Para-Command. The doctor there is able to control my movements as a werewolf, so you could say I'm the good guy."

"Let's not get carried away."

"Fair enough. Listen, about that belt he wears… just like he said, while wearing it he can keep his consciousness while a werewolf. If you get free, try to grab it and take it off him. He'll still be dangerous, but at least be unable to think like a human."

"How do you suppose I'm going to get free?"

"I'm still working on that. You keep doing the same."

The electronic door to the Command Center slid open and Skorzeny came back in. He was nude, save for a black ceremonial cloak clasped across his chest by a gold chain with a gold Wolfsangel medallion, and der Wolfsgürtel.

"Pardon the interruption. My Wolf Pack are just eating the rest of Ferenc's men. They have been quite famished, and some red meat was in order." He wheeled the piece of machinery around and brought it near West. "Before we get to this, I want to tell you of my plans."

"Here we go," West groaned.

"What? You don't want to know why I am doing all of this?"

"Not particularly. I've heard it all before. Besides, your plans don't matter because you will die tonight." West didn't like to think he was just bluffing, but in his current situation, he wasn't so certain.

"So self-assured, right to the end." Skorzeny was disappointed that West didn't want to know what his master plan was. "Nein. You are a captive audience and I want you to know what will happen after you are dead."

"That couldn't possibly matter to me."

"You will listen. After being tricked into the 'Wolf Trap' prison by the traitors Heinrich Himmler, Dr. Josef Mengele, and worst of all, my own cousin Bluto, I spent all my time in an endless dark limbo since 1945. All that time, I thought of nothing but the day I would be set free. Then I would enact my plans, the plans I would have enacted in 1945. The coming of the master werewolf race, the Wolf Reich. Thinking of this, hour after hour, day after day, decade after decade was all I could do to keep sane."

"Didn't seem to work."

Skorzeny violently backhanded West across the face. "Insolent turd! Now, shall we continue?"

He did not wait for a reply from West. "The Wolf Reich will replace man as the dominant species—the apex predator, if you will. I, as the Alpha, will lead my Wolf Pack to recreate the World War II directive of Operation: Werwolf. We will turn civilians—starting right here in Transylvania—into werewolves, who will then in turn bite others, and all will be under my command. The army will continue to grow and spread throughout the nations of this world, all of these werewolves coming to heel under me, the Supreme Uberwolf, der Wolführer."

Skorzeny paused his rant for a moment to wait for West's response. "Now you know the plans I have for everyone."

"I'm sorry. I wasn't listening."

Skorzeny's eyes blazed, and he flexed, transforming into the great beast that was his werewolf form, and unleashed a thunderous growl. He regained his composure and exhaled, shapeshifting back to his human likeness. "I suppose you should know there are other plans as well. One of the things in the train car containing Dr. Mengele's laboratory equipment was a vial containing the cultures for a virus bomb. It also contains the cure for the virus, in vaccine form. My werewolf venom will be replicated and added to the vaccine, making all who take the vaccine, one of my werewolves, under my command."

"That will never work. No one will ever fall for that—taking an experimental vaccine without even knowing what's in it."

"Silence!" Skorzeny shouted, livid at West's comments. "There is one other piece of Mengele's laboratory equipment that you will find works all too well." He pointed to the machine he had wheeled over by the table to which West was strapped. "This device is known as the Extractor."

Whatever the Extractor was, West was sure it was something he wanted nothing to do with. The machine had a number of gauges and lights on the front of its box-like shape. On top was a glass dome with rubber tubes running out of opposite sides. The ends of the tubes had long needles surrounded by clamps. Skorzeny took the two tubes facing West and brought them near his face.

"When we first started Operation Werwolf, through vivisection Mengele was able to determine the 19th century Transylvanian werewolf we had resurrected was able to create more werewolves with his bite by a venom produced through the fangs. He built the Extractor specially to extract the venom—much like milking the venom of a cobra. This is also how a cure could be generated. However, that does not apply to you. Under low power the extraction process is extremely painful. I will be using it on you at full power.

"By absorbing your werewolf powers, I will be increasing my own strength and transcending beyond the alpha wolf I already am. Der Wolfsgürtel will also fuse into me, making us one, on this beautiful Halloween night. You know, I would have used your friend Wildebeest for this, but because you killed him, it will have to be you instead. This is just as well, as you don't appreciate what you have become and do not deserve to wield such power."

Skorzeny grabbed West by the mouth and pried his jaws open. He took the sharp needlepoints of the hoses and pushed them hard and painfully into West's gums, just behind the incisors, then cranked the clamps tight around the teeth.

"That was the easy part," said Skorzeny.

Leaving the writhing West to his pain, Skorzeny powered on the Extractor and began adjusting the controls. The level of pain coming from his teeth covered the added agony from contorting his right wrist to aim straight forward. Now, he hoped he could launch the razor-sharp shuriken throwing star loaded in the gauntlet of his suit. While this weapon would produce no more than a short delay if it hit Skorzeny, West thought it would be better used in a different way.

He steadied himself as much as he could and squeezed his glove. The spring-loaded shuriken embedded into the wall near Tanya, just narrowly missing her head. Skorzeny saw what had happened and paused for a moment to laugh.

"Dummkopf. You almost killed the girl with your stupid toy. Do you really think your secret agent gimmicks would have an effect on me, even if your aim wasn't so bad?"

At first Tanya was alarmed, but then saw the possibilities. The shuriken was sticking in the wall, with the sharp spiked edges pointed toward her. Skorzeny went back to his work of preparing the other end of the tubes. Watching him working with his back turned to her, she slowly began moving her chair closer to the wall.

The brightness of the full moon was shining directly into the Command Center through the large open-air window. Skorzeny let it shine on him, his features rippling back and forth between man and wolf as he drank in its power, reveling in the control he had over his own lycanthropic powers. West also felt the power of the lunar WLF rays. The pull was so strong, but as awful as he already felt there was the worse feeling of being unable to shift into a werewolf when it was all his body wanted to do.

"Not until I say," Skorzeny said, holding command over West, preventing him from transforming. Taking the two ends of the hoses connected to the other side of the Extractor, he sunk both needles into the veins on the undersides of his wrists. He gazed straight into West's fading eyes. "Now," he said, raising his hand to release his control. His body chemistry freed, West quickly changed into his werewolf form. LoneWolf gnashed his fangs, fighting against the clamps attached to them.

Then Skorzeny powered on the Extractor.

A crackling static filled through the Command Center and West, as the LoneWolf, now felt the full tooth drilling, jaw-cracking pull of the machine.

Tanya was making slow progress sawing through the ropes binding her wrists with the sharp edges of the shuriken buried in the wall. She looked on, horrified, as West's face would switch between werewolf and his own, the Extractor pulling out his werewolf venom. The unbearable pain brought terrifying sounds, and she could not bear to listen.

West was mostly conscious now, which was worse. As the machine extracted away, he thought about the only option, one he never would have otherwise considered: the kill switch. It was designed by Borge and Commander 7 to send all the colloidal silver used in the suits veining, the silver used in carefully measured dosages to transform him back from LoneWolf. As a failsafe, the kill switch could be engaged to inject all of the silver, killing him by sending a lethal dose straight into his werewolf glands. If he did this now, once the silver destroyed him it would then travel through the tubes of the Extractor to Skorzeny.

The shock of the extraction was so great he was not numbing to the pain, which was what normally happens after being tortured for a time. The thought of what he had to do was all that drove him, and he jammed his shoulder into the side of the table repeatedly, dislocating it. He slowly bent his twisted arm, trying to make his fingers reach close enough to place his thumb on the chestpiece of his suit. Once his thumbprint had been placed on the sensor for three seconds an alert would happen. Three more seconds and the kill switch would be activated. Just like the cyanide he used to carry in the false tooth as an agent with International Command, this was that last choice he had to make in the line of duty.

He would not be bringing Skorzeny back alive. He would not be bringing himself back alive, either.

23: DEATH MOON

Where the hell was Val West? Commander 7 had just called in to Dr. Borge at ParaCommand headquarters and he had no answer for him. Since arriving at the Transylvanian Alps, they had been in regular communication, all the way through his infiltration of Otto Skorzeny's Wolf's Lair base in Wolf Mountain.

Borge had respected West's wishes to wait until contacted, and not interrupt while West was sneaking around. Too much time had now passed between check-ins, and Borge felt he had to open the communication line through the NeuraComlink. Nothing. His monitor showed 'connection failed,' over and over. Was West dead? If he was, the link must have been damaged in the process. And, perhaps, it was just that the NeuraComlink had been damaged and West was still alive after all. But in what condition?

***

Val West wasn't dead. He was only wishing he was. The agonizing pain from Skorzeny's Extractor machine was on a level he never conceived of existing. He had managed to shoot his only gauntlet shuriken into the wall near Tanya, hoping it would be within reach for her to use the sharp edge to cut the ropes binding her to the chair. Time was running out and he couldn't hold on much longer to see if she could be freed. Even if she was, he would rather she take the opportunity to run away, and not attempt to take on Skorzeny.

While West's werewolf venom was being painfully pulled from him, Otto Skorzeny basked in the glow of the moonlight shining through the window onto him. He was in his full werewolf form, glowing with the increased power of the werewolf venom now flowing into his veins.

Tanya moved the rope binding her wrists against the sharp edge of the shuriken in the wall. Her fingers had found the razor-sharp edge first. Even though Skorzeny was in his own zone, she had bit her lip to not cry out from the sudden pain of the cut and cause him to look over at her. She was doing her best to remain calm and stretched her bound wrists backwards to keep them on the blade's edge.

West's dislocated shoulder had given almost enough space in the restraints to move his thumb over the top of the biometric sensor on his suit's chestpiece. He was already in such excruciating pain that adding this additional level would, he hoped, if not successful in reaching the kill switch, at least finally send him into unconsciousness. No, he had to reach it. It wasn't enough that he would surely die from this. Skorzeny also had to die, and the lethal silver injection from the kill switch would do the job by killing them both.

**

General Ferenc was cornered. Just minutes before, he was pacing the polished floors while his remaining men started the arduous process of loading the gold bars onto the helicopter. Ferenc supervised, ordering them to hasten when they were already moving as fast as they could. Soon, they would fly out with a 200 million dollar cargo.

The echo of a distant howl had come from one of the tunnels surrounding the complex. Ferenc stopped to wipe the sweat off his brow and chug some antacid for his pulsing ulcer. He still wasn't sure what those things were or even what Skorzeny really was, but as a native Transylvanian he knew the lore, even if he had dismissed it as superstition. All he knew was it was past time to get out of there and yelled again for his men to hurry, as the howling grew louder… and closer.

Only the four troops remained, and he inched closer to them as he saw flashes of something moving in the dark shadows of the far walls. Ferenc ordered one of the men to investigate and shoot on sight. The soldier moved out with machine gun at the ready, walking into the creeping darkness along the wall.

The sound of gunfire, growling, screaming, and the snapping of bones came back from the shadows. Ferenc strained to see what was happening and did not notice the silhouetted figures looming behind him. The three soldiers still loading the gold became a feast for the Wolf Pack. Ferenc turned around, let out a high-pitched squeal, and then fled in terror, the pack of hungry werewolves trailing him as he ran.

The steps to the walkway were straight ahead and if his heart didn't give out from the running, he might be able to get up in the stairs in time to make it to the Command Center. His heart and lungs pounding, he was forced to stop by the large industrial vat near the steps.

Now, he prepared for the worst. While wheezing, he noticed the creatures backing away. They were scared of the bubbling silver in the vat and kept their distance. They continued to circle, licking their chops as if readying to pounce on a succulent fat pig.

Ferenc kept close to the large vat of molten silver. Even though the vapors surrounding the vat were enough to keep the werewolves at bay, they still attempted to get closer, lunging near him, and then backing away as the silver fumes reached them. He would have to hold out until daybreak, with the hope that the coming of dawn would send them scurrying back into the shadows. He looked above, over the walkway to the wall of windows of Skorzeny's Command Center. Inside were flashes that looked like lighting, along with torturous screams and a howling that also sounded like it could be a wicked cackling. As soon as he had a chance, he would take it and make a move. He would also be taking as much gold as he could carry.

***

Borge didn't know what to do, until he remembered the drone. It wouldn't have much power left after carrying LoneWolf to the edge of Wolf Mountain, but he had to do something. He wheeled his office chair over to the monitoring system and checked the drone's status. It was just as he had thought—low power. If he could just get enough out of it to see what was happening in the Wolf's Lair, he could hopefully report to Commander 7 that West had the situation well in hand.

The drone powered up and lifted off, Borge watching through the viewfinder as it flew past the trail of destruction left in LoneWolf's wake. The entrance cargo doors of the Wolf's Lair had been sealed shut and on the ridge above was the opening where West had entered.

What about this large window around the side past the cargo doors? He piloted the drone toward the window, past the series of small, barred cell windows. He pulled the drone back as he neared the big window. It was carved out of the mountainside, like the rest of them, although it was much larger and was completely open, with no bars or window glass. The brightness of the full moon was behind him, shining into this opening. Borge felt it afforded him a bit of cover, with the light shining directly at whomever might see the drone outside the window.

Holding the drone steady in hover mode, Borge zoomed the camera in closer to see if he could make out any details of what was going on inside. The power light began flashing furiously, and the drone only had a matter of seconds before it would lose power completely and crash down the mountainside. Borge was startled to see the werewolf Skorzeny grinning with sadistic delight while West struggled against the Extractor.

He had only one shot at this, and by the look of it, so did West.

***

Tanya felt the ropes finally beginning to fray. The slow, laborious process was not going fast enough for her as she watched helplessly while West was being destroyed. Once she was free, she wasn't going to just run away. She was going to get that wolfskin belt off Skorzeny first.

Skorzeny, in full werewolf form, was absorbing LoneWolf's energy and the feeling was one of pure electric vitality. He could feel his own power increasing, his strength growing with each second. He paused to look out at the beautiful Halloween blue moon and saw the silhouette of a dark, bat-like shape in front of it. It was curious, this thing. It looked like a bat, but perhaps too large.

Skorzeny continued to stare at it, puzzled. West felt himself going into deep shock. He knew he couldn't stay conscious much longer. His thumb hovered over the small circle in the center of the chestpiece. Just six total seconds of courage is all it would take for the kill switch to activate... if he could last that long.

With no weapons to fire and the power supply almost dead, Borge had only one chance. Building up to full speed, he launched the drone toward the window opening. Skorzeny looked up as it zoomed toward him, uttering, "Was zur Hölle?"

To deflect the attacking drone, Skorzeny threw the operating table, with West still strapped to it. He missed entirely, the table and West splintering against the wall. The drone crashed into the Command

Center control panel in an explosion of sparks and flames. Danger alarms sounded, and an enraged Skorzeny moved to the control panel, desperately trying to power down the system before it overloaded.

Under the window, the remains of the broken Val West lay hanging off the remains of the broken table. The full moon streamed through the window, illuminating his mangled body. Under its blue light, his nearly dead body felt the full power of the WLF rays and began its natural metamorphosis. A savage and re-energized LoneWolf rose up, tearing off the straps and pieces of the broken operating table. Without Borge to control him, he was in his purest, most natural state. Following only his instincts and his scent, he knew who Otto Skorzeny was, and he wanted his blood.

Tanya's bonds broke loose and she sprang out of the chair. Skorzeny saw this and grabbed her by the throat pushing her into the wall.

A furious growl came from behind him. Skorzeny turned and came face to face with LoneWolf. He dropped Tanya and responded with a savage snarl. Tanya was unsure what to do as these two huge werewolves stared each other down. The Command Center was on fire and the equipment was overheating, with small pops turning into large explosions, shaking the foundations of the floor.

LoneWolf's eyes blazed red and he lunged at Skorzeny. The two beasts locked up in combat, smashing what was left of the flaming Command Center as they clashed. Possessing super-strength from the extraction the power-charged Skorzeny whipped LoneWolf into the cavern wall, bouncing him off the rocks. Skorzeny sprang at him with a direct hit, the momentum sending the two of them crashing through the Command Center's wall of windows. Both combatants slowly got to their feet, shaking off the broken glass covering them.

The werewolves faced off again, their hair and hackles raised, fangs bared. Skorzeny stopped and sniffed the air. LoneWolf turned around to see the Wolf Pack prowling down the walkway behind him. Skorzeny took the stance of the Alpha and barked at them.

Underneath the walkway, General Ferenc was watching. Once he saw the Wolf Pack leave to climb up the scaffolding to the walkway, he knew it was time to make a break for it. Tremors rumbled throughout the base. The overloaded system was responding with a series of catastrophic explosions, each growing more intense.

Ferenc ran across the floor toward the helicopters and stacks of gold bars. He wasn't leaving empty-handed. He rushed over to the control bank by the main cargo doors and opened them, the doors struggling under the raining rubble. The bridge groaned trying to push itself out, the metal track slowly pushing out to the cliff across the gap.

Running back to the helicopters, he was stopped when a large falling chunk of rock crushed the copters. He scurried like a rat to the racks of gold bars and began shoving the near thirty-pound gold bars into his pants and shirt. The increasing tremors opened a large crevasse, the cracks spidering across the floor. Ferenc ran for the bridge and tripped on a large crack opening under his feet. Grabbing hold of the edge, he struggled to pull himself up, the weight of the gold bars pulling him down. Getting his fingers in a groove, he began climbing out. He looked up to see the tall rack of gold bars toppling over. The last thing he saw was the pile of gold falling down onto him, as the crevasse opened up wider, swallowing all.

The Wolf Pack climbed on and around the walkway framing, licking their lips. The werewolf Skorzeny gave a beastly grin of triumph. He was now reunited with the soldiers he commanded, and nothing could stop him. He barked out an order to attack LoneWolf. The Pack didn't move and an angered Skorzeny barked again. The Pack moved and began circling around LoneWolf.

They stopped when LoneWolf raised his hand and pointed. They slowly turned toward Skorzeny. He continued barking at them but knew he was no longer in command. He was no longer the true Alpha. Suddenly terrified, he let out a pathetic yelp and attempted to flee. The Wolf Pack moved in for the attack, flesh and fur flying in their midst.

Skorzeny fought back, tossing two of them over the walkway, with one falling into the silver pit below. The molten silver splashed up into the air, licking the bottom of the walkway.

One of The Pack sunk its rotting fangs into Skorzeny's arm, taking a chunk of flesh with it. The panicking Skorzeny ran back into the Command Center.

The room was now filled with thick choking smoke and Tanya was certain she was going to die. Now, with Otto Skorzeny standing right in front of her she was even more certain. That is, until she realized he hadn't seen her through the smoke, so she quietly tiptoed behind him. With a gulp of courage, she reached toward Skorzeny's back and un-buckled the Wolfsgürtel, ripping the belt off him. Without the Wolfsgürtel, he instantly lost his human consciousness and went full savage, thrashing and clawing.

Seeing the rabid werewolf reaching its claws toward her, Tanya's instinctive reaction was to put on the wolfskin belt. Instantly, she felt a rush go through her and the feeling of growing larger and stronger. A raw animal power pulsed through every fiber of her being. She saw her arms raise up to defend against the attacking Skorzeny, and saw they were covered in fur. Her talon-like claws struck hard, scratching Skorzeny across the snout.

The huge werewolf Skorzeny reeled from the bleeding claw marks. Tanya growled in an animalistic voice, "Now you're dealing with a real bitchwolf!" while he howled from the smarting pain. Tanya leaped across the room with a wild energy. She marveled at the abili-ties the Wolfsgürtel gave her.

251

The enraged beast charged at her, and she leapfrogged over him, letting the monster crash through the opposing wall onto the walkway. Skorzeny lay on the metal grating, LoneWolf and the remaining members of The Wolf Pack standing over him. Tanya ran out through the hole in the wall, the last of the Command Center collapsing behind her. She looked at all of these other creatures and knew they were operating on pure primal instinct and could easily overpower her, even as a werewolf. She decided it was time to get away from the fray.

As soon as the Wolf Pack caught scent and sight of her, their eyes bulged and their lapping tongues dripped with drool, snapping at each other over which would pursue her. She gnashed her teeth at them and ran off, The Wolf Pack right on her behind.

Skorzeny looked at LoneWolf with pure ferocity and launched at him in full attack. An explosion rocked the walkway, the force throwing them over the edge. With claws dug deep into the edge of the steel rail, LoneWolf and Skorzeny dangled above the silver melting pit some thirty feet below. The chain which held the cage was hanging just above and LoneWolf made a leap, catching it and bounding upward. Skorzeny followed with a jump as the stressed walkway collapsed, falling down into the red-hot silver below. Skorzeny followed Lonewolf up the swinging chain, furiously slashing with his claws.

Skorzeny snapped and bit, struggling to reach Lonewolf, who held on with one hand and feet claws hooked into the chain links. Engulfed with rage, Skorzeny pulled himself up the chain and reached toward LoneWolf, ready to pull both of them down if necessary.

LoneWolf gnashed his teeth and lunged down to meet Skorzeny, sinking his sharp fangs deep into his attacking hand.

Skorzeny instinctually recoiled in pain and lost his grip. In his long fall down into the molten silver, his final howl of defeat rang throughout the base. Covered in melting silver, the thrashing Skorzeny let out a demonic shriek before sinking into oblivion.

A massive explosion rocked through the base interior and part of the cave ceiling crumbled down in a stream of rubble. From the ground floor, Tanya made a howling shout to LoneWolf. He launched off the chain with a powerful leap, clearing the other side of the pit. The ceiling continued to collapse, the steel girding and chain plummeting into the molten silver below.

With the still-aroused Wolf Pack clawing at her, Tanya backed into the wall of the silver vat. She backed into something hard—it was the spigot drain. Grabbing the wheel, she opened the pressure valve, spraying molten liquid silver at the pursuing Wolf Pack. The scorching silver melted their half-decayed carcasses, sending them to hell along with their former master.

She found LoneWolf and grabbed hold of his hand. Together they ran toward the cargo bay doors. A large, tumbling rock crashed down in front of them, trapping Tanya underneath the debris. LoneWolf stopped running, his instinct telling him to come back for her. Pushing through the torrent of falling rubble, he plunged his hands down into the rocks until he found her hand and pulled her free.

They ran on, diving through cargo bay doors just before they disintegrated under the collapsing mountain. They rode the plunging bridge down the mountain, leaping off when spotting an overhang. Darting down the steep mountainside, Lonewolf and Tanya jumped and skipped from each tumbling rock to the next, an avalanche of mountain debris following ever closer behind.

Finally on even ground, they ran along the edge of a cliff overlooking a deep river gorge. Still moving with great momentum, and with a wave of flying, crashing rocks and wreckage coming up fast, the two of them were pushed to the cliff's edge. They stopped their momentum by holding on to the side of the cliff. A tumbling boulder struck the cliffside, causing the edge to fall away.

As they let go, all they felt was the feeling of falling into the darkness far below.

24: SHADOWS IN THE MOONLIGHT

The river's icy waters flowed fast, sweeping the two werewolves down the canyon. There was no fighting against it, and when the current finally slowed, the two battle-worn wolves swam to the nearest wooded shore. Above them, dust from the collapse of Wolf Mountain hung in a haze under the bright full moon. Now in the safety of the forest, LoneWolf and Tanya ran free, danger no longer racing behind them. Surrounded by the purity of nature, they were the apex predators here and all other animals gave way to their presence. Pausing in a clearing, they howled at the moon, partly in triumph and partly in relief.

Animal instincts ruled over LoneWolf, and Tanya, still clad in der Wolfsgürtel, allowed herself to be overtaken by the feelings of what it was to be a pure unrestrained animal, one both natural and supernatural. It was the feeling of true freedom, freedom to roam, wilder than the wind. Together, they lapped up water from a trickling creek, and looked at each other with a deep longing, one that reverberated through all they were.

The time to fight was over and now it was time for other natural instincts to run wild. Looking up at the night sky, Tanya realized she felt more real than she had ever felt before. She felt the call of the wilderness fill her. LoneWolf nuzzled against her, dominant in his mount. Keeping the forest awake, the two dark silhouettes moondanced the night away, tied to each other, the way that young wolves do.

Faint streaks of sunlight painted the horizon when they finally bed down in the soft meadow grass of the clearing. LoneWolf fell into a deep sleep and in the morning twilight, Tanya watched his features slowly become those of Val West. In the first rays of light, with the first birds singing a sweet song, Tanya took off the wolfskin belt. She felt the strange rush of shapeshifting once again, back to her human form. Without the cover of fur, she shivered in the chill mountain air. She placed the belt across West's shoulder and huddled up next to him, falling into a deep slumber, the most restful she had ever known.

The morning air was crisp, but the sun was shining down into the valley beneath the ruins of Wolf Mountain. Awaking first, it took Tanya a moment to realize it had not all been a dream. She felt the softness of the forest grass on her naked underside. Looking around her, she saw shreds of her clothing strewn about and only scraps of the spysuit still adorned West's body. It had been quite a night.

Val West awoke feeling a sense of calm. The horrors of the torture inflicted by Skorzeny were now just a nightmarish memory, his body healed after its transformation back from being LoneWolf. He had not been consciously aware at the time, but he somehow knew Skorzeny had finally met his doom. Knowing this comforted him, even with all that had been lost—Cedric's death, the sad fate of Thomas Hedison, and his own chance at a cure. Skorzeny had taken that possibility with him, and he had to reconcile himself to the fact that this was now who he was. He also realized he and Tanya were both nude. While he couldn't recollect what happened as LoneWolf, once he saw der Wolfsgürtel laying across his shoulder he began to put it together.

"Good morning, Tanya. Glad to see we're both unscathed, apart from our clothing."

"I thought you could use a new belt. Quite fashionable."

"Indeed. Thank you, and I'm looking forward to hearing the details in your debriefing. You know, we could use someone like you in ParaCommand."

Tanya looked at him for a moment then let out a sigh. "I've seen things I thought only existed in movies or folktales." She looked away, staring at the bright blue sky. "I think that after all of this, the most dangerous thing I want to deal with is being a history teacher at my old high school back in Ohio."

West looked at her and nodded. He understood her want for a normal life, a life he would never have a chance at again. Now, he would have to make the curse of the werewolf into a blessing in disguise.

"I thought I knew what normal life was… or what it was going to be once I left the secret service," West said, unsure of his words. "I used to be a man. Now, I'm just a beast."

Tanya shook her head. "You are a man. But you are also more than that." She placed her hand on the golden faceplate of the wolfskin belt slung over his shoulder. "You have this now, and with it you will always be more than just a beast."

West thought about what she said and knew she was right. He could control his werewolf powers now with der Wolfsgürtel and would learn to reconcile his beastly side with his human side. He looked around for scraps of their clothing and decided there wasn't enough to make any sort of cover. "Looks like we're going to go for a hike in the buff. A little chilly, but at least the sun is shining. "You can cover up with the belt if you like."

"No, thank you. I've worn it as much as I would like to."

"I thought as much. No instant fur coat, then? And I do certainly approve of your current state of undress."

She smiled and gave him a kiss. They walked hand-in-hand together down the grassy hillsides of the mountains. It was a new day, for both of them, and the way they saw each day going forward would never be the same as it once was. In the distance on the road below, dust clouds kicked up from an approaching covered wagon. West noticed the mark on the side as the secret logo of ParaCommand.

Tanya was covering up as best she could and elbowed West as he brazenly walked down the hill with all of his extremities in view. He called out and the wagon came to a stop. Dacia Zabor, also known as Double Agent Gypsy, did a double take when she saw West come bounding down toward her.

"Guess the cold morning air doesn't have that much effect on you, Mr. West," she said in her thick Transylvanian accent.

"Now, Miss Zabor, a nude hike in the morning always gets the blood flowing. But please, if you have something for my more modest travelling companion, I would be very grateful."

Dacia thought for a moment. "If you don't mind wearing Transylvanian Oktoberfest lederhosen, I have enough for both of you in the back of the wagon. You can also use the secure channel to send a coded message back to ParaCommand. Commander 7 and Dr. Borge have been wondering if you made it out."

"Yes, although I lost my shirt in the process. Won a belt, though." Tanya was still attempting to cover herself, so he helpfully lifted her up into the wagon while continuing to converse with Dacia. "What's the latest word on the street?"

"Well, it seems an unprecedented geologic event took place late last night. A rare earthquake occurred, causing the collapse of Wolf Mountain. No comment from the Transylvanian National Alliance authorities, and so far, calls to General Ferenc's office have been unanswered."

"Ferenc's a bit indisposed. Or more like, disposed of. I would not expect a reply to be forthcoming." West climbed into the wagon and began dressing in the traditional Transylvanian garments of the

258

chemise shirt, with vest and trousers. He looked over at Tanya, garbed in ruffled sleeves and apron, and thought she looked quite fetching.

West moved up to the front of the wagon where Gypsy sat on the buckboard wagon seat. As they trotted along the winding dirt trail, she told him that Borge had sent her the coordinates of the ThunderBird and they would be there soon.

"I can make room for three if you'd like to come back to London with us."

"I'm sorry," Gypsy replied with a hint of not-so-well-hidden sadness. "I would love to, and will someday, but I am needed here now. The fallout from all of this, plus Ferenc's demise means there will be a power struggle."

West understood the sense of duty and nodded to her. "You're a good and brave woman, Dacia. I never did say thank you for the silver dagger."

She gave a warm smile. "Do you believe in superstitions now?"

"Not necessarily, but it seems they are a big believer in me. Next time I'm in Transylvania, I hope you'll tell me more of them, so I know what to avoid."

"It's a deal. I'll bring the garlic." She reined the horses in, and the wagon slowed to a stop. "Looks like this is where you get off."

"With any luck," West replied with a wink.

West and Tanya bid thanks and farewell to Gypsy, and then scrambled over a field of large rocks to find the hidden landing spot of the ThunderBird microjet. West located the keypad to deactivate the camouflage projection and slid open the bubble canopy. Tanya came closer and examined the craft's interior layout.

"So... we're going to have a few hours flight back to London," West said. "Could be a bit boring."

Tanya moved closer and ran her hand down his arm. "Somehow, I don't think that will be the case."

"On the other hand…" West looked into her eyes. "It could be a bit of a wild ride, with a fair amount of turbulence."

"I wouldn't fly any other way."

"Good thing I have autopilot," West said, giving her a swat on the dirndl as she climbed into the cockpit.

Tanya gave him a wolfish look "Splendid," she replied.

***

It was a sunny, but icy November day at Highgate Cemetery, the day Sir Cedric Erle Kenton was laid to rest. While Cedric's daughter gave a moving memorial, back among the old oak trees, clad in dark shades, were Val West and Dr. Hector Borge. Cedric's casket was interred in the family crypt, where he would always be at rest just across the cemetery from the ParaCommand base. It was fitting, in its own way.

West and Borge walked back to the base in silence. Looking around them to make sure all was clear, then entered the secret entrance to the subterranean base of ParaCommand, beneath the time-worn tombs and stones of old Highgate Cemetery. They sat down in the expensive lounge chairs next to the control console, chairs Cedric had insisted on installing, along with his secret bar.

West opened the hidden panel in the wall and the bar extended out, with glasses, ice and a mixture of very expensive whisky and liqueurs. "Carrot or potato juice, doctor?" West asked.

"Ultra-smooth vodka made with hard winter wheat. It is $5,000 a bottle."

"Cedric would approve," West said, handing Borge his glass. "Except, he would be insulted he wasn't here to join us when you finally decided to have a real drink."

As they went to toast their drinks, a glass fell off the bar to the floor. West and Borge looked at each other, neither one a skeptic anymore when it came to supernatural occurrences. "Good show, Cedric," West said, and they toasted each other and drank up.

THE LONEWOLF

After many more drinks and stories of Cedric, it was getting dark. West still didn't have a London apartment, but he thought a nice hotel would do, especially when the other option was to sleep in the dank catacombs of ParaCommand. He had seen Tanya off on a flight to Cleveland the day before and now with all of the day's remembrances at an end, he was looking forward to a hot bath and a long, restful sleep.

Static crackled through the speaker above the control console and the waveform signal of the monitor signaled Commander 7 was tuning in.

"Gentleman. Pity I couldn't join you today. You know Cedric and I, of course, went way back."

"Yes, sir," Borge said. "Completely understood."

"Mr. West," Commander 7 intoned, "for what it's worth, I am sorry you were unable to bring Skorzeny back alive to try and create a cure. If it is of any consolation, the world is a much safer place with him gone... and you still in it, as you are."

West had resigned himself to this fate, but hearing it again made him wince. Still, to receive such a compliment from Commander 7 was high praise indeed.

"I do hope you will stay with us," Commander 7 added. "We do believe you now to be the only werewolf in existence."

"Here's something to help seal the deal," Borge said, handing West a small box. Inside was a vintage Enicar Ultrasonic wristwatch. "Just like Cedric's, but with a few modifications," Borge noted.

"Sure beats having another hole drilled into the back of my head to implant a communicator," West replied. "Thank you. I accept. Both the gift and the job."

Commander 7 began briefing West on a number of things he would like him to begin looking into. "We've intercepted CIA cables reporting recent unsubstantiated UFO sightings in Wisconsin. There's also the matter of a missing realtor in Transylvania that could have some teeth to it. I'm also concerned about the Russians possibly having weaponized an intergalactic sasquatch, among other items of interest."

West listened on as Commander 7 put those aside and gave him an immediate directive. With this new order, he packed his new spysuit engineered by Dr. Borge, put on his wolfskin belt and ran off into the cool dark London night.

He was a shadow in the moonlight, the only one of his kind.

He was the LoneWolf.

Made in the USA
Columbia, SC
23 June 2023